A Silver Ring

A Silver Ring

By Nathan Carriker

www.asilverring.com

Published by Karcher Prince
Printed in LaVergne, Tennessee, USA

International Standard Book No. 978-0-9836419-0-2
Library of Congress Control Number 2011910177

14   13   12   11   10   9   8   7   6   5   4   3   2   1

Cover design by Cassandra Marshall and Jennette Green
Cover image courtesy of the U.S. Air Force Museum

1

Levi Hutchinson arrived home from work Monday evening hungry as usual. But when his sons Wesley and Samuel waylaid him to proudly confess what they'd done instead of school that day, his appetite vanished. Before he could decide what to say, the boys' mother Charlotte called out to them from the kitchen window, "I think this chicken's been through enough already, you boys. Now quit tinkering with that car and come get it while it's at least hot."

They had to tuck it away where brave men keep their horrible secrets and go make a show of eating supper.

Charlotte had just begun cooking the chicken for an early Sunday supper when their neighbor burst in, frantic with the news. She finished cooking it, alternately trying to hear the radio over the sizzling and trying to ignore it to pray for her family and her country. By the time she was finished, no one was hungry or even thought to ask about eating. The family all sat around the radio, and the chicken sat out until bedtime, when Charlotte carelessly put it in the icebox, uncovered, and went to bed.

A bad night's sleep hadn't done her or the fried chicken that would now forever remind her of Pearl Harbor any good. With Levi at work and the kids supposedly at school, she had the time and privacy to sneak it outside and quietly bury it, as she sometimes did with things that cast her meager cooking abilities in a bad light. But with the war on, it just didn't seem right. When the kids came home, she just fired up the stove, tossed a few extra potatoes into the pot, and let the chips fall.

When their unusually quiet meal was over that Monday night, only one dry piece of meat remained—a leg which sat, with one tiny bite out of it, on youngest son Jim's plate. His four siblings had managed to swallow their unsavory portions, and all of them were now conspicuously looking at him with expressions ranging from mild amusement, in the case of eighteen year-old Wesley, to middle brother Jacob's condescending disappointment, to the overwrought hostility and insult sister Eileen's face wore for her mother's pride's sake.

"I'd eat that chicken with a smile if I were you, Nubs," she taunted him.

Clenched teeth permitted an, "I told you, stop callin' me that!"

Charlotte's worry and embarrassment over their inadequate supper cut deeply into her tolerance for the sibling rivalry normally saturating their household. "Eileen, I don't care what that boy says or does, he don't deserve to get picked on by his sister for that. Now you apologize."

She picked up her dishes and dropped a pallid "Sorry…James," as she carried them into the kitchen. "Nubs" was a name she usually reserved only for defense against her prepubescent brother's jabs about her accursed "female-ness." The Hutchinsons' only daughter, she'd suffered immeasurably at the hands of her five brothers for sixteen years now, but she'd learned the precise location of each of their underbellies and knew just where, if not always advisably when, to strike.

Jim had had an accident in an Oklahoma oilfield a few years before that cost him half his left hand's middle finger. It had happened on Wes' watch, and Eileen knew intuitively that he had never gotten over the guilt, so hurling that one epithet at Jim not only put the eight-year-old on the defensive but also ruffled Wes.

At the head of the table, Levi Hutchinson had apathetically cleaned his breast piece down to the bone and asked, "Don't want your meat tonight, Jim? You know that chicken'd probably love to be eating your leg right now." Jim struck an accommodating, strained smile but didn't even make a feint for the drumstick. Without another word, Levi dutifully grabbed the leg from Jim's plate, devoured it, sucked on each of the dark, greasy bones in turn for a few minutes, then quietly belched into a fist and pronounced, "Right proud supper, Mom, thanks."

At this, the boys all quietly echoed a half-hearted thanks to Charlotte and got up to carry their plates into the kitchen, where it was Eileen's turn to spend the next half-hour giving her own thanks by washing the dishes, while the rest of the family gathered around the radio for a news update.

Charlotte's attention was spent, however and, sitting on the floor between Levi's knees while he slowly ran his callused fingers through her hair, she drifted into a reverie about the last time they'd made love—the last time things had been normal, the morning of the seventh—and marveled grimly at how much life could change in just one day.

After firing up the stove to make breakfast that peaceful Sunday morning, she'd crept back to their bedroom and lay down on top of the blankets beside her husband for a few decadent minutes of Sunday morning laziness. As she did, a chill ran through her, shaking the bed slightly and popping Levi's bright eyes open. Without a hint of panic or even displeasure—twenty years spent living hand-to-mouth with this woman had taught him nothing if not that problems were both inevitable and solvable—he asked, "What's wrong?"

Charlotte blink-smiled warmly and shook her head a little, then leaned over and gave him a long kiss. Then, stroking his graying sideburn with a finger, she whispered, "Not-one-single-thing."

Life had been as hard as anyone could have imagined for them during the Great Depression, but now Levi was a lead mechanic for Sinclair Oil, in charge of a whole shift of men maintaining scores of state-of-the-art electric-powered oil wells across five counties in Oklahoma and Kansas. He had been re-hired by his old boss after a two year furlough, on the condition that he train himself and pass a battery of tests on the new electric motors powering the wells. The massive diesels had had their time, and now the cost savings associated with electricity as well as the simplicity of stringing wire instead of cumbersome mechanical rod lines across miles of rolling countryside made the change inevitable.

Levi had fallen asleep at the table many nights during the weeks he pored over the electricity textbooks. More than once, Charlotte awoke to an empty bed and went out to find him asleep at the table, his eyeglasses all bent up on his head as he'd simply exhausted himself at his task.

"This is the new thing, Shug," he'd told her. "I've got to either be part of it or die yesterday."

Like much of the country, the family had thus optimistically gone about its business that Sunday morning. After breakfast, they went to Sunday services together, and when they returned home, Levi and the older boys went out to the garage to finish the clutch replacement they'd begun on the family's old Ford the day before, while Eileen helped Charlotte in the kitchen and young Jim played with his friends.

As they worked, Levi talked again with Wes and Samuel about their plans should America enter the war. Both boys had inherited their father's love for and talent with complex machinery, but bookish Samuel's interests ran to the design and construction side, while Wes' eyes didn't really light up until something started moving. Wes and Levi had talked many times about airplanes, both trying to imagine what a thrill flying one might be. Levi was openly jealous of the opportunity Wes seemed to have to become a pilot, and he truly felt his son's pain when Wes learned that, at 6' 1", he was too tall to fit into the cramped cockpit of a fighter and thus, in classic military logic, too tall to be inducted into the Air Corps to fly anything, even a huge bomber.

Wes had asked a recruiter if there weren't some way, any way he could fly, but the Sergeant just apologized, said rules were rules but that if he "just" wanted to fly, he could become a bomber crewmember—either an engineer, radio operator, or gunner. Wes carefully read the Army's glamorous description of each job and concluded that being a flight engineer would be the next best thing to piloting, but he'd follow his father's advice and just wait and see if that silly policy might not change by the time he finished school.

As Levi's second son, Wes seemed predestined to be relegated to obscurity in eldest brother Lee's shadow, but when that hellion left home, at sixteen, Levi was working day and night, sometimes gone from home for weeks on end; he didn't even know Lee was gone for five days. Wes became an indispensable vice-dad to the brood, a clown in good times and a minister in bad. Like any father, Levi loved all of his children equally, even Lee. Each was special for his or her own gifts, talents, and senses, and he openly doted on only daughter Eileen more than any of the boys, but Wes was, often literally, the one who got Levi up in the morning.

What Wes and Samuel had proudly told Levi and their sister, but were still waiting for a good time to confess to their mother, was that they'd ditched school and went to the Army recruiting office in Coffeyville together that Monday morning. By the time they got there, over a hundred men were in line to enlist ahead of them. The recruiter recognized them when their turn came, and Wes asked again about becoming a pilot, hopeful that a real war might bring some flexibility to the rules. It didn't.

"If flying's really your bag kid, we can get you on a bomber crew easy as pie. Why, you could be helping remodel Tojo's palace in just a few months!"

Wes' lusty hate for Japan roared in his mind and carried his hand through a signature on the enlistment form next to the title "Flight Engineer." Then he handed the pen to brother Samuel, who'd make his own contribution to the war in a non-combat engineering battalion.

Thus preoccupied with their own tiny roles in the country's headlong plunge into war, none of them noticed Eileen slip out the back door and into a'29 Chevy driven by a young man smoking a cigarette. Eileen barely had the door closed before it sped away, bald tires leaving fresh ruts in the dirt alleyway. Hearing the noise, Levi got up from his chair next to the radio, flashing Charlotte a practiced "trouble" look, and went to look for their daughter.

Once they were a few blocks away, Frank Lawton reached across the seat to take Eileen's hand as they drove out to the river. "Did anyone see you leave?"

"No, they're all glued to the radio, like everyone else in the world. I tell you, Frank, I'm scared to death. Wes and Samuel signed up for the Army today— they're going off to training next weekend. You do anything foolish like that, and I swear I'll hurt you so bad you won't pass the physical! I know my folks'll be proud of them, but I could see in Mom's eyes how scared she is. She said she never dreamed the whole world could go so crazy as all this."

Frank squeezed her hand and smiled accommodation. "I think the physical's pretty much over when you walk through the door now, sweets. So unless you plan to break both my legs…"

He looked at her playfully, took the last drag off his cigarette, and flicked it out the window. It was unseasonably warm, nearly sixty degrees, and though the winter air lacked the living seasons' sweetness, with most of the town's night fires just getting started, it did have a certain pungency like no other's. It made him feel like a man.

"Would you put that window up if you're through?"

"Crank's broke. Sorry."

He turned the car onto a long lane that led to the river. They pulled up to their usual spot, turned off the engine and lights, and sat in silence for a long minute. Eileen whispered, "Please tell me you're not going to do anything rash, Frank. I'm going to worry myself sick over Wes and Samuel, and if you get wrapped up in this too, I really don't know what I'll do."

Frank looked out the window, trying to give the appearance of considering her plea but, in truth, trying to think of the best way to tell her it was already done.

They'd met outside school earlier that, his senior, year, as Eileen was walking home. Frank had noticed her the first day and asked if he could see her home only three days later. She was new in town, having moved in over the summer.

Frank and Wes sat at opposite sides of their own classroom, both in the back row, each with his own reasons for sitting there. Their teacher had said at the beginning of the year she had yet to meet a student in whom she couldn't find some quality to appreciate, but Frank was trying hard to make this the year. His humor was unusually crude, and he seemed to have an inexhaustible supply of unanswerable cut-downs. He was both class clown and town bully, playing both parts to the hilt at odd, unpredictable intervals that made nearly everyone around him uncomfortable.

Frank and Eileen kept their burgeoning relationship above board at first, but when Eileen's father first met Frank on their front porch, he noticed the boy had a black eye and asked him jokingly what the other guy looked like. Frank was truly proud of very little about himself, but fighting well was one such thing. Looking directly into Levi Hutchinson's still laughing eyes he said, "A hell of a lot better than you would if you'd been him, mister."

This insolence stuffed Levi's sympathetic chuckle into a nervous smirk, and he turned back into the house, certain his prim little girl would soon enough notice the dirt and tarnish covering this once-white knight and send him packing. She hadn't yet, however, nor did she pledge compliance when her father forbade her to see Frank any more after he brought her home late one Friday night in November with whiskey on her breath.

Eileen never found the right time to tell Levi that the "other guy" who'd given Frank that shiner was his own father.

Frank wrestled with how to tell his love that he was, even as they sat by the river with night's chill just beginning to seep through his open window, already U.S. Government property. The eighteen years he'd spent alternately holding his position against a superior foe at home and seizing the offensive to exploit Weakness at school had prepared him well for the infantry.

"Eileen, them slant-eyed sons-of-bitches are a couple of ships from being able to just walk onto California. Would that be too soon for me to go too, or do you want me to just sit out on the porch and wait for them to come down Wood Street?"

He was doing it again—putting on a big act as if he didn't give a damn what she thought he should do. She sat silent for a long moment, shaking her head almost imperceptibly as her eyes filled.

"What do you think the chances are that you could get into a good outfit with no business in combat?"

"Honey, that stuff's best left to the kind of guy that can't fight anyway, don't you think? I mean hell, I've been in combat more than about anybody I know my whole life. This way it's just the right thing to do for once—I'm made for this stuff, hon."

"This way? This stuff? You're already in, aren't you?" She began to break down as she saw the guilty look spread across his face.

"I should have known if Samuel joined you sure as hell wouldn't stay out of it." She leaned into his shoulder and clutched his shirt in her fist as she sobbed unevenly, trying to retain her composure but getting overwhelmed by a tide of stress, worry, and confusion.

"Any man in this country that hasn't already's going to do it soon, Eileen. We've got to get those pan-faced bastards back. We shouldn't stop till they're spit-shining our boots in downtown Tokyo! Bobby's in too, and he ain't even seventeen yet. Told the recruiter he was, then got my dad to sign the form while he was drunk, thinking it was a thing for school. This is the real thing. You'll see."

Eileen Hutchinson pulled herself up away from him but held on tighter than ever to his shirt, shaking him gently as she spoke. "You go fight your damned war then, Frank Lawton. As long as I've known you the devil's had you by the tail, so maybe it'll do you and the Army both some good to stick a rifle in your hands. But it's not going to help me one bit to sit here worrying over you out there fighting your damned crusade—not when my brothers are doing the same thing. I swear everybody in this world's ready to kill each other over something, some of it's over me, and I just can't stand it. You and my family are all probably secretly hoping the other will get killed before it's over."

"Well, taken prisoner and tortured long enough for us to get married, at least," he joked. She stared at him for a moment, looking for a chink in the armor he'd put on. Finding none, she let out a sound that was both a sob and a nervous laugh, wiped her nose with the hand that had grabbed his shirt, and kissed him hard on the cheek.

"I love you, Frank. Please don't try to kill the whole damn Jap army yourself, ok? I know you can, and you know you can, so let's just leave it at that, alright?"

They held each other and kissed for several minutes but stopped when they noticed a light shining on them from behind. It was Leon Darby, the town cop, driving up about a hundred yards behind them, sealing off any escape.

They quickly separated, Frank mumbling obscenities while straightening his shirt where she had wrinkled it in her grip, and Eileen fixing her hair and face as best she could with no mirror or light.

"Frank? Frank Lawton, that you in there?" came the voice from behind them in the dark, shining a flashlight through the rear window. Darby approached the driver's door tentatively, hand just touching the butt of his revolver.

"Why, hello, Leon. How's the night find you, old buddy?" Frank pandered.

"Nothing big enough to complain of, I suppose, Frank. Say," he shined his light into the car, hitting the floor first to look for bottles, and then Eileen's face, "that wouldn't be one Eileen Hutchinson in there with you, would it?"

"You don't forget a face that sweet once you've seen it, do you? Eileen and I were just talking about the war and stuff. Did you hear I joined up with the Infantry, Leon?"

"Nope, but I'm sure you'll do us all right proud in the Army, Frank. Can't think of any better thing than for a young man to go fight for his country." Darby was hedging his bets on getting Frank to let him take Eileen back home with him and figured a few well-placed compliments might help get what he had to say to go down a little easier.

"I hear a lot of boys joined up today. Town's not going to be the same without you all. Heck, I just might not have a job to do without all you miscreants and ne'er-do-wells mucking up the works," he kidded.

Frank managed a fake laugh for the middle-aged cop, but before a good break in the banter that Darby needed to broach his point could fully bloom, he interjected, "Well, I guess we've about used up our time together for one night, Eileen. What say we take you on back home and pick this up tomorrow after school?"

Leon Darby took a deep breath and pretended to pinch the bridge of his nose, as if what he was about to say pained him, and said, "Well, now, Frank, I think you probably know Eileen's daddy really don't want to see her running with you at all, much less getting brought home by you after dark on a school night. He told me it's been made real clear to Eileen that she's not to be going around with you, and I just think it'd be best for her and you if you just let me take her back home and you just head on back to town by yourself ahead of us. I can't tell Mr. Hutchinson a lie about this, but I don't have to tell him the whole truth, either. Now you see where I'm going with this, don't you?"

"Yeah, Leon, you're going down the same old road Eileen's dad and lots of other folks have gone down with me, and some of them's not looked too good at the other end of it."

"Frank, don't," Eileen interjected, "you can't be doing this kind of thing in the Army, or you're going to spend the war behind bars. Let's just take Leon's kind offer here and I'll see you tomorrow at school, ok? Plenty of time to talk more then."

"Smart girl you got there, Frank. I'd listen to her if I was you. Them sergeants are going to break you if you don't learn to bend a little—maybe somebody's trying to tell you something."

Lawton paused, clenching his hands around the steering wheel. He hated getting boxed in like this. He felt the same sickness in his guts that his dad made him feel every time they'd argue. He could either betray himself and walk away with nothing damaged but his pride, or have his ego be the only part of him that didn't hurt in the end. Sure, he knew Leon Darby couldn't hurt him, but the law was on his side and the Army stood towering over all of them, waiting to see what its newest recruit would do.

"I suppose that's probably the best thing, Leon, like you said," Frank leaned over to kiss Eileen, but she politely turned her cheek to him. He kissed it, held his posture leaning for a moment, then sat up in his seat again and bade her goodnight. Eileen got out, walked back to the police car and got in.

Leon Darby held out his hand to Lawton, saying, "I don't imagine I'm going to be seeing much more of you around here for a while, Frank, but good luck."

Frank Lawton acted like Darby wasn't even there, much less speaking to him. He leaned forward to hit the starter, put the car into gear, and began to turn around on the narrow lane. Only after the last of the four-step maneuver did he so much as look at him—a sidelong, bloodcurdling glare that made Darby jump when Frank let fly with an obnoxious honk as he sped past the police car with the only thing on Earth he cared a whit about inside.

2

Justin Prator stood there holding the razor, wondering if he really had the balls to do it. He'd kept them around all eight years he'd been sober. Seeing them every day had helped him weather the anxiety of his second career change—from his old identity as a swashbuckling corporate pilot and jack of all winged trades who'd allowed one too many near misses between the bottle and throttle—into just another eight-to-five drone. But enough was enough. He'd departed Comfortable a few years back, cruised over a year or so of Boredom's bland landscape, and had only recently realized he'd arrived somewhere vaguely familiar, deep into Burnout. If something didn't change soon, he'd go nuts.

Justin's ex, Gloria, never could understand how much his apparent inability to find his place in life frustrated him. Their daughter Sarah was still in high school, but she'd clearly inherited his love of music, and their son Paul had been one of Ohio State's most driven flight students ever. He took classes year-round to graduate early, began working as a Flight Instructor in his freshman year, and was hired by commuter airline BlueSky at twenty-one. He'd been there just over a year when the major airlines' hiring boom delivered him from the poverty-level life of a copilot and into a Captain's seat at age twenty-two. Now *that* was finding your place.

In his forties and overweight about a pound for every year, Justin's sleep apnea wasn't helping his mental state. He only slept well early in the morning, when his body finally became weary enough to ignore the intermittent suffocation, and his job only allowed that to happen on weekends. He'd slept through Paul's first call, but the second one woke him.

"Hey, Dad. You asleep still?"

"Umph. No, no, just dozing. Dog woke me up earlier," he lied.

"Well, I just got into Chicago, and I should be leaving for Wichita at 11:15, so probably be there about one I'd say. I'm on the list for the jumpseat, but I could still get bumped. If you don't hear any more from me, you'll know I'm on. You *are* buying me lunch for this, right?"

"Yeah, kid. I have to do something for you I suppose, for risking your good name on a desk jockey like me."

As an airline Captain, Paul would never again have to earn a living as a flight instructor, but he dutifully renewed his license every two years anyway, partly out of pride but mostly as a favor to his dad. Whenever Justin came due for his FAA-mandated biennial training, he'd call "Mr. Hotshot," as he called his son—with occasionally equal parts pride and envy—to ask if he'd spare him the indignity of having to fly with, and possibly fail to satisfy, a less "invested" instructor. Today was another such occasion.

Justin's no-longer-new title with his old employer, Cessna, was Central Regional Director of the company's Pilot Centers, a franchise/dealer program conceived to increase the company's market base by making pilot training simpler and more accessible to "average" people. Justin was well suited to the job, with his background as an educator and love for and experience in aviation but, unlike the job he'd lost to drinking, it didn't pay him just to fly. Still permitted—but not financially disposed—to fly privately, his considerable skills were in atrophy.

"You coming in on Universal?"

"Yep. So, do you want to do it today or tomorrow?"

"I've got the plane reserved at four o'clock. Figured that'd give us time to talk a little, or a lot, depending on when you got in, and then talk some more after if we need to. It's a nice, later model 172, so it shouldn't be too tough, unless you're one of those black-hat types." Justin used some of his limited airline jargon with Paul, trying to show off. "Black-hats," notoriously too-tough check pilots, could turn a routine route check into the beginning of the end of a pilot's career.

"Ok, well, the flight number's 822, and I'll look for you outside the ticket counters around one, then, ok? I'm looking forward to it, Dad, really. How long's it been since we flew together now, a couple of years?"

"Pretty close, I'd say. Must've been right after you graduated."

"Well, we'll find out if either of us can still fly a Cessnoid, I guess. I'm not sure I know what VFR means anymore. That's where you just go up and flop around without any direction or purpose, right?"

"I'm pretty sure it stands for Visual Flight Rules. Nobody tells you when or where to land anyway, I know that much."

"I bet you're right."

"Can we call that my oral exam?"

"No."

Justin drew an exaggerated sigh. "Sounds like this could turn out to be a pretty long day. Alright, I'll see you then, kid, and thanks."

Paul wasn't nearly so impressed with himself as his father was. Like him, he'd wanted to be a pilot since he was a boy, but he got his first pair of glasses in fourth grade. A few years later, when he learned the military only allowed men with 20/20 uncorrected vision to become pilots, he went into a frightening depression from which he never fully emerged. Paul's career as a "bus driver"—his auto-derisive term for airline pilots—was but a frigid surrogate for his Life's dream: to reach the top of the pilot food chain, flying fighters.

The mental effort of conversation had awakened him too much to go back to sleep, so Justin hauled himself out of bed, gave his Boxer dog a pat on the head and a "Good morning, Double-Ugly," and went to the bathroom.

Sneering at the brittle, yellow list of "Just for Today" positive morning affirmations taped to the mirror, he added a dubious, "I will not be a fuck-up with my kid," and grabbed the razor.

He didn't need them anymore. He'd come close to doing it before, but always chickened out. Why did he cling to them so? It's not like they were still serving any purpose in his life. If anything, they now only reminded him of those first few years he'd been so weak that to take life *One Day at a Time* was still asking too much. He'd risked his family to get his commercial license, only to lose it, and them, to alcoholism. He'd had to break the days down to hours, sometimes minutes, to cope with his soul's throbbing craving for the poison that had left him needing it worse than ever in the aftermath of ruining his life.

But he was past that phase now, thank God. And he was sick of them, truth be told. Sick of steering clear of them, sick of taking care of them, sick of grooming them, sick of the nagging itch. It was time. He was going to do it. He was going to shave the now-graying beard he'd grown as a daily reminder of his most recent trial identity.

Justin took a few extra moments after shaving to splash the last long whiskers clinging to the sink down the drain, then studied the vastly different face in the mirror—cleaner, younger looking at a glance, but more aged under the new scrutiny permitted by having shaved. Concealed by his beard, lines had been carved into the pale face of a man who still wasn't who Justin wanted to be, whoever that was, but was now way too old to do much about it anyway.

He put on a jacket and tie and spent an hour over breakfast, thumbing through his stained, dog-eared copy of the Flight Training Manual, Federal Aviation Regulations, and a few other dusty flying tomes. He really wanted to be "on" today and maybe regain some of the respect he was certain his son had lost for him. He knew he'd never again be able to out-fly his prodigy, but perhaps if Paul's expectations were anywhere near as low as he feared they were, he could still impress him with some half-decent advanced maneuvers and smooth landings from solid, stable approaches.

A Silver Ring

If he'd had the usual trouble finding his car keys, he'd have been there to answer the phone. But today he'd gathered everything he'd need to take well ahead of time, including the car keys buried under the previous Sunday's newspaper, scattered across the coffee table.

Holding the door open with his foot, Justin stooped to grab the weathered leather attaché containing his worn, lime-green David Clark headset, some obsolete charts, and owner's manuals for all six of the Cessna Employee Flying Club airplanes—five of which he'd never flown—and walked out in plenty of time to meet Paul's flight.

So as he half-collapsed into his eight-year old AMC Ambassador, spilling a little bit of his fourth cup of coffee on his pants and growling a brief curse in response, the phone in his tiny apartment rang twelve times, eight more times a few moments later, then fell quiet for the rest of the day.

3

Charlotte had eaten what had to have been one of the chicken's thighs, with a modest serving of the potatoes she'd boiled for filler, and her hunger was still reasonably sated when Darby brought Eileen home Monday night. By the morning of the ninth, however, her worried stomach didn't know anything about any chicken or potatoes and growled ferociously as she cooked breakfast with Eileen behind her, scolded and silent, putting away the dishes she'd washed the night before.

Levi ate his breakfast in his own angry silence, trying to think of a way to keep his family from being torn completely apart. Realizing he was out of both time and ideas, before everyone got up from the table to start their day, he looked sternly at Eileen and pronounced, "You won't be going around with that junkyard dog anymore, understand? You're too good for him, and he knows it. He'll move on, I promise.

"You will too." It wasn't a prediction.

Their eyes locked until she got up from the table, saying, "I'm old enough to know who's good for me and who's not, Daddy.

"And right now," she hissed as she turned to storm out the front door and down the street, crying, "You ain't making the cut."

With a frown and a twitch of his bald head, Levi dispatched Wes and Samuel to see to her return.

The Lawtons lived on a cross street a few hundred yards north. Wes and Samuel caught up to her just past the turn, behind a hedge that bordered an abandoned house on the corner lot.

"Eileen, stop! Dad sent us after you. I don't think you want any more of what you've got coming than you already got."

She didn't even slow down. Wes and Samuel flanked her.

"Eileen, listen to me!" Wes made himself a wall in front of her and grabbed her arms, expecting her to stop.

"Get the hell out of my way, Wesley."

"Right now it's just your ass. If I don't bring you home soon, it's mine too. Forget about Lawton. He ain't worth it. He wouldn't do this for you, would he?"

"You don't know anything about him. There's a whole other side to him he doesn't let out except for me. Now let go of me or I'll do something that'll hurt worse than anything Dad's ever going to do to you."

As she said this, she saw Frank and his two brothers bound down their front steps and start down the street toward them. Frank was in the lead, followed closely by Bobby, just a year younger and built like Frank but lacking his wit and guile. Behind them a few yards and along for the ride, in more than one way, was thirteen year-old Zach.

Eileen struggled with Wes, buying herself time. Wes had her wrists and started twisting them to force her into a hold. They'd been playing together their whole lives, and Eileen's practiced responses to her brother's predictable tactics made her a worthy opponent despite her strength disadvantage. But she could feel it in his merciless grip; he wasn't playing this time. She was about to be subdued, and it infuriated her. Without thinking, she brought both knees up as hard as she could, hitting her brother's most vulnerable spot as she pulled him down to the ground with her.

In a few seconds, Frank was slowing to a swagger in front of them, an amused sneer on his face. Ignoring still-uncertain Samuel, Frank looked down at normally three-inches-taller Wes and asked, "What's got Eileen so upset here, fellas?"

"Well Frank," Wes panted, "I bet even you can probably figure that one out. No sense pretending you got any manners for us, asshole."

Wes wanted a reason to hate Frank for his father's sake, but the respect he always seemed to sense Frank accorded him proved irksome. In another situation, perhaps if they'd known each other from a younger, less volatile age, they may have been good friends.

With his nausea no longer intensifying, Wes stood and felt his knees go hollow in anticipation of the brawl shaping up. Frank had never been beaten in any of his frequent scraps, and Wes knew this likely wasn't the day. But he also knew that men like Frank didn't respond to talk—only force and bravado. He'd seen it play out between oilfield roughnecks around his father dozens of times.

With this in mind, he pretended his legs hadn't turned to jelly, imagined he was already in his Army uniform, and took the last step closer to Frank Lawton, boresighting his eyes with the tip of his nose.

"We ain't lived around here long, so I don't know your whole story, but my dad don't think you're worth a cup of warm spit, which is kind of unusual. Now you're making a lot of trouble for his baby girl here, and the only reason we're here instead of him's because they won't send us to jail if we throw you in front of the train."

Frank smiled, supremely confident of Wes' bluff. "I'd like to see you, or your daddy, try. Now you go home. And you tell him not to worry about *my* girl."

"I don't tell Levi Hutchinson what to do—and I suggest trash like you don't go trying to make a habit out of it, either." Wes' expression was deadly serious, but his heart was in his throat. They stood there for a long moment, each waiting for the other to strike.

Wes startled visibly as the morning train from Bartlesville blew its whistle. Unflinching, Frank held his cocky smile and raised a contemptuous, daring eyebrow.

"Right on time. Eh, Hutch?"

Afraid of seeing things take a turn for the worst, Eileen's family loyalties made a sudden, triumphant return.

"Frank, how about I just go back home for now and let me try to handle things, ok? I want my dad to give things another look, to give you half a chance, but if you go kicking the shit out of his boy, that ain't ever going to happen, now is it?"

Wes broke his stare with Lawton just long enough to register his offense with his sister, at which Frank Lawton couldn't help but let out a chuckle, casting to the winds the ominous overtone in which he'd been reveling so throughout their exchange.

Frank saw the fresh fear and tired sadness in Eileen's eyes. He was just about to agree when a voice called from the Lawton house.

"Frank! Bobby! What the hell's going on down there? Get back here, now!" It was Boyd Lawton, Frank's father, standing on his front porch in an untucked shirt and jeans. He'd heard the commotion as his boys ran off and come outside to see what they were getting into now.

Boyd didn't know the whole basis for Frank's reputation around town, but he believed most of what he heard, and none of it was good. He'd come to see his boys only in terms of how much pride they brought him, which could have been considerable, had he stayed sober enough to appreciate it when they were young and still trying in vain to impress him. Those days were long gone now, lost in the bottomless cocktail of angry despair he force-fed everyone in the house after his wife hanged herself, in the depths of another, still greater depression, in 1935.

He stepped down to the front yard. "If I get to your asses before they're back in this house, you're going to wish to Jesus they weren't attached!"

Frank grabbed Eileen, kissed her hard, then gut-punched Wes when he tried to pull him off of her. He smiled in Samuel's face as Wes doubled over and, narrowing his eyes with arms at his sides, gave a chuckle and said, "Real roughnecks, you two.

"Tell your daddy to leave me and Eileen alone. And tell him if he's ever man enough to push his own weight around, getting thrown in front of a train's going to sound better than what I'll do to him."

With that, he and Bobby ran back to their house, Zach trailing along after giving Eileen the finger and a laugh. Through watery eyes, Wes and Eileen watched as Boyd Lawton smacked Frank on the back of his head, hard enough to sprawl him across the front steps, then kicked his rear and pursued his boys into the house, slamming the door behind them.

"I don't know what you see in that piece of shit, Eileen," Wes told his sister after the Lawton boys were out of earshot. She didn't answer but turned and started walking back home on her own, fighting the urge, the near-compulsion to try to get all of her worries and fears in front of her at once. She knew whether she failed again or finally succeeded, she'd break down right there on the sidewalk. She decided to focus on how best to handle her father.

None of her forethought could have prepared her for what awaited her at home, however. It made her father two hours late for work and put her out of school for the rest of the week. The prospect of losing another of his children, especially his only daughter, terrified him, and fear wasn't something Levi Hutchinson often experienced, expressed, or handled particularly well.

It had, of course, occurred to Levi before that his little girl would eventually have to spread her wings and fly away, but he thought he'd raised her to have standards someone like Frank Lawton couldn't meet. She'd always been such a steady, reliable child; he just couldn't see her with someone so "full of piss, vinegar, and gunpowder."

Eileen didn't see Frank Lawton outside school again until the day before he left for basic training three weeks later, when Charlotte, having said "any boy headed off to fight a war deserves to kiss his girl goodbye," allowed her to visit with Frank on their front porch for the two hours after school before Levi would get home from work.

Eileen knew when the war was over, if she didn't start to lie, to herself or to them—a lot and often—either Frank or her dad would end up in jail, and the other would be dead.

4

Two weeks after he put his father through the wringer out in Wichita, Paul Prator stared silently out the window of the Columbus Airport Holiday Inn's courtesy van, trying in vain to ignore the racket as it rattled and clattered over the same 2.7 miles of bad road it had traveled 30,000 times in its purgatorial life. He'd had a nightmare, a rarity for him, the night before. Its genesis was simple enough to figure out, but its incredible detail and realism had him reeling.

He'd been reading a book from the shelf in BlueSky's Indianapolis crew lounge, an old Bantam paperback titled "Ploesti" with a pair of World War Two-era B-24 "Liberator" bombers flying low over a burning oil refinery on the cover. An aficionado of that period in aviation, Paul read a little about the mission as a boy, but since the raid hadn't been on German soil or had any impact on the war, he'd immaturely dismissed it as inconsequential and never bothered to learn the details.

Ploesti was the tallest of orders: its plan called for just under 200 planes to takeoff badly overloaded at first light from a makeshift base in Libya, fly across the Mediterranean Sea, skirting German-held Greece, crossing Albania and mountainous portions of Yugoslavia. They would have to fly low to avoid radar detection and bomb five oil refinery complexes forming a ferociously defended ring of nearly identical targets without inflicting significant collateral damage to "soft" civilian portions of the central city. The raiders were then to fly the six hour return trip in damaged airplanes, many with wounded crewmembers aboard, trying to avoid capture or interment in neutral Turkey, which was the nearest land for much of the over-water return flight. Casualties were estimated to run as high as 50%, at which level the mission would still be considered a success. There were no fuel reserves.

When the mission was over, roughly 20% of the total force, with four-hundred forty-six men aboard, had been lost. Eight planes and seventy-nine men were interred in Turkey for the remainder of the war, 54 men were wounded but landed safely in friendly territory, and 76 wounded were taken as prisoners of war. Only thirty-three of the planes and barely more than half the men on the mission returned to service.

Paul's nightmare, like most of his always bizarre dreams, started out innocently enough with him flying at treetop altitude and high speed over beautiful countryside, just enjoying the ride and the incredible rush of high-speed low-altitude flight. What was odd was that, for perhaps the first time ever, he wasn't flying the plane, but riding on the right side as a waist gunner. Out his window, he could see at least a dozen other B-24s lined up in battle formation, all flying at top speed.

Everything seemed fine at first, but then he heard a voice in his headset telling him to watch out for flak towers coming up. The planes were flying so low, the gunners actually had to aim slightly upward to fire on anti-aircraft guns the Germans had wisely placed atop towers, to protect them from bomb bursts. The Germans hadn't planned on such a risky low-level attack, and while they struggled to realign their guns to fire horizontally, the advantage was the raiders'.

Paul was shooting at the towers, but they were going by so fast he couldn't tell if he personally was scoring any kills, though he could see some of the guns getting hit in the withering crossfire. Suddenly, there was a loud thump, and the plane seemed to jump a few feet sideways, making him lose his balance and fall backward. They'd been hit and his intercom, which had been busy with voices of his crewmembers directing each other's attention and fire, went dead.

Looking forward as he struggled to his feet, he could see daylight shining into the forward fuselage through a hole where the radio operator and navigator stations had been. Then he caught the unmistakable odor of 115-octane aviation gas and spotted the source, a steady dribble curling around the forward lip of the left side waist gunner's window. For the volatile fuel to make it the thirty feet or so from its tank in the wing to there without evaporating there had to be a massive leak.

Perhaps oblivious to the fuel leak or just too scared to stop firing, his partner, who he didn't recognize, at the left waist window was still firing his .50-caliber machine gun as targets came into view. As Paul stood up, he leaned forward and shouted to his friend to cease fire, pointing to the stream of fuel saturating his uniform, but the man wouldn't stop. Paul resumed firing out his own window, hitting a man running toward a gun tower. It seemed as if he physically knocked the man to the ground, and he felt indignant and powerful.

Miraculously, the strong and chaotic airflow around the opposite window and gun somehow kept the muzzle flash from igniting the fuel, but ahead of them he could see what might soon do the trick. Spread from just ahead of the airplane's left wingtip as far to the right as he could see were buildings and oil storage tanks ablaze. Where inside that mess their target lay, he wasn't sure, but what was about to happen to them seemed certain.

He knew they'd passed through the ring of the city's defenses now, for the flak had stopped completely, so he began making his way forward to tell the pilots about the fuel leak. As he approached the bomb bay amidships, he was almost overcome by the heat welling up from beneath the plane and pouring through the bomb bay doors, which had been open for some time. He could see occasional flashes of undamaged city, but much of the view through the doors was smoke and fire, passing what seemed like only inches or feet beneath the plane.

Just ahead of the bombs was the top turret, in which another man he didn't recognize was staring straight ahead, guns quiet. Directly to his left was a gaping hole from where the shell had pierced the plane, and through it he could see the number two engine closest to the fuselage on the left wasn't turning. Covering the inside of the fuselage to his right he could see some kind of liquid glistening in the smoky daylight, and that whole side seemed to be littered with small bits of material he couldn't identify. Reaching out to touch a piece, he realized it was—seconds before—

part of the radio operator, whose other remains were in a lump on the floor to his right.

Peering beneath the floor of the elevated cockpit, he could see the bombardier in his "greenhouse" at the nose of the plane, pounding on the bomb release switch and its housing, trying to get it to work. The bombs were motionless in their rack. The wire that ran from the switch to the release on the bomb rack had been cut clean by the shell, and the plane was now carrying 3,000 pounds of armed bombs over a series of flaming oil refineries—with a fuel leak and a dead engine.

As if he didn't already know how dire their situation was, climbing the three-rung ladder up to the cockpit confirmed his fears. Half of the gauges in the instrument panel were dead, nearly every red warning light installed was aglow, and the engine controls confirmed what he already knew about the number two engine–it had been euthanized by the pilots before it could shake itself off the wing.

"The bombs are stuck in the bay, and we're leaking fuel!" he screamed at the pilot, who he felt he knew in the dream but couldn't identify afterward. The man didn't respond, but he had his hands full of airplane and perhaps couldn't think of much to say at that moment. Looking out through the windshield, which was covered in wet soot and had been cracked by debris exploding from below, he could see nothing ahead over the plane's long nose but blue ocean at some distance. The pilot turned to him and said "We're gonna make it after all, just you wait. Jar of flies got it made now, buddy!"

That last comment was the biggest mystery. Was he referring to the crew as a jar of flies, which made no sense at all, or could Paul just have misheard him? The dream ended there, and Paul had just shaken it off as another weird dream, though they were seldom so vivid. He'd been reading the book for a few days and had just finished it, so there was little doubt in his mind he was just living vicariously through the dream. Long and detailed as it was, he didn't see any sense in mentioning it to anyone, except maybe his dad. He wouldn't want it to seem like he still harbored fantasies about flying in the military, much less twenty years before he was even born.

As much as he hated getting up early, Paul loved to fly in the morning, especially on glorious ones like this. The airplane, all covered in dew, looked like a succulent red, white, and blue Bomb Pop just starting to melt in a midsummer sun. He took his sweet time with the cockpit preflight, savoring the sounds his plane made as he slowly, deliberately awakened the gyros, instrument vibrators, cooling fans, and each electrical bus, savoring the intricate, handsome, some might say cramped cockpit he lovingly referred to as his "office." By the time his copilot, Mitch Russett, returned from his exterior inspection, Paul had had several minutes of quality time alone with his plane.

The Brasilia was a handsome design, not quite as long as its ample wingspan, with a high T-tail and a 1,800-horsepower Pratt and Whitney turboprop engine, driving a fat, four-bladed, reversible propeller, on each wing. Capable of going well over three-hundred miles per hour, it was one of the fastest non-jet airplanes in the sky, but not the least bit unforgiving or squirrely, like most pilots would expect of such an overpowered, capable machine. Paul adored it.

Picking up on the churchlike vibe, Russet almost whispered, "It's good outside," as he contorted himself through the tiny cockpit door.

"Matter of fact, this thing's cleaner than a convent - you could eat off the gear legs."

Paul acknowledged with a look over the dirty, scratched, mirrored-brown lenses of his trademark gold Ray-Ban aviators, adding a William Shatner-esque, "That's—not—a good—sign…and I'm not sure I'm comfortable sharing a 'cock-pit' with a guy who just put the words 'convent', 'eat', and 'legs' in a single sentence that wasn't part of a joke."

Paul was a big believer in the axiom that the most reliable aircraft are typically the dirtiest, and vice versa. The good ones don't spend much time in the shop, and all manner of grease streaks, sooty exhaust stains, faded or peeling paint, worn decals, crazed windows, minor fluid leaks, and the like tell a long tale of faithful service.

This particular plane had good reason for being so clean. Its left engine had quietly reached its service life limit and been exchanged six weeks earlier. Then, a chronic problem with the fuel control on the right had developed, leading one hapless crew to a "hot start" two weeks before, which necessitated a thorough inspection of that engine. No damage was found however, and the aircraft had been released for service just the day before. Neither pilot, nor any others outside the airline's maintenance department for that matter, could have known any of this, which was by design. As far as the pilots knew, they were getting into an airplane that had been certified as airworthy by a highly qualified mechanic with his livelihood, if not his life, on the line—nothing more, nothing less.

"Yeah, I know, but hey, what's the worst that could happen?" First Officer Mitch Russett asked glibly as he tossed his flight bag into its place beside his seat and folded his six-foot frame into it, sighing as he surveyed the instrument panel. He didn't look over at his Captain, knowing well there would be no response and that to look for one would show an amateurish amusement with their banter. The really funny guys are the ones that never laugh.

Russett was a newbie as airline pilots go, at only 22 years of age and with scarcely 1,400 total hours in his logbook. But he did understand the complex psychological dance pilots performed together better than most such inexperienced pilots, thanks to the mentorship of his father, a captain for Eastern Airlines.

Russett had flown with Paul Prator for most of the past three months, and the rapport between them could hardly have been better. Spending ten to fourteen hours a day working exclusively with one other individual in a tightly confined place like an airplane cockpit, often without any breaks longer than a few minutes, could be a challenge for even the most flexible and upbeat personalities. The perceived length of a day could vary widely depending on how well each crewmember got along with their partners. Pilots' personalities run the gamut from antisocial intellectuals, known as "slam-clicks" for the only sound ever heard from them on layovers—that of their hotel room doors locking—to the beer-swilling, skirt-chasing fraternity types who could find trouble on a Monday night in BFE. Either of the pilots or the lone flight attendant could end up being anything from a welcome partner in some good-natured hijinks amongst a well-matched crew, to a human buffer between people who'd otherwise have no love lost between them, to a persistent irritant to either or both of the others, making the entire trip drag for everyone, including the passengers.

Paul Prator and Mitch Russett had no need for any interpersonal buffer, which was a good thing, because their flight attendant, an older and well-kept but not particularly attractive woman named Doris, just didn't get it. She took her job far too seriously, perhaps because this was the third "career" of her life, and always seemed a little unsure of herself in her work even though she'd been with the company for two years now, and the Brasilia was the only airplane she'd ever worked.

Boarding and startup were uneventful, and Russett ran briskly through the checklist as Prator taxied to runway 28 left at Port Columbus International. With everything done but to turn on every light on the airplane for takeoff, a few thousand feet remained in their long taxi route. In shameless violation of an oft-ignored regulation against non-essential conversation at "critical" times, Paul picked up the conversation they'd had to pause when Doris showed up in the hotel lobby for their ride to the airport.

"So, what was the deal with Blue Legwarmers last night - did you get anywhere with her?"

"Nah, she wasn't going anywhere with me. I don't know what went wrong; I lied about what I do and everything. She probably just figured I was out of her league." Prator particularly appreciated the droll irony in that. Russett's father had definitely imparted to his son the critical knowledge that being a pilot was no longer a ticket to anything but mistrust from any woman worth having, courtesy of their forebears' burning the glamorous veneer off of the profession with reckless philandering and false modesty about a job they were clearly proud to have.

"At least you got some sleep."

"I can sleep when my dick goes limp."

Paul smiled, looking out his side window, away from Russett, to ensure he had the plane completely stopped behind a 727 ahead of them before pulling up on the parking brake's red-handle. An emergency backup for the normal brake system, it was either on or off; there was no gradual way to apply it, as many less careful captains had learned the embarrassing way.

"Well, maybe when you're flying for them." Paul pointed to the big jet ahead of them. "Chicks dig Ferraris."

"Yeah, that'll be the day."

"Oh, come on. You said your dad flew there, right?"

"Yeah. And they've got a firm 'no-nepotism' policy. I could be the second coming of Chuck Yeager and they'd still toss my app away."

"Well, at least you'll get out of here eventually. Your dad only worked for one airline—that leaves a couple dozen. At least you're not a 'lifer', like me."

Russett had flown with Paul a lot and considered him a mentor, someone he'd probably end up calling later in his career to get a leg up for a better job. There were several reasons a pilot might consider himself doomed to the sometimes angry sub-caste of pilots considered unhirable by the major airlines, and Russett didn't see how any of them applied to Paul Prator.

"Why would you be a lifer?"

"Because I can't squint hard enough to see 20/20."

"Oh. Yeah, they really need to change that. I mean, I know the FAA's the king of ancestor worship, but we haven't had to wear goggles for quite a while now. How close are you?"

Paul didn't answer right away, trying to guess at how much of his dirtiest secret he wanted to spill. He'd only been allowed to fly commercially by virtue of a career-killing waiver the FAA would issue to pilots whose natural vision was worse than 20/200, but fully correctable.

"If I ever lose both contacts, I may never find my spare glasses."

"Oh."

"You know, I wouldn't care if they just said, 'Whoa, you need glasses? That's it, you're done. No 20/20, no flying. Have a nice fucking day.' I could deal with that. I'd just go smuggle cocaine or fly food to Congolese refugees or some shit. But a guy can do exercises and go on a carrot juice diet for a week and whatever else to get through the physical and then show up for his first solo or his first trip wearing glasses and they just say, 'Gee, that came on awfully quick. Be careful out there, 'k Lieutenant?' It's just a total double-standard. Boys' club bullshit."

Paul's face flushed as he finished his tirade. "I've been flying my whole life—I can fly circles around any swingin' cheese dick with 20/20 who just decided he might like to be a pilot after he stumbled into a recruiter's office to ask directions to his Aunt Lucy's. But I'll spend my career here, doing the same fucking thing for ten cents on the dollar, because they're too lazy to cull the pile on something that actually matters.

"I'm sorry, man. I just have a thing about bullshit blanket policies. It doesn't matter if you wear contacts and they know it. They're just using it to weed people out, and I wish they'd look at something else. Like ability, maybe."

Mitch Russett felt terrible for having cast a pall over what had been a great start to their day. He had to say something, and "I'm sorry" wasn't going to cut it.

"You thought at all about getting that surgery or those special contacts that can get you to 20/20 for a few hours or days at a time?"

"Yeah, I looked into orthokeratology, it's called, but my eyes are too fucked-up. The doctor says he'd be surprised if I got to 20/20 at all, and it costs eight hundred per eye, per year. That's a big gamble. And radial keratotomy, the surgery, works in almost all the cases, but it hasn't been around long enough to be considered safe, and they're onto it. Most of the airlines now ask if you've had it done, and if they do any kind of serious physical, they can see the scars. And it's five-thousand per eye. That's an even bigger gamble.

"As bad as flying a turboprop for thirty-grand a year the rest of my life sounds, shelling out serious cash to end up not even able to leave, or going blind and then having them come out with some no-risk, undetectable way to correct vision the next year sounds a hell of a lot worse."

"Yeah."

The 727 taking off ahead of them was breaking ground, a cloud of kerosene soot pouring out behind it.

"You ready?" Paul quickly surveyed the cockpit, his mind comparing the position of every switch, dial and annunciator light to the file photo in his mind labeled "pre-takeoff," as the tower cleared them. Russett did his own last minute "big stuff" check as he acknowledged the clearance and replied, "Hit it."

Paul advanced the throttles as he lined the plane up on the runway centerline and scanned the engine gauges for any abnormal indications as they accelerated. Having seen nothing unusual by the time his copilot called "V1, rotate," indicating they'd reached the speed at which aborting the takeoff was no longer safe, Paul applied, then gently reduced, back pressure to the Brasilia's control yoke. Simultaneously, he pressed the right rudder pedal just enough to counteract the complex set of forces that would otherwise pull the plane's nose to the left as it pitched up and, with the smooth grace of a ballerina, 26,000 pounds of airplane, worth about eight-hundred dollars a pound, was climbing at 2,000 feet per minute and accelerating through one-hundred fifty miles per hour.

Climbing through 1,500 feet in a rare cloudless Ohio sky, they had switched from the tower controller to departure radar control, raised the landing gear and wing flaps, and just reduced power on the engines when there was a muffled "poff," followed immediately by a mumbled, "What the fuck, over?" from the pilots, neither knowing who'd actually said it out loud.

The airplane banked slightly and yawed hard to the left; Prator countered, and looked at the engine gauges, which were showing textbook failure indications. The autofeather system automatically aligned the stricken engine's propeller blades with the slipstream, eliminating the biggest source of aerodynamic drag, and both men heard a tiny voice in his head say, "Cool - a real engine failure - I get one!" Outright failure of a turbine aircraft engine would occur only once in hundreds of thousands of hours; many pilots could retire having never seen it happen. It was, for young pilots like them, a revered badge of proven competence to successfully handle one, though none would tempt Fate by actually wishing for it.

Designed to be safe after any statistically possible malfunction, an airliner experiencing a simple engine failure was not, by itself, considered an emergency. The standard drill was to run a checklist or two to close fuel, hydraulic, and electrical connections with the affected engine, taking note of lost redundancies, and land as soon as possible with emergency vehicles standing by, just in case something else went wrong.

But as Prator trimmed the controls to make the plane fly straight on one engine, something else did.

A loud synthetic bell sounded in the cockpit, along with a calm but insistent female voice saying, "ENGINE FIRE." With little thought and even less discussion, Mitch silenced the warning and used a single word, "verify," to get Paul's concurrence in selecting the correct, illuminated one of the plane's two "fire handles" sticking out from the center of the instrument panel. Pulling it shut off the engine's fuel and hydraulic supplies and generator if they weren't already isolated and armed two fire extinguishers for discharge into the engine.

Now the little voices inside the pilots' heads that had said "cool" about the engine failure were nowhere to be heard, having been replaced by hysterical ones screaming, "FIRE? HOLY SHIT, MAN! NOT COOL!"

A seal for one of the engine's main bearings had blown, starving it of oil and causing the smallest of the engine's three concentric rotors, spinning at well over 30,000 RPM, to literally weld itself to a halt, igniting an inferno in the engine's core. In the seconds it took the autofeather computer to do its job and for the pilots it was coddling to get the most basic awareness of what was happening, the engine was destroyed and a two-hundred mile-per-hour wind was force-feeding the fire.

In the cabin, twenty-two passengers sat transfixed in fear as they watched the engine disintegrate from the inside out. Flames and smoke trailed as far back as any of them could see, with molten engine dripping from the massive tailpipe at the wing's trailing edge. One of the passengers, a pilot for another airline on his way to work, got out of his seat and moved all around the cabin trying to get a read on the situation, stressing his fellow passengers all the more.

Doris remained in her jumpseat at the front of the cabin, trying hard to appear composed with all eyes scrutinizing her expression as she reviewed her emergency evacuation drill, praying she'd live to use it.

After seeing the fire continue unabated for what seemed like minutes, Doris couldn't keep quiet any longer. She picked up the interphone to call "the boys."

"You guys know about the fire, right?"

In the cockpit, the "boys" knew, indeed. By the time she called, they'd already performed the immediate action items they had to have memorized for an engine fire in flight, and were in the middle of a 30 second waiting period after "blowing" the first fire extinguisher into the engine. If the warning remained after that, they would turn the fire handle the other way, discharging the other extinguisher. The "engine fire in flight" checklist ended there, Mitch advised Paul, and the two looked at each other. They'd both trained for this situation in the simulator dozens of times, and in each case the first bottle put the fire out.

Paul couldn't help but recall a sick joke his dad once told him. They'd been discussing emergency procedures, specifically engine failure in a single-engine airplane at night. Justin said, "About all you can do is trim for best glide speed, head for the darkest patch of ground you can reach, and try like hell to get the engine running again. When you think you're getting close to the ground, you turn your landing light on. If you don't like what you see, turn it off."

The thirty seconds seemed like an hour, but that glowing-red fire handle didn't so much as flicker.

Russett asked, "You ready?"

"Do it."

Mitch twisted the handle the other direction, and watched with some relief as the indicator for the second bottle's discharge "squib" lit up. They'd turned back to the east by this time and were pointed directly at Rickenbacker Air Force Base, just south of Columbus, just about eight miles ahead.

If that light doesn't go out pretty quick, but the light flickered once and went out before Paul could finish the thought.

"Call Doris and make sure the detectors didn't just burn away."

Mitch already had the interphone in hand.

"Doris, we don't show any fire indications up here anymore. What do you see?"

"Um, there's a lot of smoke still coming out of the engine, but I don't see any more fire. Are we going to be ok? I mean…"

"We're ok now that the fire's out, but we've got a lot of cleaning up to do up here, so I'm going to go. We'll get back to you in a minute, plan to land back at Columbus in about 10 minutes."

"Well, should I, um…hello?" Doris asked, but realized Mitch had hung up on her. She pretended to talk for another few moments, let out her best fake laugh, then hung up and stood to make a seat belt check in the cabin. The passengers were clearly shaken, and with the fire gone they were now giving her their undivided attention; it made her uncomfortable.

"The pilots said we'll be landing back in Columbus in a few minutes," she repeated as she walked through the ten rows of seats, looking at everyone's seat belt, but not really seeing anything. The pilot who'd been out of his seat said he wanted to talk to the pilots. She told him they were very busy and couldn't even talk to her right then, but she'd see what she could do in a minute.

With the fire warnings stopped, Paul called for the single-engine approach and landing checklist. The third item on that checklist was to consider leaving a backup electric hydraulic pump on to replace the one normally driven by the now deceased engine. At that point, Mitch looked up to the overhead panel for the switch controlling the pump and noticed both hydraulic fluid quantity gauges read zero.

Numerous other relatively low-priority warnings and annunciators were going off in a cascade effect unlike anything either man had ever seen in simulator training, except for some doomsday scenario hatched by a gifted and sadistic instructor during occasional "free time" after a particularly clean checkride. On those occasions, anything and everything was fair game in a macho contest between instructor and pilot, with the instructor playing the part of cruel Fate, trying anything within the realm of possibility to kill the pilots, and the pilots doing anything, orthodox or not, to survive.

"Paul, look here real quick." Mitch was pointing up at the hydraulic panel and tapping on the left system's fluid quantity gauge.

Prator stole a glance. "You think that's real?"

"I don't know. There's still power to the right gauge."

"Yeah."

Paul had noticed the rudder seemed to be moving itself to the left and was impossible to move back to the right. "Rudder's jammed, it feels like."

"Rudder's jammed? What do you mean?" Russett's not long-changed voice cracked, and he swallowed nothing from a mouth gone dry. This was some kind of multiple failure, and now they seemed to have some structural damage too, which was his personal aeronautical "boogieman.". As a kid, he'd read accident reports about planes that had been literally torn apart by thunderstorms, overly aggressive pilot technique, or both, and he had no trouble imagining the terror of riding a fluttering piece of wreckage for some eternal seconds to a sudden and gruesome death.

"It's not moving. I'm pushing as hard as I can to line the nose up, but it's not moving at all."

Mitch Russett noticed the plane was literally flying somewhat sideways through the air. Paul had to hold about twenty degrees of right bank to keep from turning left.

Unable to deflect the plane's rudder to counteract the asymmetric thrust from the good engine, the only other way Paul could keep the plane from rolling over was to reduce power or use the ailerons to bank the plane's wings in the opposite direction, creating an uncomfortable, crooked maneuver called a slip. Already low on airspeed and altitude, reducing power was the last thing Paul wanted to do.

Flying in a slip increased the minimum speed they'd have to keep for the wings to create enough lift and reduced their climb rate, which had been a healthy 1,000 feet per minute just after the engine failed, to an anemic six-hundred feet per minute. Putting the landing gear down would negate most of that, and with no hydraulics they wouldn't be able to raise the gear once they let it fall into landing position. They would have to land with no rudder, wing flaps, nose steering, or brakes—or Mulligans.

"Actually, I don't think the rudder's jammed, or we wouldn't be sitting here talking right now. I think it's just lost pressure and the air load on it's just too strong for me to overcome manually."

Russett nodded.

"What do you think about the brakes?" Paul asked.

"What about them?"

"You think we're going to have any?"

Russett puzzled over the question. It wasn't as easy to answer as it seemed. The Brasilia had hydraulic brakes, like any other large plane, but it had the added redundancy of the parking brake, which could tap pressure stored in a small shock absorber for the hydraulic system called an accumulator to instantly lock the wheels. In training and even in their Quick

Reference Handbook, "QRH," it was made clear that, when all else fails, the accumulator will always work. "You'll stop *right now*, and probably blow the tires; it won't be pretty, but you *will* stop," went the conventional wisdom.

"I'm looking at the 'loss of both hydraulic systems' procedure, and it says that even in the event of a total failure on both systems, the accumulator will retain enough pressure to hit the brakes up to three times, depending on preload."

"But if we don't have any fluid for it to push with…"

"How's it going to work?" Russett shared Paul's concern.

"I don't know. Doesn't sound like it is, does it? Get maintenance on the radio and let's get a ruling here, can we?" Prator's leg was starting to fatigue from pressing on the rudder pedal, so he stopped. Nothing changed.

After a few minutes on the radio with a crisis team hastily convened at company headquarters, the verdict was that the parking brake accumulator would in fact stop them, hard and fast, if they used it. With that or an uncontrolled swerve off the runway after touchdown as the two possible scenarios, Prator picked up the interphone and briefed Doris. He then punched up the P.A. system and addressed their passengers for the first time since before they'd started that sick pup of an engine that had just drizzled Pratt and Whitney over half of Franklin County.

"Folks, we've obviously had a pretty unusual thing happen here this morning. I'm not going to tell you this isn't an emergency, because it is. The situation is that the left engine failed, we had a fire, and it appears now that the fire knocked some other components out, including some or all of our hydraulics. Now, that's not the end of our story, because we have some manual flight controls on this airplane, and I'm not even sure we don't have some residual hydraulic pressure. The reason I'm not sure is that the fire seems to have taken out a good chunk of our lights and gauges up here, but we have to assume the worst-case scenario is valid. We are going to land at Rickenbacker Air Force Base, south of Columbus, because their runway is longer and wider than Port Columbus. I know that isn't the most convenient option for any of you, but it is the safest course of action. I've asked Doris to prepare the cabin for an emergency landing, with the remote possibility of an emergency evacuation. I need for all of you to follow her instructions and mine explicitly, and I have every confidence that what's going to happen is going to be a normal, uneventful landing. If it's not, however, we have to be ready."

Paul kept his microphone keyed for a moment more, wondering if he should say anything else, but decided against it and released it.

"Well, I'm sure that made a big impression back there," Prator said aloud, but mostly to just himself. "So, you ready for the approach?"

"I don't think you're going to like this no-flap approach speed."

"Mitch, I'm a pilot. I don't like anything but money and time off. What's the damage?"

"151."

"Yep. This is going to be interesting."

Their inability to extend the wing flaps meant an increase to their minimum approach speed of over 30 knots, increasing the pressure Prator would have to overcome to use the rudder, the likelihood of a fire-damaged tire blowing out on touchdown, and, obviously, the amount of speed they would have to dissipate before going off the end of the runway if the brakes didn't work as advertised. It also gave him a general idea of where their minimum flying or stall speed might be lurking. It wasn't as far away as he'd hoped.

All of this also meant that, once the landing gear came down, a missed approach, or "go-around" would likely prove fatal. They would have a Hobbson's choice of descending gradually and under control into the ground, impacting at around one-hundred-seventy miles per hour, or attempting to maintain altitude at great risk of losing control and turning into what an old friend of his liked to call a 'smoking hole'.

"I'd like to get about a fifteen-mile final so we've got plenty of time to get the gear down. Sure as shit something in that left wheel well's going to hang up. We may have to get creative. When you go to drop the gear, make sure you do the left one first. Don't drop the others until it's down."

The emergency gear extension controls were on the right side of the cockpit, beneath a panel in the floor under Russett's left leg. There was no way for Paul to help him with the crucial task.

"That's not a problem, man. You take as much time as you need, let's get it right."

Keying his microphone, Paul said, "Columbus Approach, Bluegrass 514's requesting the visual to 21 at Rickenbacker, and we're requesting a fifteen-mile final and all the equipment." "Equipment" was jargon for having fire and rescue vehicles standing by their landing runway. Paul was acutely aware that, from the time Mitch declared their emergency on the radio after the engine failed, every crackpot wanna-be-pilot with a radio scanner and every television station in Ohio was listening to every word he said.

Extending the Brasilia's landing gear without hydraulic pressure was procedurally simple. The copilot, using a tool resembling a straightened tire iron with a flared fitting at one end and a handle at the other, would slip the flared end over each of four metal fittings beneath the emergency landing gear extension access panel. The fittings all normally pointed up and forward at a 45 degree angle, and the tool was used to pry each of them backward roughly 90 degrees. Moving the first fitting would vent all the hydraulic lines to allow the landing gear to fall freely once they were released from the mechanical locks holding them up in their wells. The other three fittings released those locks for the nose, left main, and right main landing gear legs.

"Blue 514, roger, you're cleared for any approach to any runway at Rickenbacker, and they've already rolled the equipment and a chase plane for you," the Columbus Approach controller replied.

Slipping the extension handle over the return line fitting, Mitch said, "OK, just say when."

As his glidepath to the runway approached the normal three degrees, Paul pressed his lips together and, trying to prepare for any number of new crises when the gear came down, reset his grip on the yoke. "Do it. Go."

Russett pulled on the handle, but felt a resistance much stronger than he'd experienced in any simulator session. He released pressure and pulled again, still feeling as if he wasn't really moving anything, but only applying torque.

By this time, they were less than 12 miles from the runway at 3,000 feet, and Paul had been wrestling an airplane that was never intended to fly in this configuration for half an hour. Mitch tried the fitting again, and it felt as if something actually moved this time, but when he released pressure on the handle, it still sprung back to the starting position, which was not as it had been in the simulator. He pulled again and felt only the previous odd resistance.

Having neither seen nor felt anything like a gear leg coming down, Paul impatiently asked his copilot, "What're you doing over there?"

"This thing doesn't feel right."

"What do you mean?" The strain was showing on Prator's face.

"Well, I pull back on the return line thing, but it feels like nothing's moving, except one time, but even then it didn't stay in position once I got it back.

"I don't think it's going to come down."

"Did you follow the procedure?"

"Yes. Exactly. I've done this in the sim, but the fittings always stay in the position you pull them back to, they don't spring back like this."

Prator reduced power to keep from getting too high to land, since none of the landing gear drag had been added yet, and the airplane straightened out somewhat. He looked down at the panel on his copilot's floor then back out the windshield at the ever-closer runway a few times.

"Just try the uplocks and see what happens."

Russett pulled back on the left main's fitting, and felt the same odd torqueing sensation he'd felt with the return. Then he tried the other two uplock releases with similar results. Nothing was happening. The landing gear position indicator, a set of three green and three red lights, was totally dark, indicating gear up and locked, but it also failed to light up when he tested it, so there was no trusting it. Still, there was no different sound, no sensation of any change taking place to the airplane at all. By now they were less than five miles from the field and 1,500 feet from the ground.

"Tower, Blue 514. We're having a gear indication problem. Can you take a look and see if you see our gear down?" Prator asked. The stress in his face was unmistakable, yet he seemed almost resigned to what was now looking like an inevitable gear-up landing, which would likely total the airplane and hurt a few people, not to mention the huge fire hazard.

After a short pause the controller responded "Bluegrass 514, Rickenbacker tower, you appear to have a nose gear down and all others up, but your gear doors are all open. Fly-by is approved. Maybe we can get a better look as you pass."

"Shit. Well, what do you want do now, man?" They were three miles from the runway at 1,000 feet.

"Can we climb at all?"

Prator paused, looked at his airspeed and said, "I think so."

"I say we go around then. We can try a few more things."

"Tower, 514's going to fly by and take you up on that look-see." Prator gingerly added power on the good engine. The airplane swerved drunkenly and began to climb at 300 feet per minute.

As they passed over the airport, the tower controller confirmed his earlier report. All gear doors were open, having no hydraulic pressure to hold them up, and the nose gear was extended. This configuration explained their paltry climb rate, and narrowed their margin above stall speed even more. With the good engine at full power, Prator now had two hands full of airplane.

"What do you want to try?" he asked Russett.

"I think, if I can just get this return line to come back for me one time, I can hold it open with just my hand and then use the handle to pull the uplocks. You think that'll work?"

"Beats the shit out of me. If it doesn't, we're going in like a one-handled wheelbarrow, because I don't know if I can keep this thing upright much longer."

It took another five minutes to reposition themselves, and in the mean time Prator had Russett call their company again and explain the problem in his own words. The mechanic started to respond, but was asked to hand the microphone over to the airline's director of flight training. A former Air Force and major airline pilot who'd come to work as an instructor at BlueSky after his mandatory age-60 retirement as a pilot, he was well respected by BlueSky's pilots but had never faced such an odd, compound emergency.

"Mitch, this is Jim Stevenson. You guys are having a rough day of it up there, aren't you? Listen, you're doing a terrific job. I just want you to check to be sure you're on page 18 of the QRH with the emergency gear extension - *hydraulic* failure checklist, and not the page before that where they put the procedure for an *electric* or gear control failure. If you do that one, you're not going to get your gear down without hydraulics."

"Don't answer that" Paul barked. His stress meter pegged, Paul keyed his mike. "Jim, we're on the right page, we know what we've got up here. The procedure isn't working; the gear's not coming down. I'm pretty sure I'm not buying the line about the parking brake accumulator either. Mitch thinks he's got a way to get some wheels down, and it sounds pretty good to me, but when we land if we don't have nose steering or brakes and either of those left main tires is blown, I don't think we're going to care much. We're almost back on final now, so we've got to go. 514 out." He reached down and turned the number two radio off. The glad-handing about what a great job they were doing had tweaked his last remaining well-frayed nerve, and he wasn't about to let anyone think they'd succeeded in blowing sunshine up his ass right before he got killed.

Lined up twelve miles out, Russett began feeling for a good release on the return lines, and after a dozen or so false pulls, he got one. He reached down with his left hand and grabbed firm hold of the return fitting, then slowly released the pressure he was holding on the handle. It stayed back. Quickly he slipped the handle off of the first fitting and began yanking away at each of the two main gear uplock releases, feeling both resistance and movement, but nothing positive.

The tower had sent up an Air Force trainer to fly chase after their first approach, and it was directly behind and beneath the Brasilia on the right side, watching. Its pilot reported all three landing gear now appeared to be down.

Still not convinced this bad day was over, both men mentally prepared for the collapse of one or more landing gear legs, since the extension procedure had gone so poorly. They knew for the gear to lock down, it had to fall freely, and it was anybody's guess if that had occurred. Landing with a single main gear collapse would be more dangerous than a belly landing. Then there was also the likelihood that the fire had blown one or both of the left main tires, which would also make for a swerve upon landing they'd be helpless to counteract. In any event, the odds looked pretty slim for an uneventful landing, which made Prator feel all the more wise for having chosen to come to Rickenbacker instead of going back to Port Columbus. If they were going to become crash test dummies, it'd be far better to do it at an Air Force base than a major civilian airport with lots of airplanes, buildings—and witnesses—around.

At five-hundred feet, Russett made the standard call out of airspeed and sink rate, both of which were right on the money. Paul was holding about half-power on the good engine in the descent. There was no way the airplane was going to climb in this configuration. The approach had to be right.

Paul's heart was about to beat out of his chest as he gently stopped descending over the runway and kissed the pavement with the main gear. They held. He gently lowered the nose, and it held as well.

The good news was they were down and rolling straight. The bad news was they were doing over one-hundred and fifty miles per hour with no nice way to slow down. Prator tried the normal brakes, just for the sheer hell of it. Nothing.

He said he was going for the parking brake, locked his shoulder harness, counted to three, and pulled. Nothing.

He pulled three more times in quick succession, if for nothing else than to take out some frustration on this pig of an airplane that was trying its damndest to end his career, if not any longer his life.

"I'm going to try some reverse on your side. Hang on," he said, easing the right throttle backward into the reverse thrust range.

Then, giddy with adrenalin, Russett struck the tone of a sportscaster and said something very strange.

"We're going to make it after all, just you wait. Our guy's got it made now, buddy!"

Paul couldn't believe his ears, but he didn't have time to dwell on the déjà vu. He was kicking ass and taking names, and everybody was going to walk away now for sure. Not hurting the Goddamned airplane was icing on the cake though, and the icing always was his favorite part.

The 'whoosh' of the propeller blades going into reverse pitch was unmistakable, as was the yaw the airplane took to the right. Paul quickly went back to idle with the right throttle and shrugged. "Well, we're just along for the ride now."

He tried to steer with the rudder, now that their speed had dissipated enough that he could move it, but it was like trying to steer a car with power steering and a dead engine.

They drifted ever so slightly to the right of centerline as their speed dropped below the sixty knot bottom of the airspeed indicators. Everyone's survival was now assured, but Paul wanted more. He wanted the bitch to stop on the runway.

He shut down the right engine to eliminate what little thrust it made at idle, but the laws of physics were unyielding, and the 12-ton airplane trundled off the paved surface of the runway and about 100 feet into the clearway weeds, where it came to a gentle stop.

When Paul and his crew arrived at the base commander's office thirty minutes later, having used every inch of "his" 12,102-foot runway (and a few dozen feet of his weeds beyond), Paul's first instinct was to call his dad. He was no airline pilot, but he could certainly appreciate the crucible through which Paul and his career had just passed unscathed and would be very proud of him. Even though there was no privacy, and knowing it was strictly forbidden to have any conversation about the incident with anyone before speaking with his company, the FAA, and the NTSB, Paul couldn't resist excusing himself to use the restroom down the hall and picking up the pay phone next to it, "just to let him know I'm ok."

Justin said he was glad, and he'd be going out for dinner but would be back home later to get a full rundown and for Paul to just keep trying if he didn't answer at first.

Paul wondered about what his father said about dinner. *Who's he having dinner with? Dad doesn't "have dinner" with anybody—he's always 'fed up with humanity' by the end of the day and likes to be alone. That's when he used to do his drinking. What if it's a woman? Jeez, he's not dating, is he? Am I ready to have a stepmom?*

"What's the occasion, you got a hot date or something?"

Please, God, don't say "Well, as a matter of fact,"

"Are you kidding? No, it's, well, I'll tell you about it later. You better get back to your deal there, Captain." Paul reveled in the pride in his dad's voice.

Just then, the base commander's secretary came out of the office and said Paul's Chief Pilot was on the phone for him.

"Captain Prator, sir, they need to speak with you right away. I'll tell them you're in the restroom, but you should hurry."

Nice old doll – she runs interference pretty well. Wonder why. Paul mused, pretending he already knew some of the stupid things the General had her do to cover for him.

His father had always told Paul he'd likely make more money than a military pilot and get to fly a lot more, especially as he got older, since the military tends to put pilots past their prime behind desks to set up hoops for the younger, less experienced ones to jump through. Now, looking through the open doorway into the General's office, he imagined how frustrated he would be in that position. Back when he was a kid, he'd have gladly signed on for his entire career, just to be able to look into the mirror and see a superhero in a flight suit and one of those cool helmets with the tinted visors standing utterly invincible in his place, but that time had clearly passed from the General's life, if not yet altogether from Paul's.

Now, eyeing the General sitting at his desk like some...*drone,* for the first time, he didn't have to remind himself; his dad had been right.

"Yeah, they're looking for me right now—got to find some way to pin it on the pilots, right? Good luck's all I can say—we kicked ass."

"Good job, Paul. I'm so proud of you! Don't let them get to you now; you know you did right."

"Thanks, Dad, I'll talk at you later." Paul hung up the phone, feeling smug but a little nervous, as if he'd just taken a test and had no difficulty finishing it ahead of everyone else in class. Could they have done anything wrong up there? The only thing he could imagine them throwing at him was the length of time they spent flying around on one engine, but he really didn't see what choice they'd had. If he'd gotten into a big hurry and landed unprepared, there might be nothing left now but some recyclable aluminum and a big patch of scorched grass out there.

"Looks like you did a decent job with a bitch of a situation, Captain," the General said as Paul returned to the office. "I'd like to see more pilots like you in the Air Force. May I ask if you've ever considered it?" His handshake was firm, and there was genuine respect in his face.

Paul cleared his throat to say, "Well, yes, General, I did 'consider' it. I 'considered' it for a lot of years, actually. Unfortunately, I also had to 'consider' selling my soul to the devil to give me 20/20 vision long enough to get through training at Lackland, which I hear is all the further you need to get without corrective lenses."

There was nothing subtle about Paul's words, but had there been any, his expression would have cleared up any confusion about his message.

"Well, you could come in as a back-seater and probably get a transfer later, if you did well." Then, striking a conspiratorial expression, he added, "I could help you."

"I've heard of that, yes sir. I just don't know how many years of my life I'm willing to throw away just for a chance to do something I already know I'm better at than a guy whose corneas are his best qualifications."

The General pursed his lips and nodded. "They say 'Life's a bitch,' Captain, but that's not entirely true. It's just one long hand of poker. Some of us get dealt good cards, but some of us have to bluff. Time is our chips, and everybody buys in with the same amount, so if you put enough in, sometimes you can win with a hand that's nothing. You follow me?"

The General took a business card from the brass holder on his desk and handed it to Paul.

"Yes, sir, I think I do. I'll mull it over." The General's stature in his blue uniform was almost overwhelming to Paul, and he felt an urge to salute the man but managed to satisfy it by just bowing his head slightly as he turned to leave, before he made a total ass of himself.

The Air Force had done Paul and BlueSky a huge favor by whisking them to Headquarters after the passengers had deplaned. They hadn't seen so much as a microphone yet, despite the fact that news of the bloodless and anticlimactic "accident" had already pre-empted the soaps on all three network affiliates in Columbus, Cleveland, and Cincinnati.

After the initial slew of questions, phone calls, and paperwork, they were free. BlueSky 514's crew was placed on administrative leave and would be taken to a hotel to rest and recuperate before deadheading back to Indianapolis for a debriefing the next day.

Their layover hotel was unable to accommodate any more than the two crews already scheduled to spend the night there, so the company arranged accommodations at the upscale Hilton Downtown, a welcome change. An orderly took them there in an Air Force staff car, and they were able to get checked in and to their rooms without any contact with the press.

"You guys going to come downstairs and let your grateful Captain buy you some brewskis, or you think we've had enough excitement for one day," Paul asked as they approached the hotel. He was hoping, as was Mitch, that Doris would take the graceful exit offered her, stay in her room and bathe or something like that, and let the two guys get some quality "debrief" time at the bar.

To their surprise, Doris piped right up with a "Hell, yes. It's fucking Miller time!" She realized how unlike her that sounded and looked around as if taking note of the time and place she'd finally been freed. Mitch, sitting opposite Paul with Doris between them, rolled his eyes discreetly, but Paul couldn't contain a chuckle. With that, all the stress of the day suddenly broke like a landslide, and the trio finally had their first real laugh of the day.

5

Downtown Columbus was all but deserted when Paul Prator and his crew met at 7 p.m., so they decided just to go to the hotel's faux Irish pub. As promised, Paul put the whole crew on his tab, and they ate dinner and rehashed the whole day for a good couple of hours.

Having had a few more than her usual glass of wine, Doris got "a little tipsy" and said she wanted to go on up to bed. Ever the gentleman, Paul had Mitch hold their table and escorted her as she zigzagged her way to her room, slurring through what few would recognize as Gloria Gaynor's "I Will Survive."

He then started back to the pub but stopped by his own room first to call his dad, just in case—or perhaps to ensure—his big night ended early. An answering machine, something his father detested and swore he'd never buy, picked up the call. Paul left a message for "whoever's taken my father and replaced him with someone who'd use an 'ass-ream machine'."

When Paul returned to the pub, a group of nearly a dozen people were sitting around a larger table where only a few had been before, and Paul noticed one of them in particular. Tall and athletic, but still very feminine, with shoulder-length dark hair and eyes the brooding gray-green of a summer squall line rolling across the plains, her youthful beauty stood out from the party of mostly older people.

"What's going on over there?" Paul asked Mitch when he returned.

"I don't know, but they're having a good time, seems like."

Paul watched the young woman for a long moment then turned to order another beer from their waitress.

"Did I tell you about the dream I had last night? Nightmare, really." He laughed a little, finished his beer and said, "Maybe somebody was trying to tell me something."

"No, you didn't mention it. Let me guess—you were at work, and you had this hellacious fire on number one, and the bitch just would…not…go…out."

Paul looked up at the ceiling, giddy, and shook his head, "No, no, no, no.…"

He stole a glance at the girl, headed for the ladies' restroom in the back of the pub. "It was actually worse, but along the same lines, if you'd believe that. I've been reading a book about this bomber mission in World War Two, and I guess I've been getting a little too into it.

She was going into the restroom. "I was in one of the bombers in the book, but not flying it. I was a gunner in the back, the "waist gunner," they called it. And we were in the middle of this nasty raid these guys did, down on the deck right over the target, and all hell was breaking loose. We had an engine out, a fuel leak, we were getting the shit kicked out of us by anti-aircraft, and then to top it all off, the bombs wouldn't release."

"Wait, I think I've heard this one. You're about to say, 'So there I was, flat on my back," Russett quipped, but Paul wasn't indulging him this time.

I should be there when she comes out, he thought. "I've got to take a leak. Be right back."

Paul headed for the restrooms, hoping to God he'd get there just as she was coming out so he could get in her way; get a whiff of her perfume, perhaps a word with her. He walked fast at first but then slowed his pace noticeably as he closed the distance to the restrooms until, when he was less than ten steps away and there was still no sign of her, he had to stop and feign interest in the dart board on the back wall.

"Come on, sweetie. Come on out and talk to Paulie," he mumbled half-aloud. The dartboard was out of order, according to a sign, and there wasn't a soul around to pretend to talk with while he waited. He did have to urinate, but the ladies' room door was opening and there she was, taller than she'd seemed from a distance, and even prettier. Those eyes, barely any makeup, and lustrous chestnut brown hair, thin and not at all busty, all the ways Paul's taste ran. Sure, he'd had a hell of a day and was more than a little drunk, but *Jesus.* He was literally dumbstruck.

"You the dartboard mechanic?" she animated somehow before his eyes.

"Uh, yeah, yeah," he play-acted, "this one here's got, uh, big problems. Yep. You guys won't be playing on this one anytime soon. *I'm so screwed.*

"Seems like you're having a pretty good time without it, though. You guys all work together or something?" *Nice save.*

Across the Mississippi and several state lines in Wichita, Justin Prator and a petite but stately old woman had arrived separately at the Scotch & Sirloin on East Kellogg Avenue, just a mile or so away from Justin's house near Cessna's headquarters.

She'd finally reached him on the phone a week before, just after Paul's visit. After making sure it was really him, she began the conversation bluntly, saying "Justin, I don't want you to think this is someone's idea of a joke, so I'm going to get right to it. I'm the woman who gave birth to you and then gave you up for adoption. I'm your real Mum."

Justin had been home for a few hours, eaten his dinner, and was just getting into a particularly good episode of "Miami Vice" when she called. Thinking it was probably Paul, his only frequent caller, he answered the phone in the overtly presumptuous "what must I do for you now" voice he liked to use to tease his son when they'd recently spoken and he wasn't yet craving his company.

When the voice on the other end was female, his mind immediately went into defense mode, since the only women that ever called were his secretary, reminding him of something he'd forgotten, or his daughter Sarah, asking for money.

That it could have been a friendly call from a prospective romantic interest didn't cross his mind for a second, and having someone with a soft, pretty English accent call just to say "Hi, Justin. I'm your real Mum," wasn't exactly something he had any turn-key plans for handling, either. He stood there in silence, holding the phone and staring, blind, at his dog apathetically licking himself in his spot on the sofa, and tried to figure out what he should feel.

The woman on the phone waited.

"Wow. Well, that is quite a little bomb you dropped on me there, um, what did you say your name was?" Calling a stranger "Mom," or "Mum," was out of the question.

"Oh dear, where are my manners? Melody. Melody Thompson was my name when I, when you were, well, oh my, this is positively dreadful, isn't it? I'm so sorry. I thought I had rehearsed at least the first minute or two of this conversation much better."

"No, no, please. I don't know what this is, but nothing like "dreadful" is even close to what I'd call it, ma'am. I mean," he started to inhale deeply, then caught himself and tried to feign nonchalance as he, for the first time in his life, addressed someone as, "Mom."

Suddenly he realized that this could all still be some smart-ass's idea of a joke, and he felt foolish for calling her that."You're sure about this, what you're telling me and everything?"

"Yes, Justin, I'm quite certain. It's taken me quite a bit of research and no small expense to be sure, but I have all the documentation now, and it's rather incontrovertible, I must say."

So much for the joke idea, he thought. *Who says 'incontrovertible'?*

"Where are you? Where do you live?"

"I'm home at the moment, in Austin. Austin, Texas."

Were there any other Austins?

"Well, that explains the accent, I guess." They both laughed, a little more than his quip warranted, trying to be nice to each other.

"Justin, I'm calling because I'd like to meet, I mean, see you, again. You can say 'no' or take some time to mull it over, and I promise I won't be hurt. I know your head must just be swimming at the moment."

Actually, she has no idea, he thought, but Justin was instantly taken with the sweet lilt in her voice. He would wonder later if perhaps the sound of a mother's voice can't help but sound sweet and trustworthy to the child, even if it's never been heard before. He didn't know how, but he somehow felt as if he had missed her all those years, and he couldn't wait to see her again.

She arrived slightly ahead of him and recognized him the moment he walked through the door and approached the hostess' station near the cash register. Their eyes met immediately, and he figured the odds of two old women coming to this place alone for dinner on a weeknight had to be astronomical.

"Might you be Mr. Prator?" she asked, and her accent brought to Justin's face the same mischievous, bemused smile she remembered from the young man in an old photograph she carried. She hadn't seen it except in her mind for forty years, and she'd forgotten what it did to her insides.

Back in Columbus, Paul couldn't believe he was actually talking to this girl, or more like it, that she was actually talking to him.

"Well, I feel like I work against them a lot more than I do with them. *That*," she said with sincere pride and feigned disgust, "is my family."

"Oh. You guys having a reunion or something?" The televisions mounted above each end of the bar, tuned to MTV and, as if by law, turned up too loud, barked the "Hi there!" at the beginning of Peter Gabriel's "Big Time," but only the girl looked up.

Paul had felt the crowd at her table watching him, and all conversation there had stopped, perhaps to grade his performance with her. Following his gaze, she noticed her family watching her; her younger brother Marty puffing out his right cheek, miming fellatio.

Sick fuck, she thought, grimacing at him with seething eyes.

"I love this song, but the video's just too weird," she said, looking back up at the TV, hoping he'd mimic her and somehow not see her brother. "Yeah, we do this every year, usually at somebody's house, but there's some babies this year, so we decided to meet in the middle to give everybody more space, which is fine by me."

"Babies like 'Pampers' or babies like 'whiners'?"

"Both, really," she chuckled, "but I meant like Pampers. My sister-in-law and my cousin both had babies this past year."

"So, does that make you one of the whiners?"

"What, about the babies? Oh, no, I love kids. I mean they're not for me, not yet, but, they're fun. I'm still waiting for my boyfriend to come to his senses and ask me to marry him, but I think he's a little threatened."

Ahh, the boyfriend reference, he thought, *right on time. Blow-off play number 4, textbook performance. I give her an 8.5 out of 10.*

She'd seen the look on his face before, and decided to toy with him a little. "Of course, I could always meet someone a little more secure and ditch him. Serve him right," she said with a coy smile that seemed to mock space and stop time. No doubt about it—head over heels would be a step back. He was *gone.*

"They're going to send my troglodyte brother over here to get me if I don't get back, but it's nice to meet you, Mr. Dartboard Game Repairman." Raising an eyebrow over a wry smile, she added, "Keep up the good work."

Glancing at the game, he offered his hand. "Paul Prator. I know absolutely nothing about dartboards. But I'd love to maybe play some foosball later, if you're going to be around."

"Christina, or Christy, if you like that better, but not Chris. Chris has smaller tits than I do and he belches the national anthem after his fifth beer—every fifth beer," she said, offering her hand, which he noticed had short but well-kept fingernails and a grip that just didn't want to hurt him. "Maybe we can get a game going with your friend and one of my entourage, if you don't mind really gross firemen."

"Well, as long as they don't try to..." Paul started, but she was already walking away. She gave a quick look back when she was about halfway back to her table, but he didn't see it, having turned to finally go to the men's room before he pissed his pants. Along the way, it dawned on him that she'd noticed Russett, which meant she'd been watching them, or him, at least a little. He wondered if it was his better-looking partner in crime she was after, but he knew Russett wouldn't intentionally cock-block him with a girl he really liked.

As he urinated, he felt a familiar dizziness. He'd be full-on drunk soon. "That would explain such reckless behavior!" he pretended to scold himself aloud. "Get to meet the family before you even go out with the girl this time, eh, Paul? Gooood plan."

Paul habitually talked to himself, sometimes pretending to talk to the toilet, whenever he got drunk and no one else was in a restroom he was using.

"Druuunk, druuunk, drunk, drunk, drunk, drunk, drunk...Jesus, I hope this girl's just half as hot as I think she is now when I get these beer goggles off..."

Back at his table, Paul brought Mitch up to speed on his brief chat with Christy.

"Man, you couldn't get me to hit on some chick with her family right there watching like that. You've got balls of steel."

"Balls of barley's what I've got. Besides, I didn't know what I was doing until I was already doing it. She said she might be into a game of foosball later - you up for that at all? Maybe she's got a cute cousin…"

"All I see over there with her are oldies, fuglies, and old fuglies. Plus, I'm getting a little tired actually. I think the day's festivities might finally be taking their toll, man. I could go to sleep right here." Paul struck an expression of overacted utter despair. "But, I guess I could, under professional duress, give my poor Captain who's buying my beer, an assist, just in case it might help his loser ass get laid."

Paul perked up. "That's the spirit. Anybody asks me, I say you're ready to upgrade."

"Yeah, sure. Ready, willing, and able, but notice how 'senior' isn't in that list? So what about this nightmare you had? I'm curious how you got out of it, or if you just woke up drenched in sweat. And I can't believe I just painted that mental picture."

"Ah, it's just a dream. Hell, I can't even remember much of it anymore. I know it was just because of that book I'm reading. Pretty amazing what the guys on that mission did though. Talk about balls. A bunch of guys our age, fresh out of college, flying friggin' B-24s from Libya across the Mediterranean, then dropping down on the deck for a couple *hundred* miles and trying to find this town full of oil refineries Hitler needed to fight the war: *Ploesti*." Without a hint of self-consciousness, he pronounced it the Rumanian way, "plo-YESHT-e," and his gaze went nowhere for a second.

"Some of the planes that made it back had fucking corn stalks caught in their bomb bay doors. That's *low*—and those things weren't exactly easy to fly, either. Overloaded four-engine bombers? Probably flew like shit-on-a-stick.

"The whole thing ended up pretty much a disaster, because they lost their lead plane, with their lead navigator, to a mechanical before they ever saw European soil, and the next guy in line made some big mistakes. That, and they had some old planes and some brand-new ones, so the formations got strung out and separated, and by the time they arrived at the IP, nobody knew where anybody else was anymore, and some of the navigators turned at the wrong IP in the first place so they ended up approaching the target from two different directions. It looked to the Germans like this incredibly well-planned, Swiss-watch coordinated attack, but in reality…"

Paul had gotten utterly lost in his own story and, catching his mouth running like a little boy's after an airshow, decided he'd best summarize and shut it.

"…it was total clusterfuck."

"Paul?"

"What?"

"What's an 'IP'?" Mitch had been politely listening, but took his chance to bring the unsolicited debriefing to an end by asking the question in a Ben Stein monotone, hoping Paul would take the hint.

"Oh, sorry. Stands for 'initial point'. It's where the bombers commenced their target runs." Paul took a gulp of beer, and Mitch saw he was gathering his thoughts to begin anew. So much for hints. He had to be stopped.

"You're really into this stuff, aren't you? World War Two, I mean. You've talked about it before."

"I always have been, I guess. My dad learned to fly when I was a little kid, but I was way into it even before then. We lived in Wichita for a while, so there was always a lot of aviation stuff around, but for some reason World War Two planes just grabbed my attention. It's like," Paul stared at the saliva smear on the rim of his Guinness glass and said, almost to himself, "It's when aviation saved the world."

Justin and his mother were on their best behavior as they tried to catch up on the past forty years of their lives. Like two Pentagon supercomputers communicating with an eighties-era modem, both had so much to share, but they could only talk, and listen, so fast.

After a few minutes of small talk, Justin began the real conversation, asking his mum to explain her accent.

"I was raised in a little town about 85 miles northeast of London. When you came along, I knew there was no way my life would ever be the same if I stayed; you must realize that a woman becoming pregnant out of wedlock was an absolute scandal in those days, at least in the Kingdom. My family would have been outraged, justifiably. My whole life was upended at once.

"When your father," she started to well up ever so briefly, but stopped it. "When I lost him, I had no one to turn to, no one who would accept and understand. So, I borrowed money from an Uncle I knew would be more happy to see me leave than to stay and embarrass the family. He suspected what was afoot and asked me no questions. I came to the United States, and I've been here ever since. It seems the accent is still hoping I'll return home someday, but most people here don't seem to mind. If anything, it gives them the misinformed impression that I'm the product of some prestigious breeding. But very little of my life afterward has any bearing whatsoever on you. I didn't go looking for you to tell you about me. I want to know about my son. Please. So, do you fly for Cessna then? Are you a test pilot for them, or a delivery coordinator, or something like that?"

"No—nothing so interesting, unfortunately. I'm in charge of a flight school program they began a few years ago hoping to increase the number of people learning to fly and, in turn, the number of planes they'd sell. It's mostly a desk job, but it's more stable than any flying job I ever had. The pay and benefits are good, and I suppose I'm helping other people find the joy I did in flying, in a small way." His initial contented, if not quite proud, expression faded and he poked at the ice in his drink as the voice in his head added, *and you were a little too drunk a little too often to be anybody's pilot.*

Even drunk, Paul Prator's heart climbed quickly, effortlessly into his throat when he saw Christina get up and start toward him. She seemed even prettier somehow, and he resolved silently to himself not to overdo it, but not to let her get away either.

"None of my deadbeat family says they want to play, but I'm getting no end of crap from them for talking to you. The more I try to get them to shut up, the longer they'll go on, so what do you say we just go play a game or two and see if they'll get bored enough to let it go?"

"Sounds fine to me—anything to piss your family off." That gaff got out ahead of him, and he feared she'd take it badly, but the look of conspiracy on her face put him instantly at ease.

Paul looked vaguely at Mitch, going through the perfunctory, uniquely male ritual of pretending to be torn about abandoning a friend in favor of a female.

Unlike the females' counterpart, the concern a man exhibits in such cases is always feigned, understood to be, and the deceit is always forgiven in advance; a mini-drama staged entirely for the benefit of the female audience, who is to be moved by the actor's concern for his pitiful friend, and thus more amenable to the idea of having his hand going down her pants.

With any luck, the reward for the abandoned friend is that occasionally another female notices and takes pity, and with a lot of luck, the duo can pull off a "double-header." With no hope of such a glorious outcome that night, Mitch still played his part to a tee.

"Uh, I don't know man, I'm pretty thrashed myself. I was just thinking how good that bed's going to feel, you know?"

"That's cool, I hear you. Go get some sleep," Paul said, almost unable to conceal a smile at getting his conquest all to himself without even having to work for it. He was definitely going to put in a good word for Mitch Russett with their Chief Pilot when they got back.

"I'll buy the first game, loser buys the next two, worst two out of three buys a round," Paul offered. He was fishing alright, but in a cute, dignified way.

"Are you sure you can afford all that? I don't want to hear any crying about having to buy drinks after I skunk you," she said as she turned to lead the way. This girl had attitude—and a great ass. No one ever talked to him on his level right off like that. *Ass and attitude, she's got 'assitude,'* he mused.

"You skunk me and I'll buy your whole fam damily a round."

She wheeled around on him, with a look of utter astonishment. "My whole fam damily, huh?" She was putting on a good show of disgust, which wasn't altogether insincere.

"What?"

"You said you'd buy a round for my whole fam damily..."

"I did? Oops. I meant your whole fang damily. Sorry." *Drunk, yes, but a cute drunk, right?*

"Oh, my God. Now I know I'm going to kick your butt."

"Cut me some slack, I've had kind of a rough day," he said while trying to nonchalantly rise to the oddly formidable challenge of getting two quarters into the foosball table's coin slots.

"Oh, yeah? So what exactly do you do anyway, if you don't really repair dartboards?"

"Nothing quite so important, really. I'm a pilot."

"You mean, like, airplanes?" She burst out laughing at what she'd call the 'bimbosity' of her question, covering her mouth and closing her eyes as she hung and shook her head. After a moment, she looked back at him, uncovered her mouth and held up the hand that had been covering it, saying, "Ok, now you're probably wondering if I'm drunk—or secretly blonde!"

"I can think of one way to prove that one," he mumbled with a ventriloquist's smirk.

"No, that's a fair question, really. There's balloon pilots, helicopter pilots, even guys who drive boats call themselves pilots, but we fight that when we can. You ready?"

She nodded, and Paul dropped the ball through the chute in the middle of the table.

"So, who do you fly for? Are you one of those guys that fly executives around in Learjets, or in the Air

Force, or what?" Christy had the ball well into his side of the table, and was maneuvering for a shot.

"I fly for a commuter airline, you might have heard of them, BlueSky Airlines." Paul's right hand was making his goalkeeper pace in his box, his defense still in their positions under his left, awaiting a chance to steal the ball.

"I've heard of them, but I thought you had to be older to do that, I mean, no offense or anything, but how did you get that job at your age, or are you way older than you look?" She flicked her left hand, and one of her attack figures slammed the ball to Paul's goal, but it glanced off the side of his goalkeeper's foot.

"How old do I look?" His defense passed to his midfield.

"I'm not answering that." She smiled, coy again. "But am I wrong about thinking you're young for an airline pilot?" Christy's own midfield tipped Paul's wayward pass, and she passed it to her attack.

"No, I am young, but I've had a few breaks, and I knew what I wanted to do since I was a little kid." Paul's defense and goalkeeper were getting fidgety as Christy's attack maneuvered for another shot.

"Were you ever in the Air Force, or Navy or something, because, I mean, well there I go again."

She started to lose the ball again, realized it, and fired off a quick and dirty kick that her relatives even heard hit the back of the goal box. She'd taken an early lead.

"You don't have to join the military to become a pilot, if that's what you're wondering."

She could have been stone deaf and still known—she'd hit a nerve.

"I would have loved to, but I started wearing glasses in 4th grade, so obviously I could never handle an F-14." He pointed at his eyes, "Contacts. I'm 'living a lie'." Sarcasm ran like blood down his chin.

"So I did the next best thing, and now I'm kind of glad I did, because I'll get hired at a big airline like Universal years earlier this way and be a captain by the time they can even hire a guy my age who's in the military now. Then we'll see who can fly and who can't.

He finally noticed how Christy was hunkered down, waiting for the storm to pass.

"I'm 23, by the way."

Paul wasn't a habitual liar, and it surprised him that he was would stoop to exaggerating his dim career prospects to her, just to help his case. What the hell was he so ashamed of? He'd just saved almost two dozen lives in his little "puddlejumper."

"Wow. Well, that's cool. But, you might want to stop talking so much and concentrate on your game, if you don't mind my saying so."

"Really? Ok, why don't you serve, smart-ass, and tell me your life story while I tie this thing up, unless you don't think you'll have time."

She held the ball up before serving it, chiding him, "Oh, I think I'll have pllllenty of time."

Paul made a face he usually reserved for his sister and hadn't used since junior high.

"Well, I'm a firefighter, like them. Only, hopefully, not *much* like them." Christina dropped the ball into the chute, and fought to gain control of it, but it angled quickly to Paul's midfield, and he swung hard for a goal immediately but was stopped by one of Christy's unattended defense.

"I tooold you," she almost sang. Paul thought he'd never heard those three words sound so damned good.

"So, you're a pilot. I always wondered how people get started doing that." Christy dribbled the ball between two of her defense, waiting for Paul to start talking again.

"I hear that a lot. In my case, I think I was just made for it. Except for the nearsightedness, anyway. That was a pretty short life story, by the way. It's almost as if you need me to do all the talking to score on me."

Christy passed the ball straight from her defense to her attack, saying nothing in response.

"I don't remember ever not loving airplanes, which is what my dad says, too. I think it's just in our blood."

"Ok, so your dad got you into it then. Is he an airline pilot or something?" Christy dribbled as he spoke then, as she began to answer, spun her attack handle hard, sending the ball past Paul's goalie and hard into the wooden chute behind it with a "crack." So much for her needing him to talk.

"Something," Paul resolved with a sigh and straightened himself as he fished in the chute for the ball. "I'm worthless at this game, in case you haven't figured that out."

"I'm getting that picture. And I'm glad to see your attitude coming around a little bit. You give up or what?"

Yeah, I give up. You get to do whatever you want to me.

"I don't know. What if I do? I hate to make you go back and face your family, the gross firemen, so soon."

"We could just talk for a while if you want. I won't even tell anyone I kicked your ass at foosball." She winked playfully at him.

"Wow. Now that's what I call a friend. Sounds like an offer I can't refuse. Where do you want to go?"

"I'll make a feint for the ladies' room, and you go over and sit down at the table behind you to wait for me. When I get out, I'll come sit down with you and 'voila,' we're 'just talking'."

"Damn, you're good. You must have to do this kind of thing a lot—are they that bad to deal with? Your family, I mean."

"Don't even get me started. You wouldn't believe it. OK, well, game over and now 'I have to go to the ladies room,' ok?"

"Didn't you just go a little while ago?" He winked back. "I mean, um, yeah, sure. I'll just wait over here for you."

While Christy was in the restroom, Paul studied her family acutely out of the corner of his eye while staring at the television. MTV was now playing Bruce Springsteen's "Dancing in the Dark," with a beautiful, barely driving-age Courteney Cox playing a star-struck groupie in the front row of a concert. Christina was prettier.

An older man at Christy's family's table was talking, much too quietly to be heard from the distance, but Paul got the feeling that not only was the man Christina's father, but that Paul himself was the subject of the conversation, since every few seconds one of the other people at the table would look his direction, study him for a second, then return their focus back to the man talking.

It was her father, but in actuality the subject was a woman found unconscious from a heroine overdose in her burning apartment the previous week, whom one of the firefighters in his command remembered having rescued under similar circumstances once before.

His insecurities running away with him, Paul was almost angry enough to walk away by the time Christina came out of the bathroom to get to know this cute, smart-assed pilot guy better.

"So exactly who is it over there, I mean, is that your dad or somebody, or more distant relatives, or what?"

"The old guy's my dad, Doug, the woman next to him's Alice, my mom, and then there's my older brother Larry and his wife Paige, and my younger brother Mick, who's totally gross most of the time. By him's my Aunt Emily, 'Auntie Em'—cute, huh—and her husband Jake. The rest of them are cousins and a couple of friends that are like family to us. Firefighters are a pretty tight-knit group.

"Kind of figures they would be. Where, which city?"

"Cleveland. Ever been there?"

"Yeah, sure, I've been to Cleveland. I went to high school in Marion and college here at OSU. I even landed there a few times when I was instructing. Seems like a nice town, although I never left the airport." Paul realized how stupid that sounded. Christina didn't.

"It's ok. Not big enough to be crazy, but big enough to be fun. My family's been there since the 1940's, when my grandparents came."

"What, like from overseas or something—immigrants?"

"Not quite," she said sharply. "Kansas. It's a big, long Romeo and Juliet type thing, only not as dramatic, and with a way happier ending."

"Well, if you're here, it's obviously better than Romeo and Juliet."

"This is true. So, what about you? You lived in Ohio your whole life?

"Wait a second. Am I crazy, or is firefighting about as male-dominated as flying? Is it some kind of family tradition, like you couldn't have even tried to do anything else?"

"Try the opposite. I'm the only woman in the CFD, thanks to my grandpa, the Chief, and he wouldn't even have me there if he had his way."

"I always thought the word 'Chief' implied some pretty absolute authority. How'd you get on then?"

"Well, you're not the first one that's had to fight an established system of bullshit, you know.

"I grew up in the shadow of the men in my family, who, in turn, grew up in his. He always tried to treat me like some little China doll, to be kept clear of all the soot and sweat, maybe taken out and admired every now and then, after the hoses were dried and put away, the tanks refilled, the trucks washed, and the men fed and rested; just long enough to get dusted off and put back where I belonged, safe in my little showcase."

"So what'd you do?"

"I called 'bullshit'.

"I'm the only girl of his three children and four grandchildren. I love the man, but he's a walking penis, literally. His entire ego, all of his pride, all of his control comes from being male, and all of his threats, all his head games, all of his dominance only work on men.

"He got a Medal of Honor for singlehandedly taking out a German machine gun nest on D-day, for God's sake, but my grandma could tell him to go sit in the corner and I seriously think he'd start to do it before he realized she couldn't make him.

"His mom died when he was really little, so I'm sure that's part of it, but I swear it's like he uses that thing between your legs like some bizarre kind of handle, so he's literally got no way to 'handle' women. He's been busting balls his entire life, but with us he's like a parent with a kid who's finally done believing in Santa Claus. He's just lost.

"I don't think he's ever understood that you don't have to be able to beat the shit out of someone to have authority over them. To the boys he's just this impenetrable fortress that's always loomed over them, with guns and towers and slings and burning pitch and a moat full of burning oil and all that. But for my grandma and me, well, he's just a boy whose mama left him all alone in the world without saying goodbye.

"So, what did you do?"

Christina, and all the beer, had Paul completely mesmerized. She was so incredibly beautiful, and so beyond headstrong, he had no trouble at all imagining her poor old grandfather struggling with what to do with her—and how desperately he'd want to just protect and cherish her if she were his.

"I applied and was interviewed by a woman in personnel who—duh, it's 1986—didn't think twice about another Lawton getting into a CFD uniform. Three days after that, he called me to his office, sent his secretary on some stupid errand, and closed the door behind him. That's usually where the guys all start to wet their pants.

"He started off real sweet, as usual, telling me how much everyone in the family loved me and couldn't bear to see me get hurt doing what I knew was a very dangerous job, but I guess he saw I wasn't buying it, because then all of a sudden he just stopped. He stood up from his chair, leaned across his desk— trying to scare me—and swore he'd be six feet under and have worms crawling up his ass before any God-damned woman, his granddaughter or any other, would carry a hose on 'his' department."

Paul was transfixed. He'd never met a woman even remotely this self-assured, this animated, this well-spoken, this ridiculously hot.

"So what'd you do then?"

Flirting shamelessly now, Christina stood, leaned across the table at Paul, pantomiming the scene and, with the same lightning in her eyes that had taken her grandfather down, brought them so close Paul could smell the ozone as she reenacted pulling a cassette recorder from her breast pocket and said, "I said, 'Would you care to repeat that for the WCLE News at Six investigative team—and the EEOC—*Chief* Lawton?'"

Paul thought seriously about taking her hand and telling her if she'd walk out of the hotel with him right now, he'd go wherever she wanted, and do whatever she said, from then on. You couldn't even get a fork into him, he was *overdone*.

Twenty minutes had gone by, and Christina's mother took it upon herself to come meet the man who'd so stolen her daughter's attention. She was rather taken with Paul herself but, because of his obvious "impairment," was more than a little uncomfortable with how close to kissing they appeared to be.

The three of them chatted for a few minutes, then Alice politely asked if the two could perhaps exchange phone numbers and part company for the night, so Christina could spend some time with the family, and Paul graciously accepted, promising to call Christina after his trip, and their reunion, was over.

Trying not to hurt his mum's feelings, when she finished telling him how she came to America, Justin glossed over his awful childhood with a simple, "Well, it obviously wasn't any lost episode of "Leave It to

Beaver," but I guess it was about as good as could be expected.

"The Prators lost a son in Korea, and I think they were still grieving when they adopted me. They never made any direct comparisons or anything mean like that, but I just always felt like I was competing with his ghost, and I had the oldest parents of any kid I knew. They were in their sixties by the time I was in high school, and they gave me a lot of freedom, so I started drinking recreationally with some other juvenile delinquents in Atchison. They never knew I was doing anything wrong because I got decent grades, the high point always being the 'A' every kid gets in Band."

"What did you play?"

"Sax. Do you play?"

"Saxophone? Oh, heavens no. My family wouldn't have thought it 'proper' for a girl to play a wind instrument, and none of those dreadful violins or anything like that ever interested me. Playing music always seemed a very daunting proposition to me."

"Well, you pick it up quick." Justin hadn't had a woman listening so intently to him in a decade. It made him terribly self-conscious, but he loved it.

"I graduated in 1962 with no better idea what to do, so I joined the Army band. I should've just gone out to the airport and said, 'How do I become a pilot?'

"In the winter of that year, I met this pretty Italian girl who was apparently supposed to marry a nice Italian boy—like there's any such thing, right? Move to the suburbs, inherit or maybe start a business and raise a dozen or so children with names like Rocco and Theresa. She was certainly expected to steer well clear of some musician/soldier whose origin and destination were equally obscure. I guess she thought I was worth a gamble, that I'd figure things out eventually."

"Did you?"

"Well, yeah, I guess. But not nearly fast enough."

"Her family never did accept me, but they threw us a huge wedding and welcomed our son, Paul, into the family just before I announced that three years of the Army life was going to be it for me, and I was going to take my little family and my G.I. Bill back to Kansas to study music—just to teach, I tried to tell them, not to perform.

"A newspaper ad led me to a night job riveting airplane wings at Cessna while I took classes during the day. I started work as a junior high school band director in 1970, but I quickly learned that teaching music and playing music were two entirely different animals.

"I'd heard about a pilot shortage, but I had no idea how to do it, except joining the military, which I was too old for by then. The idea kept haunting me, though, and I started to think, 'could I be making this harder than it really is?'

"I'd already given Gloria her big dream: a family. Did I not have the right to provide for that family however I chose? She didn't understand, mostly because I didn't even know before then, that flying was the only thing I'd ever wanted so badly.

"She didn't have much choice but to try when my flight instructor called one afternoon to cancel my flight lesson for that day. He'd tried to reach me at school, but I was out 'sick' that day. I'd driven to the Cessna factory to talk with my old boss about becoming a pilot for the company, and I'd told no one, intending to be back for my lesson and dinner with the family.

His mum was wincing, not wanting to hear how the plan unraveled.

"The whole ugly picture landed on her at once. I'd been coming home late a few days a week for some time but claimed to be giving private lessons to kids after school. Privacy's always been important to me, so she hadn't dared question me or look for the extra money. What I'd been doing was, to her, infidelity—just with an airplane instead of a woman. As a bonus, my principal called to ask how I managed to take flying lessons while I was sick, like I'd claimed to be.

"Getting caught faking sick was grounds for termination for a first year teacher. There was nothing left of the fan at the end of that shit storm. He told me my contract wouldn't be renewed, which is the "clean" way to get fired as a teacher.

"What followed was what Gloria, the kids, and eventually even I realized was a series of flailing attempts to make a living as a pilot outside the airlines.

"I resumed my job at Cessna while I earned my commercial and flight instructor licenses, and from there I went from job to job, first as a flight instructor, then as a corporate pilot, with an occasional stint flying traffic or pipeline patrol, towing banners or gliders, or dropping skydivers. Eventually, I became the Chief Pilot for a large heavy-equipment manufacturer in Ohio, Marion Power Shovel, but I think I've done almost everything you can do to make very little money flying airplanes at one time or another.

"All the instability and moving took a financial toll, but that didn't bother me, and Gloria seemed to be ok because I was so happy. We had a car to drive, a roof over our heads, and food to eat, and all the moving bonded us well as a family.

"Paul was interested in flying right away, too—I used to bring him toy airplanes I made from scrap now and then at Cessna, and he'd go nuts. It was pretty cute.

"What made things bad was my drinking. I'd always binged socially, but I hardly drank alone at all before I taught band. I was often up late simplifying music too difficult for the kids to play, and I'd always say a few beers helped me 'decompose'."

His mother smiled politely.

"What the next few after that were for, I never really knew, but I quit almost completely again when I started flying, so I just assumed it was just that I hadn't been doing what I wanted with my life.

"Whenever I'd start to feel secure again, though, it was as if I'd never stopped. The occasional, quiet indulgence in a six pack of beer, either in my hotel room or at home after the kids were in bed gradually got to be a rigid, merciless habit of having a twelve-pack in one sitting, sometimes chasing bourbon, and then staggering off to bed or occasionally passing out on the couch, waking up with a headache that would take four or five cups of coffee and Tylenol to kill.

"One day I missed a call to make a short-notice trip, and the boss showed up at the house and found me out cold at two p.m. on a Wednesday. Fired me on the spot. Next day, I fell on my sword and finally admitted, to myself and everyone else..."

His mother covered her mouth as he admitted, for what seemed the millionth time to the thousandth person, "I'm an alcoholic.

"Well, Gloria'd finally had it. She filed for divorce later that week, and I was packing my stuff to leave the next day. I moved back to Wichita, but Gloria stayed in Marion. She had a good job there and she didn't want the wanderlust that had made their lives with me so miserable, for her or the kids."

"Drinking cost me my job and my family, but it didn't quite get me."

"It didn't get all of your family, either, did it? I'm sure your kids still love you. Just like I know your father would have. " At this, she completely broke down.

"Justin, I'm so sorry."

"Hey, hey. You don't have a thing to be sorry for, come on, now." He got up from his side of the booth and sat next to her, hugging her warmly. "You did what everybody else here does—the best you could."

"No, no. I didn't. I tried but I didn't try hard enough."

"What do you mean?" A sliver of suspicion, alternately imperceptible and excruciating, poked at Justin's heart.

"I came to the U.S. hoping I'd be able to find your grandparents in Kansas, but I had neither the money to buy a car nor sufficient reason to travel so far by train from New York. Rationing was still in force; we were still at war with Japan. So I had to work and live there until the war was over. I didn't get to Kansas until you were nearly a year old. By that time, I knew you so well it was absolutely impossible to think I might have to give you up, but there was simply no other way without help. I was so terribly, wretchedly poor, the only way we survived those first months was by charity. We lived in a home owned and tended by a convent, but it was never intended as a permanent solution."

She was crying, but still fully in control of herself, as if she could stop but simply didn't care to.

"So, we went to Kansas in November of 1945, to your father's home, and…"

"And…what?"

"It wasn't much, Justin. Your father had told me he came from a humble upbringing, what with the Great Depression and everything, but I really didn't fully grasp his meaning until I saw their house."

Justin's face wore concerned amusement. He, too, was no stranger to hard times.

A Silver Ring

"It was very small and old, and looked well kept overall but there were some things that looked like they needed attention and weren't getting it. The grass looked like it had gone the entire year without a mowing, the paint was chalky, the windows dirty, and there was very little wood in the crib next to the house, though it had already snowed once the week before. And it was eerily quiet.

"I couldn't summon the courage to knock on the door at first, though I'd spent weeks, months even, rehearsing what I would say. I just couldn't imagine anyone asking the people living in that house to take on more obligations, knowing they were already burdened with grief for losing their son. But I had six dollars. I knew they were my only hope left of keeping you.

"It took some time for them to answer the door; I must have knocked five or six times. It was as if they were hoping whoever it was would just go away. A boy opened the door a little, just enough for me to see his face, but then I heard his father call after him and he disappeared back inside. Then his father, your grandfather, opened the door and was very brusque with me. He asked me what I wanted, but I was so taken aback by his manner, and he was such an imposing figure. I completely forgot what I'd planned to say."

The distance in her eyes told Justin it had been a long time since she'd told this story to anyone, if indeed she ever had. Her memory's staggering detail made the intensity of this episode in her life obvious, and knowing the story's ultimate outcome, his heart ached for her.

"I stood there stuttering and stammering like a bloody fool for some time, and then I just came out with it. I said, 'I know you're going through a difficult time right now, and I don't imagine this is going to assuage your pain one bit, but Wesley and I were in love, and I believe would have married if…' and he cut me off right there. You were asleep, bundled up in my arms, so he couldn't see you, but he knew I was holding a baby."

"He said, 'If you knew my son, then you probably figured out what a good heart he had, and maybe that's why you think you can come over here now and try to get us to help you solve your problems. Well, I got news for you. My son knew better than to take up with some tramp that'd let something like this happen to her, so I suggest you go nose around some other boy's family if you're looking for help from whoever you think might owe it to you. My boy just wasn't that kind.' Then he shut the door and locked it. I thought about knocking again and showing him your face so he could see for himself, but I was too afraid.

"I took my six dollars and bought a bus ticket to Kansas City, took you to the orphanage, and worked in Fairfax until I met my husband, who was from Texas. This is the first time I've been back in Kansas since.

"I don't blame them anymore. As my other children grew and I saw how keenly biased you become about your kids, I began to understand and forgive them, though I never again tried to contact them. I've no idea where they are now, or even if they're still alive."

She collected herself and, trying to lighten the mood said, "You know, your father loved airplanes too, though he never got the chance to become a pilot."

Justin had wanted, more than anything, to ask her about him, but he was afraid to appear disinterested in her. Now that she'd finally broached the subject, however, it would be odd not to ask.

"Really? Who was he, what was he like?"

6

Sergeant Wes Hutchinson stepped out of the tent and, taking care not to look around, went to the leeward side for a smoke. Between two gusts of the warm desert wind, he struck a match using only one hand, a trick he'd learned in basic training, and lit a cigarette. He stared at a small rock 10 feet in front of him, wincing slightly as he took a drag, until the sound of an engine starting got his attention. He looked in the direction of the sound, knowing the plane was invisible behind the tent, but listening somehow more intently nevertheless. The engine fired quickly, but began missing badly for far longer than the 10 or 15 seconds the huge Pratt and Whitney radial normally took to reach consensus and idle reliably, though never smoothly.

"Nature of the beast," Wes said aloud to no one, bouncing his cigarette wildly in farcical imitation of his instructor from Air Corps engineer school. "Show me a radial that idles smooth, and I'll show you one that's gettin' ready to make Jerry's day with you."

Wes knew well the problem his friend, mechanic Mike Lewis, was having with their plane. Before they'd left England, he and Lewis had talked about the radical climate change they were going to encounter in Africa, and came to different conclusions about the problems they could expect.

Worried most about the searing heat and dust, Lewis insisted on retrofitting *Barfly*'s oil coolers with larger ones stolen from a sister squadron's parts room. The 328th's new J-models seemed to have a better, stronger, faster, or smarter version of nearly everything on their D-models, and no job was too big for gearheads like Mike and Wes. Wes discounted Mike's fears about the oil but, as "just" the plane's assistant flight engineer and, as Lewis loved to further insult him, a gunner, Lewis didn't have to listen. Wes had personally seen the plane stagger as high as 30,000 feet, where the air temperature was sixty below zero and the supercharged engines' oil would stay almost as hot there as right after takeoff. Years of experience working with machines had left Wes with many such anecdotes his minimal training couldn't explain.

Wes wanted to spend the 3 days notice they got before their detachment to get fresh grease into all the plane's hinges and joints and replace any ignition leads that weren't in absolutely new condition. He'd learned years ago that ignition wires were prone to shorts when they got hot, potentially taking a spark plug out of action, causing a miss. The effect was worse in thinner air. Lewis had vetoed his ignition wire idea, mostly for lack of time, but agreed with Wes that the re-lube was a must-do, along with the illicit oil cooler upgrades.

In assisting Lewis' crew with those tasks, which was far beyond his assistant engineer's responsibilities,

Wes had gotten a long look at each engine. While his friend was absorbed, and under the guise of making idle chitchat he knew would irritate his friend and slow his work, Wes counted over two dozen questionable ignition wires. Then without telling anyone, he'd slipped back to the 328th's parts room the night before they left and snuck two complete ignition harnesses, enough to replace twenty-eight bad wires, back into his personal gear.

That was a week ago, and now *Barfly* was a petulant child in the care of her now-exasperated father. He'd tried everything he knew (except to follow the plane's mother's advice) to get her to mind. Wes smiled to himself as he heard that engine shut down then another, similar but uniquely different, crank and fire but refuse to idle. He mused at how best to broach the subject with Lewis, knowing he'd be furious over getting outmaneuvered by a "damned gunner" without a single day of formal mechanic training.

Next came the unmistakably human sounds of Lewis' caustic mouth and steel tools being thrown against aluminum engine cowlings.

"You miserable piece of shit! What the fuck!" Mike roared.

Hearing his beloved airplane being abused, Wes' amusement turned to fear and anger. He tossed his half-spent cigarette to the lifeless dirt and started off in a run, which the desert quickly melted to a jog and then just a fast walk, to the hardstand where his plane was being tortured.

"What seems to be the problem here today, Sergeant?" he asked with the condescending tone of an officer as he looked up at Lewis, perched on his crew's lone rickety ladder. Lewis refused to offer even a turn of his head to validate Wes' appearance in his "shop."

"You know Goddamn good and well what *seems* to be the fucking problem, Hutchinson. Problem is, that's not what the problem *is*."

"Well, what do you think? Dirty carbs, bad ignition wires, shitty gas, or just too much oil going through those big new coolers?"

Two of Lewis' crew barely choked back laughter.

"Yeah, Hutch, ok, fine." Lewis still hadn't looked at Wes. "Maybe you had a point this time. Maybe there's some shorts. What can we do about it now though, huh? Wrap tape around 'em? Or maybe you assholes would just rather take the spare tomorrow. I can arrange that, you know." No one ever wanted to fly a spare. They were the squadron's most bedraggled, ragtag aircraft, basket-case organ donors left intact only to be cannibalized to keep the better airplanes airworthy.

"What would you say if I told you I could set you up with not one, but two whole new spare harnesses for this here aircraft, without having to undo a single cowl latch on that hardstand whore over there?" Wes asked, vamping a salesman as he motioned to the spare.

Lewis' tense expression froze, then slowly melted into open consideration, which morphed quickly into decadent complicity as Lewis looked past Wes at the inebriated cartoon insect painted beside a garish, bloated "BARFLY" on the side of the bomber. After a few seconds, he finally looked at Wes and quietly muttered, "You fucking thief..."

Wes' feigned outrage at the epithet, then abruptly went back to his trusty smirk. "I'd rather be in the stockade at Hardwick than grounded with you in this Godforsaken sandbox. Besides, those damned rookies' planes are so cherry, they'll never miss them."

Lewis was shaking his head and looking down at Wes; Wes was looking alternately at the plane, his friend, and down at his shuffling feet.

Mike retrieved the ratchet he'd thrown at the cowling and returned his attention to the engine for a few moments of silence, removing a badly fouled spark plug. Shaking his head almost imperceptibly as he squinted at the plug in the bright sun, he yelled to one of his men, who was sitting between the two engines on the other wing.

"Myers! Escort Sergeant Capone here back to his stash, and don't come back without two ignition harnesses and any other non-issue Army Air Corps property he has tucked into whatever maggots' nest he hides all this shit in." Then, quieter, looking first at Wes but then back at the fouled plug, "I swear to Christ, Hutch, they ought to just drop you into Germany and have you steal Hitler for us. Get us all home a lot quicker."

"Yeah, but I bet he'd probably just surrender if he only knew how much cooler our oil is now," Wes said, at first walking backward away from the plane, but then turning to run as Lewis pounced from his perch and threw his filthy 5/8" socket and a fresh stream of obscenities at him.

Only when it was unavoidable, Wes reported to Flight Engineer Randall Twomey. Despite being shackled with such a horribly stuffy name, Twomey managed to live up to the utter void of personality it implied. He had no known nickname, no demonstrated sense of humor, and even less interest in either of his jobs: manning the top machine gun turret and managing the aircraft's many functions controlled from its engineer's panel.

Twomey, who had joined the Air Corps only a month before Pearl Harbor, was what mechanics derisively referred to as a "switch monkey." He could follow every procedure to the letter without assistance, reference, or error, but when something happened that wasn't covered in the book, he was utterly lost. The engineer's panel was, to him, a two-dimensional screen upon which a finite number of training slides could be projected. Ask him to configure for single-generator operation, and in a few seconds he'd switch a generator off, crosstie the other, and point dutifully to the load meters to verify the change. Ask him why a generator might have dropped off-line, however, and he'd respond with, "That's for the mechanics to find out."

Twomey passed his exams and proficiency checks with high marks but was of little use in the chaos of combat. Captain Tommy Warwick and copilot Max Newhart learned quickly to bring problems to Wes, a kind of understood delegation of authority of which Twomey fully approved, since it kept his workload down.

In contrast, his mechanic friends would say Wes had "X-ray vision," meaning he could see beyond the switches and gauges to the actual mechanical components of the airplane, helping them quickly and accurately diagnose virtually every malfunction the plane ever suffered. It reflected well upon the whole crew, indeed the whole squadron, because *Barfly* spent less time having its maladies investigated, allowing more time to be spent on preventive maintenance and fine-tuning. *Barfly* was the quiet pride of the 409th squadron, and though official credit generally fell to Warwick, Twomey, and Lewis, everyone in the squadron knew the man behind the curtain who was the real "Wizard."

Running from Lewis reminded Wes of that tense final scene with his sister's would-be suitor, Frank Lawton. That day seemed so much more than eighteen months ago, but he could still remember feeling so smug for having chosen a so much more glamorous and easier path than his rival that he'd actually felt pity for the "poor, stupid bastard" for becoming a "grunt."

As he'd watched the patchwork landscapes of eastern Colorado and western Kansas slip serenely beneath his window during training, Wes could just imagine Lawton crawling through some rancid, barbed-wired mud pit down there somewhere with live rounds shrieking six inches over his head and sweat stinging his eyes, preparing to offer himself as a human sacrifice on some sticky crimson beachhead. Meanwhile, "high in the sunlit silence," as John Magee had written in his poem "High Flight" during the 'War to end all Wars,' Wes and his colleagues would bask in electrically-heated flight suits in the perpetual winter of high altitude, in near total detachment from the carnage their payload wrought miles below their thundering formations.

That was then, as they say, and this was, well, by now Wes had seen and done a lot of things they didn't put on the Air Corps recruiting posters back home. Their dispassionate natural enemies, frostbite and hypoxia, paced the deafening fuselage, waiting for a single oversight, mechanical failure, or combat damage to expose their prey. If they could take one man out, another would try to help him, and they could sometimes score a second or even third kill.

But by far the greatest risk to the men aboard the bombers was enemy fire, either from anti-aircraft guns below, or fighter planes attacking them on their own level. The profound isolation and vulnerability felt by an injured crew whose damaged plane couldn't keep up with the formation was arguably without equal in the life of an infantryman.

Wes wondered if joining the Air Corps was such a smart choice compared to Frank Lawton's after all. He figured wherever Lawton was right now, he probably wasn't sweating his balls off and getting sand in his teeth trying to keep precise machinery working in the middle of a desert.

With the final mop-up of their successful North African campaign over, however, the "grunts" of Lawton's 1st Infantry Division, the "Big Red One," had been doing almost precisely those same things for far longer. For security, none but the highest ranking officers in the 1st Infantry knew their objective, yet even the dimmest wit in Wes' 93rd Bombardment Group could figure out why they'd flown over a half-dozen missions over Sicily in less than two weeks.

Fortunately for the Army, Wes and Frank Lawton were unlikely to ever see each other again unless both managed to survive the war and return home to resume their own little war over Eileen.

"Unbelievable," Wes muttered as he fished through his pack for the contraband.

"Excuse me, Sarge?" Myers asked him.

"Oh, nothing, Bill. I just can't believe we've only been in this sandbox a week, and I've already got my own little baby desert in this pack. I didn't think to wrap any of this stuff up when I packed it, and now there's sand in everything, and no way to get it out."

He pulled a part that looked like a larger version of a car horn out of the bag and clenched his teeth and lips together, breathing only to calm himself. The part had been wrapped in two paper bags, shrouded in oiled cheesecloth, and looked clean as a whistle, but Wes didn't seem at all comforted as a hot gust of wind blasted sand against the sides of the tent.

"What is it?" Myers asked, a little self-conscious and not at all sure if he should ask how to help or just wait.

Wes didn't answer, and the young corporal knew not to press. Wes had become a microbe, crawling through the drive of the supercharger and looking around inside the gearbox to see if any little bits of the Sahara had stowed themselves away. Wes was looking for any sign sand had invaded the gearbox, waiting to wreak havoc on one of *Barfly*'s engines on takeoff, when all four of them would have to perform flawlessly to drag the overloaded bomber into the hot, thin air.

Wes held the supercharger with one bare hand, and with the other wrapped in the cheesecloth, turned the drive gear, slowly at first, then a little faster, then slower than before, his eyes closed, lower lip quivering slightly.

After a few moments, he wrapped the part as it had been, saying, "I carried this son of a bitch like a baby all the way from Hardwick, and I'll be damned if I'm going to watch it shell out from contamination. Tell Lewis he's got to make us a parts washer, or we're going to end up swimming home and kicking his southern-fried ass back to 'Alabamie'. I'm keeping this blower right here till he's got a better place to store it, a way to flush it, or an engine that needs it. I don't give a shit if Hap Arnold himself walks in and orders it to be inventoried. It's mine."

Myers looked down at Wes' hands and the precious supercharger in them while Wes was talking, then looked up at him and, forcing back another smile, barked "Wilco, Sarge. What can I carry back for you?"

"Grab the harness, mags, and that governor. I'll take the rest, thank you." Wes placed the supercharger back into his now nearly empty duffel, closed it tightly, covered the opening with his less-dirty shirt, and followed Myers outside, carrying a vacuum pump, two fuel filters, a handful of cylinder lugs, and a bag of assorted switches and fittings, none of which had been missed yet at Hardwick.

As he tried to sleep that night, Wes wondered if he himself had been missed yet at Hardwick. The "Circus" had relocated there from their first base, Alconbury, in February, 1943, after an earlier deployment to North Africa, for which the men had been told to pack for ten days, but which ended up lasting just shy of three months. Once settled in at Hardwick, the men had had a relatively civilized duty schedule until their June return to the desert. Those weeks provided ample opportunity for socializing.

They met at one of the more popular pubs in Hardwick, the "King's Ransom," on a rainy Sunday night in March. Wes and his best friend, *Barfly*'s other waist gunner, Ed Worley, were mourning the death of one of their gunnery school classmates who'd been killed in a takeoff accident. They'd all made an informal pact that survivors would honor their fallen brothers by taking the deceased's memory to town, make a single, final toast to him, then never speak or think of him again. This policy had been spontaneously liberalized to include a series of final toasts, made not only to the most recently lost, but also to all those before him.

The Ransom was dead that night, and with the typical English gloom particularly thick, Wes and Ed wanted just a quiet dinner and a few drinks rather than the more typical frontal assault on their livers.

While sipping their after-dinner Guinness, a pretty, decidedly Celtic woman walked in with a basket of fresh flowers for sale. Worley spotted her first, as Wes was staring into a painting of an old Sopwith Camel pulling up into a chandelle with a red Fokker triplane right behind, guns blazing.

"Get a load of this, big boy," Worley said quietly, his eyes flashing from Wes to the girl and back. She was near the door at the end of the bar, 20 feet or so behind Wes, and he knew turning around now would give her a transcript of their conversation, so he deferred for the moment.

"What'cha got?" he asked Ed in their familiar gunners' jargon, without looking away from the painting.

"On the small side, like you like, blond, blue, maybe green eyes…"

The girl spoke cheerfully with an old man at the bar for a moment, then smiled broadly and rubbed him gently on the shoulder as he paid her a compliment.

"Holy cow, pretty smile. This girl got the last good teeth in the Isles. Selling flowers on a Sunday night, though—maybe not too smart." She came toward them.

"Would you chaps be meeting your girlies here in a bit? I'm sure they'd adore you for the thought."

She laid her left hand on Wes' upper back, right below his neck, then grabbed a pinch of his hair between her thumb and forefinger and gave a playful tug. Wes startled at first, but then slowly tilted his head back until he was looking up at the girl with his head cocked back awkwardly against her flower basket.

"No girlies around here, Miss," he said with stern sincerity, then, his expression instantly changing to a boyish smile, he added, "Except you, of course. Why not take a little break here with us—for a bit?"

He'd been working on what he called his " real English," which was really Cockney, since they'd arrived in England and could now easily, almost convincingly, say "for a bit" by making the "t" sound by slamming something shut in the top of his throat rather than from the Americans' casual meeting of the tongue and roof of the mouth. She seemed skeptical, if not a little disgusted by the Yank's attempted accent, but she was clearly taken with his smile, playfulness, and intense, piercing, but not threatening, expression. That thick, wavy brown hair didn't hurt, either.

"What part of Texas are you from?" she asked, sure that only a cowboy could manage to be so brash and not completely repulse her.

"Nope—guess again, but not before you tell us your name."

Wes knew he had the fish biting, for the time being, and all thoughts of the sad business with which they came here to deal were, for now, gone. His left foot pushed a chair out from under the table.

The girl took the chair out further from the table and sat across it with its back to her side, facing Wes. She smiled faintly but maintained her well-bred condescension, keeping her cards hidden but telegraphing her bluff. "Melody's my given name, but I know how you Yanks love your one-syllable nicknames, so "Mel" will do for you. And what would be yours, then?"

So it seemed Wesley and Mel, as their pet names became for each other in allusion to that first conversation, were meant to be.

Now, sitting on his gritty cot, physically spent by the relentless, life-sapping heat of the day but pacing the floor mentally, Wes took out a pen and paper and began to write the first letter he'd ever had to write to her. He had trouble starting it, as men so often do, but by the time he was midway down the first page, he could feel the tension in his nerves easing, and for the first time in weeks the other half of his full boyish smile had slipped unnoticed back into the tent.

Dearest Melody-

Seems like I just left Merry old England, but since we didn't get to talk much lately and really didn't even get to say goodbye, I want you to know I wasn't trying to give you the old brush-off or anything. Lately it's been really crazy around here, but I have you on my mind every chance I get. I wish we could have a few more months like last spring, but I guess if not for the war we'd have never met anyway, so I really shouldn't complain.

If I hadn't joined the Air Corps, I'd probably be in some flea-bitten old tavern in Oklahoma right now, wondering where all the pretty girls are in the world, instead of just missing the prettiest one of them all.

I wonder what you've been up to the last few weeks? We've been really busy and everybody's getting a little threadbare, especially after the easy pace we had when we first got to Hardwick.

I couldn't even get into town for all the work we had in that last little bit before we left, but I heard from some other guys that your Uncle Percy may have found a gold, or maybe I should say silver, mine. I guess he's making some kind of silver rings with the Air Corps' insignia on them. Some of the guys bought them all up before he even knew what he had on his hands. They're all the rage—the guys that have them are afraid to leave them behind like we're supposed to when we fly, and the businessy guys are reselling them for another twenty pounds over what he was charging! He needs to make as many more as he can—it was a great idea. We're really starting to beat up on poor Jerry pretty bad and morale's going up. Plus a lot of these guys are looking for as many souvenirs of their time over here as they can send or carry home, and those rings are perfect for that.

Ed's over here watching me write and rearranging his stuff again. This cheeseball outfit makes a hobo's life look peaceful with all the packing and unpacking we do. I've never been so glad to not have much to carry around. I've still got all my pictures (yours on top of course and getting tattered and frayed for all the "attention" I give it) in that little wood curio box my mom gave me when I went home after gunnery school, my clothes, and this pen and some paper, but that's about it, except for a few odds and ends I brought for *Barfly* in case the old girl catches cold. Lewis forgot a few things for her and was real grateful to me for remembering. If we ever get clobbered out there after all the work we've done on her, I think Lewis might just kill the Captain himself for getting "his" plane shot up—and I'd probably have to give him a smack or two myself!

I'd tell you when to expect me back if I knew myself, Mel, but I can only tell you I'll do everything I can to be with you the first second I can. I'm missing you every minute I'm awake and dreaming of you every night, and I only hope you won't talk to any cowboys buying flowers before I get back.

Missing you always,
Wesley

Since he was with Wes the night they met, Ed Worley knew Melody better than any of Wes' other friends and was well aware of his feelings for her. He saw Wes putting the letter in an envelope and sealing it, and started a conversation with him, mostly just to break the heavy silence hanging in the tent.

"This place makes Kingman seem uptown, don't it?" Ed tested.

"Nothing to write home about, that's for sure," Wes mumbled, copying Melody's address on the envelope, remembering he was also weeks behind in writing his folks.

"Yeah. But, you know, I just wrote my mom, anyhow." Ed was fishing for what his friend was thinking and squirming around a little. "So what do you think this thing's going to be tomorrow, anyway? Getting us all up at 0500 for another damn training flight. Hell, we got all day!"

"Guess maybe they want to save the planes from having to be out in the worst of it maybe, I don't know." Wes hadn't even made eye contact with Worley yet.

"Hey Twomey, what did Warwick say this thing was going to be about anyway?"

Twomey had just settled into his cot and was reading a philatelic magazine. Not looking away from it, he replied, "'Briefing's at 0530, plan to be out most of the day, down low enough to smell the camels fart again,' is all I heard."

"Great. Guess that means I won't be needing these," Ed said, holding up his "backup" pair of skivvies. The temperature on the desert floor was going into the mid-120's, and the men missed the freezing heights and their clumsy heated suits.

"Jesus, Ed, I can take the camels' farts, but not yours," came the voice of tail gunner Dick Lindstrom, just back from their makeshift steel drum latrine. The men broke into quiet laughter, and Wes seized the moment to pass gas, getting some boots thrown at him and his arm punched by Ed Worley, which got everyone belly-laughing. It was a tiny, welcome break from the tension growing among them, each sensing all the low-level training coming to a head, and no one yet knowing its purpose.

Wes was awake before 0500 the next day, watching night's cloak slip from the desert sky in those last sweet moments of serenity before another sixteen hours of the sun's rage. There wasn't a cloud in the sky, but occasional flashes of lightning came from somewhere over the northwest horizon; a thunderstorm over the Mediterranean, where both the key ingredients for such a miraculous thing—heat and water—existed. One of them was conspicuously absent from this hellhole, Wes thought, and it damned sure wasn't heat.

He figured the temperature to be around 75 or so in the cool of the desert pre-dawn. Most of the men slept in the nude and with minimal covering, giving their bodies the best chance possible to cool off enough to get some good sleep, not to mention the opportunity to air out their stifling crotches. Wes looked at his watch at 4:57, and wondered if their Commander, Colonel Ted Timberlake, would have any characteristic surprises in store for his men today.

As Wes stood to put his pants on, he stopped to listen. He thought he heard an airplane in the distance, but it wasn't quite loud enough to believe, given the earliness of the hour and their position on the border between Hell and Bumfukegypt. Still, it seemed to be getting a little louder and soon became undeniably real. It wasn't a single engine, either. No, this was either several fighters or at least one bomber, but whoever it was they were coming in an awful damned hurry. He hadn't been awakened by any planes taking off during the night, but then again with the crews working on sickly engines all night, it was possible he might not have noticed another four engines' din over the seemingly constant belching racket of those test-runs.

A couple of the men who'd been asleep stirred, and the growing sound had Wes jumping into his trousers and quickly stepping out of the tent to identify the source. He was more than half-afraid to find out whether it was friendly, since the nearest anti-aircraft gun was several hundred miles away. No German air raids had been staged against African soil for months, with the Luftwaffe now quite busy defending Mother Deutschland against round-the-clock British and American bombardment.

Peering bleary-eyed in the direction of the sound, Wes was relieved to see not a formation of enemy fighters or bombers, but a single Liberator, down on the deck so low and fast he was kicking up a sandy rooster-tail behind him. The plane was headed straight at the camp, steady and unwavering, with a 4,000-strong herd of horses pulling it along at well over two-hundred miles per hour. Wes smiled at what a terribly pretty machine the B-24 really was.

All business, its slender wings and broad-sided fuselage could carry more destructive payload higher, faster, and farther than Boeing's pre-war-designed B-17 Flying Fortress, but, like a Bulldog, it had a face only a mother could love, which Wes did. The sound of the approaching bomber now almost seemed to fade somewhat, like a symphony dropping briefly from *forte* to *piano* just before the end of a finale, but his eyes weren't about to let him be mislead. As the bomber crossed the camp's boundary, the sound became urgent again, and well above the low roar of its engines and props, he could just make out the high whistle of the superchargers, or perhaps it was just the thick morning air getting slashed open by the 110-foot Davis wing.

A Silver Ring

Alone in that bomber's cockpit, Colonel Timberlake, wore an amused smirk as he watched the tents where his men lay sleeping grow in the windshield and then streak by in a blur just beneath his feet. Clear of the tents, he let the thought *skooch up, baby* twitch his fingers on the control yoke, and the bomber slid to 80 feet above the desert, at which point Timberlake cranked the yoke hard to the left and pulled back with all his might, throwing the hulking airplane into a nearly 90-degree banked turn, its left wingtip creating a minor sandstorm with its wake vortex.

By the time Timberlake could come around for a second pass, most of the men would be out of their tents, watching him. Knowing this, he climbed to make his second pass a bit higher and slower, made a slow roll directly over camp, then pulled the engines to idle and flew a truncated, Navy-style landing pattern to a showy nose-high landing. Anyone who'd been unsure whether their Commander could do anything no longer harbored any doubts. He tossed the B-24 around like a trainer.

Timberlake was good at coming up with unusual stuff from time to time, just to break the routine up a bit. "Spit and polish and heavy starch is fine when you're in basic and the Army's all new to you and you to it," he had said in a pep talk back in Colorado the year before, "but, just as our skills grow and evolve, and we grow and evolve, so must our habits grow and evolve. Habit's like a stake for young plant—without it we can't grow up right, but eventually we outgrow it. I'm going to make sure you men don't keep your habits any longer than they're useful. To you, or to me."

With that, he had ordered them to go to their aircraft, and take the position of another man with a similar but different job on the bomber. Captains went to the bombardier's "greenhouse" in the nose, copilots sat as captains with bombardiers for copilots, navigators, radio operators, and engineers all moved one seat, and the turret and tail gunners each swapped with one of the two waist gunners.

Once in position, the order was given to take off, join up in formation, and fly the same boring "milk run" training flight they'd all complained about having to endure the day before.

It was a mess. The copilots couldn't fly formation, the captains sent range spotters running for cover from all the off-target concrete-filled training bombs, radio communications were garbled, nonstandard, and inefficient, fuel loads became imbalanced, engines overheated or began to run cold and rough, and the engineers were so busy talking the navigators through correcting those problems that they scarcely had a mark on their trip logs at debrief and some even got lost. But at the end of the day, no one had a shred of criticism left for his crewmembers, and Colonel Timberlake had taught his men both humility and just a little bit more about their collective job: to get bombs on the target, protect each other's planes from fighter attack, and hopefully bring a salvageable aircraft back to base.

As Timberlake taxied back to the flight line and shut his plane down, the men began to gather at "ops" - a collection of empty crates arranged in a loose quarter-circle near a chalkboard jammed into the sand with a couple of sticks propping it up from the back.

Ops back in England had been a fully-functional, though miniaturized lecture hall built onto one of the large maintenance hangars, replete with projector and screen for slides, chalkboards, podium, and enough chairs for all the airmen of the 93rd's three squadrons to sit. Adjacent to this hall were the squadron and group offices, where orders were disseminated, intelligence was processed, debriefs were filed, damage assessments made, and last effects gathered and sent home with letters written by men who knew their subjects well enough, but who had never met the recipients.

The routine there had been to awaken thirty minutes prior to briefing, dress and gather their gear, eat breakfast in the chow hall, and then meet in ops for briefing, but they were not in England anymore.

Addison Baker, the 93rd's next commander, stood at the chalkboard drawing a sketch of the day's mission as the dirty, ragtag group congealed around the crates, some still scooping cold Spam or beans from their C-rations. Talk was hushed but boisterous, as with boys at camp, and spontaneous King of the Mountain games were in progress on the few crates that didn't already have officers on them. Timberlake approached Baker as he was nearing completion of the sketch, and corrected him on the position of one of its features, which looked to be a mountain or hill.

Baker furrowed his brow and peered at the chart Timberlake had unfolded to clarify his point, then looked at his own sketch on the chalkboard and dutifully erased the mountain-like mark, redrawing it about three inches further left. He then looked back at the chart and his commander with a "like that?" expression on his face. Timberlake paused for half a second, deliberating about the costs of yet another correction, both to his old "XO" and to the men he had helped train for this mission. He was a good man, professional to the utmost and a good leader, but his abilities as a pilot weren't up to comparison with Timberlake's, and the men knew it. Deciding the briefing probably wouldn't fail from the slightly incorrect juxtaposition of the mountain, he nodded, muttered something quietly to Baker, and both men chuckled. Then Timberlake addressed his men.

"Good morning, Joes," Colonel Timberlake boomed, his hands on his hips as he got the men's attention. The youngest of four sons of an Army General, each of whom had graduated West Point, Timberlake festooned all his men with the title "Joe."

"Good morning, sir." they replied in quiet unison. He surveyed them, smiling.

"I trust everyone is present and accounted for, so we'll dispense with the roll call. One thing I just love about this place is I don't have to worry much about desertion." The men laughed politely.

"I know it's a little hard to sleep at night with your cot soaked in your own sweat and your ball sacks hangin' down to your knees, but if you didn't sleep well last night, then you can rest assured, pardon the pun, that tonight will be different. Matter of fact some of you copilots may even nod off before we land, if you trust your captains that is." This brought more uneasy laughter, and someone said, "I'll never be *that* tired."

"We've had your fuel tanks topped off for this one, and your bomb bays are full of wood practice bombs so we don't have any nasty surprises on takeoff. Whoever's engine shells out, you'll still be able to climb on out and come back around to land. Your target today is the same as yesterday's, but today we'll be heading out for a bit of a cross-country nav exercise first. Whether your bombs hit the target exactly or not isn't of prime importance this time. What I want to see is navigational accuracy, a minimum of errors, and prompt corrections to those that may occur.

"Now men, we've been hedgehopping in these airplanes since before we left England, and you know as well as I that this type of mission isn't what they were designed and built for. The B-25's Jimmy Doolittle used for Tojo's little wakeup call last year would make a better choice, but they don't have the payload and range we do, and frankly, they're not here and we are, so it doesn't much matter anyway.

"My wakeup call for you this morning was an attempt to show you all firsthand the devastating surprise and nearly impossible targets that we can present to our enemy in this type of attack. In all the training we've done, none of you, to my knowledge, has ever been on the ground beneath a low flying, flat-out Liberator on a target run. I trust you all got my point."

"I'm gonna send you my laundry bill, sir" came a voice from the back, and more quiet laughter. Timberlake laughed with them, despite the nearly insubordinate tone in the man's voice, and looked out pridefully at his men, who were about to do the grim work of becoming one of the most highly decorated units of the war.

The sun melted through the horizon as Wes sat through the rest of the briefing, hoping it wouldn't take much longer, daydreaming of Melody, and wondering if Lewis had finished getting *Barfly* ready.

As Wes approached the bomber ten minutes later, Lewis said, "Well, well, if it ain't Sergeant Pocketpacker—did you get plenty of beauty sleep, sweetheart?"

Wes overacted a gaping yawn and stretch, and piped right up with, "No, not really, some poor bastard must've been having engine problems all night. About every time I thought I was out for the duration, seemed like another one would fire up, run like shit for a few minutes, then shut down. I would've come out to help if I knew who it was, but you know how some wrench-wenches get kind of huffy about having a flyboy telling them how to do their jobs."

"Hee-haw. You're just a regular Bob Hope, aren't you? That was Morris' ship. I guess their gunners didn't steal enough shit to get it to running right, but they're going anyway. You know, they're being men about it."

He stood to face the plane again, and gave number two engine's cowling a cursory wipe with his oily rag, as if it wouldn't make any difference.

"Yeah, she's ready for action again, but I don't know how number three here's going to take Twomey's ham-fisted mixture leaning. Don't expect things to happen fast - give it time to get settled in on a setting before you think you've got it right—or wrong."

"Sounds like a Ford I used to know." Wes didn't care if Lewis ever admitted the pilfered parts had saved the day for his plane and crew, and Lewis wouldn't. He sat on *Barfly's* right tire, reclined against the tall landing gear strut and lit a cigarette, and as Wes took the one Lewis then wordlessly offered him, the pair struck the picture of an amicably divorced couple who'd just seen their kid come out of minor surgery.

Wes drew on the cigarette and looking in the direction of the Mediterranean asked, "So, what do you hear, Mike? Patton and Monte ready to grab the rest of Italy yet? After what we did earlier in the month, I can't imagine it'd be long now."

"Naw, I haven't heard nothing."

Wes took leave of his friend, and began "briefing" *Barfly* as he walked around her one last time before crawling in through the belly hatch. Lewis eavesdropped, slightly amused for a moment, then resumed his smoke to wait for the pilots.

Wes didn't speak aloud to the plane until he was on the other side of its nose, just beyond Lewis' hearing, unless he was quiet. Then he began.

"Sweetheart, I know this place is giving you fits, but you gotta try to hold together for us," he said, peering up into the left landing gear well. "I don't know what these guys are thinking about sending a pretty thing like you out to this friggin' dustbowl," he rechecked a cowl flap linkage on the far left engine, number one, which was missing safety wire that held a crucial nut in place on the main actuator rod. "But I'm going to do everything I can to get you back to Hardwick safe and sound, and then we'll get you whatever you need, ok?" He worked his way back to the twin tail, grimacing at an over-greased rudder trim tab hinge that was accreting sand.

He called out to Lewis, "Did Kilborn lube this? He did, didn't he? That jackass." Wes pulled a rag out of his pocket and wiped the hinge carefully in one direction only, then inspected the rag, which he of course found full of sand. He sighed. "Just be good to us, you big ugly buzzard, and I promise we'll fix you up right when we get home, ok?"

He walked behind the right wing, eyeing the right gear leg's leaky oleo strut and stopping for a moment to consider the number four engine, whose oil, he'd found out from Lewis, hadn't been changed with the other three before they left England. Private Dan Kilborn, a bumpkin draftee from West Virginia, had been told to change its oil but could never remember from which side he was supposed to start counting, so he ended up changing the already new oil in number one. Lewis hadn't known this until he'd told Kilborn to uncowl number three and arrived back at the hardstand to find that the wrong engine opened up, prompting a sad investigation into his command of aircraft nomenclature, too late to do anything about it.

Tommy Warwick and the rest of the officers showed up just as Wes was patting *Barfly's* plexiglas nose. Warwick approached Wes alone, looked all around to make sure no one was in earshot, and asked, "So, Hutch, is this thing up for it today? Last couple nights didn't sound too good you know?"

"Yes, sir. She's got her pimples, no doubt about it, but the old girl's still a cutie underneath. She'll be fine. How much longer till we get her back to England, though?"

"Yesterday's not too soon for me, Wes." He looked around him again, and gestured to the desert surrounding them. "This sandbox's got me wondering why anybody'd fight for it, much less us. France, I could understand; Russia, I'd take their word for it—but honestly, the Sahara Goddamned *desert*?"

"War is hell, sir," Wes smiled down at his ship's captain. At 5'8" Warwick was of average height and highly skilled as a pilot, but Wes couldn't help but think of him as the shrimp that had his job. "Let's go see how the old girl feels today."

With that they sauntered over to the belly hatch and climbed aboard. Newhart, the copilot, was already busy getting the sweltering cockpit set up for engine start, setting the four engines' throttles, propeller pitch and fuel/air mixture controls. Radio operator Chuck Allred was setting his "boxes" up and waiting for the rest of the crew to sign in with him on the intercom. Billy Marshall, their navigator, was up in the cockpit telling Newhart the compass was leaking fluid, and may not make it through the day before going dry and becoming useless in any but perfectly still air, which they wouldn't be seeing at any time today at such low altitudes. Bombardier Larry Wilson was sitting at his position in the nose, but facing backward with his elbows propped up on the twin .50-cals in the nose turret, smoking a cigar with a look on his face like the father of a bride.

Wilson was one cool customer. With veterans in his bloodlines as far back as the Alamo, he was another man whose enlistment date read "8 December 41." He could think of no better way to indulge his rage at Japan than serving as a bombardier, focusing solely on toggling the switch that would release an 8,000 pound payload of bombs. Ever calm under any amount of pressure or fire, Wilson had cemented his place of honor among the men in the squadron on a mission the previous spring.

He'd just taken over the controls from Warwick for their target run, and the formation was getting pummeled by flak in the clear sky. With his face seemingly glued to the eyepiece of his Norden bombsight, he didn't even flinch when an 88-millimeter anti-aircraft shell slammed through the Plexiglas floor, streaking inches past his head and back out the top of the "greenhouse" at the nose of the bomber, exploding a few dozen feet above and well behind them. As Navigator Marshall unclenched his teeth and stole a glance to his right, afraid to see what might remain of his friend, Wilson, whose left hand continued making adjustments to his bombsight, made a fist as he raised his right and shouted out like an umpire, "BALL ONE!"

Wilson knew that very soon, perhaps a matter of days, his training as a bombardier, his experience on 18 missions with the Norden—one of the greatest secrets of the war—and all his courage and skill as a bombardier would be utterly meaningless as the airplane passed scant feet above their target, reducing any calculations about when to salvo the bombs to simple reflex. What he didn't know yet was that he'd soon be aboard that airplane for over 13 hours, all for the privilege of toggling the bomb release for perhaps a half-second as they streaked over the cracking towers of Ploesti's former Standard Oil refinery, close enough to hear the timer-fused bombs clang home and start their countdown to detonation, some minutes to hours later. The hardest thing he had to do on this mission was wait.

With the officers in their places, the gunners were also at loose ends, so they passed the time trading fictitious insults about each other's sisters and moms, in the great tradition of the young American Male. As Warwick and Newhart finished the checklists and fired up the engines however, talk fell off as the men began to consider the real mission ahead of them, and how it might, or might not, resemble the day's exercise.

7

Paul told Justin the long version of the engine fire story the next day and mentioned that he'd gotten a date out of the whole thing, but then several weeks passed with nary a word between them. In August, Paul returned from a trip to find, out of the blue, an unusual-sounding message from Justin, asking if he might be able to come to Wichita for another visit soon.

It wasn't like his dad to do or say something so blatantly needy, and his voice didn't have any tone of loneliness or depression in it whatsoever. Paul knew that sound well from when he was living with his Mom after the divorce. He meant to call his dad back, but something made him hesitate. Had he met a woman? Was he wanting Paul to come back to meet her? Did he quit his job or get fired again? "Oh God," he muttered to his empty apartment, "what if he's drinking again?"

A Silver Ring

As conventional wisdom dictated, the court had awarded full custody of Paul and his younger sister Sarah to their mother and gave Justin 90 days to find other employment and begin making payments before he would be found in default of child support. With her parents getting on in years, Gloria promised to stay in Marion at least long enough to see Sarah graduate high school but planned to move back to Chicago someday.

The divorce presented an agonizing dilemma to Paul, who loved both his parents dearly and took great comfort from his mom's abiding presence through all the upheaval over the years. He couldn't ignore that he had much more in common with his father, just as many boys do, but there was much more between them than the usual father/son stuff. They were inseparable whenever and wherever the subject of flying was about, which their obsession guaranteed to be virtually all the time. Justin's flying expertise galvanized his influence in every other arena, from cars and school work to sports, fishing, camping, and the like, to the primeval urge to sit around a fire and just talk, or not, as men have done together for eons.

Paul, then a sophomore at Marion's Harding High School, had finally made some good friends, despite yet another of many rocky starts as "the new kid" in junior high and, for the first time in his turbulent life, he felt like a real part of the school landscape. He also had an intense crush on a girl in his class.

Paul wanted nothing more than to stay in Marion and graduate from that high school, but he wanted nearly as much to stay with his father, where his love for flying would be welcome. When his parents announced the divorce, they offered their kids the choice of with whom they would stay, and the stress of the decision, added to all the other adolescent turmoil, kept him up nights.

His mother proved her understanding one night when she came to bid him goodnight and said, "I know you're having a hard time with this, Paul, and I think I know why. You and your dad have a relationship any boy would envy. You guys do love your airplanes, don't you?"

Looking up at his mom from his pillow, his eyes filled, and huge tears cascaded from them as he pursed his lips tightly and nodded his head.

"Oh, honey, it's okay, it really is. I wish I had something like that that just took me into another place whenever I thought about it, but I don't. You're very lucky."

"Great."

"Listen. Look at me." Nudging his chin, she brought his eyes up from the P-51 Mustang model sitting on the dresser by the foot of his bed to the face of the woman who had brought him into the world, in whose eyes he saw nothing but steady, selfless love.

"If you want to stay with him, I understand. You two are peas in a pod, and as angry as I am with him, I love what he does for you, and you don't do him anything but favors either. I'm not going to be mad at you or feel like you abandoned me or anything like that if you need to stay with him."

Paul's flushed face broke into a hurt, angry look as he said, "Oh, ok, that's nice. Been nice knowing you. Bye!"

"Paul Prator, you know good and well that's not what I'm saying," Gloria started crying and pulled him into a hug.

"I just know your father's never happier than when he's flying those damned planes, and you're just like him, maybe even a little worse, and I don't want you feeling guilty for my sake if you stay with him. I know you love me, and I hope you know how much I love you, and none of that's ever going to change no matter who lives with whom or where, ok?"

The two of them sat there crying for a few minutes until Paul was able to compose himself again.

"Mom, it's not just that. I don't want to change schools again. I'm so frickin' sick of being the new kid, and now I'm finally not. I go to school and people actually go out of their way to talk to me. I pass notes with people between classes. I sit with the same people at lunch every day. It's like I'm one of the gang for once. I can't stand thinking about losing all that again— it takes two years to get my bearings every time we move, and that's all I've got left in school now!"

"I know, Paul, I know. The moving's been hard on all of us, and that's why I just can't do it anymore, as much as I love your dad, I just can't. So, I know what you're saying, believe me."

"If I stayed with you, would you, like, get mad every time I talk about flying, or would you try to keep me from doing it? You know how I couldn't wait to be old enough to fly solo and everything, and now I am."

He looked at the tail of the shirt he'd been wearing on his first solo flight the month before, which was tacked up prominently on the back of his bedroom door. Bearing the inscription "1st SOLO MARCH 12, 1980 N9572Y RUNWAY 22" the memento included a bad cartoon of a pilot in a Cessna reaching his hand down below the plane, feeling uncertainly for the ground. It had been, by far, the best day of his life. It was also less than a week before the day his dad identified himself as an alcoholic and was fired.

"As much as I hate what your father's love for flying did to our marriage and our lives, I can't tell you I'm not proud of what you're doing with it. You've got something he never had—you know what you want to do with your life before it even starts. If that's what makes you happy, I say go for it. I'm behind you all the way."

He hugged her and asked, "How do you suggest I ask Dad?"

Her face showed what she'd like to say to him herself, in any of a dozen ways, but she said nothing. Then, only when his raised eyebrows and sad eyes told her she wasn't getting away with not answering, she finally said, "I don't know."

Paul found a way however, and spent hours on the telephone the next two years telling Justin about his exploits. Justin completely understood his desire to stay in Marion, and even took time off from his "new job" at Cessna to go back for Paul's seventeenth birthday, to have the honor of being his first "passenger" after Paul's private pilot check ride. As a little boy, Paul had ecstatically served in the same capacity for his father, since at that time Gloria didn't want to so much as hear the word "airplane," much less get a ride in one.

Paul took a job washing dishes at the Ponderosa Steakhouse after school, and Gloria, true to her word, was good about using some of the child support Justin faithfully sent each month to help him get a car and cover expenses so he could spend all his money on flying until he graduated from Ohio State and went to work for BlueSky.

Before Paul was finished puzzling over his dad's cryptic message, the next one played. Wingspan Airlines, a major airline serving cities all over the country with a rapidly expanding fleet of over two-hundred airplanes, wanted to interview him—contact lenses, medical waiver and all. One of the airline's check airmen was old golf buddies with the General at Rickenbacker and had heard about Paul's emergency.

Paul called his father even before he called Wingspan, and they both were so excited about the interview that Justin at first forgot, then decided against, telling Paul about having met his mum. After all, he rationalized, it wasn't like it was any big news to Paul, and Justin didn't want to gunk up his son's mind before his interview. He'd need everything he had to get through it; there'd be plenty of time for family drama later. Paul asked if everything was ok, if it would be all right if they visited after things settled down a bit. Justin said everything was fine.

The next week, Paul had the interview, worked a tense Labor Day weekend awaiting word from Wingspan, during which time he wasn't fit for conversation with anyone, and was hired September 2nd.

It was a dream job, if not exactly his, and high on life, he felt unusually sure of his intuitions. That day he bought a ring, and he proposed to Christina when they went out to celebrate that night. She'd been telling people she felt like she knew this guy better after their first conversation than anyone she'd ever known in her life, and she didn't hesitate. They set the date for the first anniversary of their meeting, June 20th, 1987.

When Paul called to tell his dad he was hired, Justin nearly spilled the beans about meeting his mum, but by then he'd been putting it off for so long, the big news had become stale. "The kid's got enough on his plate already—there'll be a better time. No big deal," became almost a mantra in Justin's mind as he listened to Paul report his hiring, his proposal, her acceptance, their wedding plans, and all his new dreams for their future.

Flying for Wingspan was surreal at first. Paul found himself looking up at the giant jet planes as he inspected them before each flight, marveling at their size and powerful beauty, and that he actually understood how they worked, if not exactly how to fly them. Having never flown in the military, Paul had only flown a jet a few times, and never as a captain. BlueSky only flew turboprops, none of which flew faster than about three-hundred miles per hour, and rarely higher than about 20,000 feet. There was a big difference between the Metroliners and Brasilias he flew there and these barely-subsonic swept-wing behemoths, and he was glad to have some time to just watch from his engineer's seat behind the pilots.

As with most pilots hired by major airlines at that time, Paul was initially assigned as a Flight Engineer on the Boeing 727, arguably the least fun job in a cockpit, and inarguably the lowest paid. In their first year as an "FNG" engineers were paid $21,000 regardless of how much, or how little, they worked. Assuming he made it through probation, Paul's pay would nearly double the second year, and then nearly double again when he moved up to copilot in a few years, but he was glad he didn't have a wife or kids to feed just yet.

As engineer, he had the inglorious responsibility for many of the functions computers control on more modern airplanes, but he was charged with determining and reporting to the captain the airworthiness status of the plane before each flight. Once that was finished, he'd fill out some forms, verify servicing was completed, facilitate and monitor the engine starts, bring generators and air conditioning and pressurization controls on line, and then sit back and watch the captain and copilot have all the fun of flying the old girl.

It wasn't a difficult job, but the boredom level did get tiresome. Paul would cycle between complacent disengagement during the uneventful cruise phase of the flight and fighting to keep quiet when the pilots did things in ways he thought were either wasteful or just plain dumb in the critical takeoff and landing phases.

In the pseudo-military culture of the airlines, his opinions were nearly weightless while on probation, and expressing himself could only do him harm. The idea of spending another five to fifteen years biting his tongue, though to a lesser degree, while accruing the seniority to upgrade to captain, was almost more than he could stand. If just one captain voiced dissatisfaction with his performance for any reason, he could be fired without cause during that probationary first year, but even then and forever after, he was required by regulation and expected, at least in theory, to speak up any time he had any policy, regulation, or safety issue. Walking that fine line was a learned art. Engineers or copilots who tended to speak up too soon or too often were branded as overzealous hemorrhoids, but those who failed to speak soon enough could be named as factors in an accident, which was a fate worse than, if not coupled with, death.

Since he'd be on reserve for at least a few months, subject to being called any time day or night to fill a seat suddenly left empty by a sick or unavailable senior pilot, commuting to Wingspan's hub in Kansas City was impossible. Paul rented an apartment just north of the river and invited the "Grand Wizard" of the Traveling Prator Clan to fly up one weekend in November, purportedly to help him move but really just to find out what that phone message had been about.

Paul arrived at Kansas City's Downtown Airport to find his dad visiting with the attractive girl behind the desk of Executive Beechcraft, the airport's transient aircraft fuel and service provider. ExecBeech, as it was known to the steady stream of corporate pilots and planes that flowed through during the workweek, was quiet as a church on weekends. Justin Prator and his rented Cessna 172 were its only patrons.

"Hey, old man, you said 11. You're early." It was 11:08.

"Big tailwind up there today," he smiled. "Almost enough to make a SkyHog even seem fast. I just got here though." They hugged, and Paul asked the girl if it didn't seem like more time had passed to her, with yet another weekend pilot indulging his Learjet-pilot fantasies at Kansas City's corporate aviation hub.

"Him? He's no private pilot. The tower didn't call to say he's in trouble when he gets in, and there's no telltale Beechcraft, so he's not a doctor."

The guys laughed at that, but she continued, a pilot herself and glad to have someone she'd describe as "real" to talk shop with.

"Lawyers fly just to impress their buddies, which is why they always fly something fast, which *that* is not." She looked disdainfully outside at the yellow and white aerodynamic atrocity that was Cessna's mediocre but legendary model 172 Skyhawk and went on, with a nod to the still, gray November sky.

"Besides, only an old pro would be out boring holes in the clouds on a good bowling day like this. He minds his manners too well to be rich, and he didn't have to ask where the men's room was," she was flirting outright now. "Nope, he might as well have letterhead tattooed to his forehead—I can tell an old pro from a weekender even on a weekend."

Justin's raised eyebrows arched as he stuck his tongue out at Paul. With false humility he then mentioned he did fly a Citation for a while, "as a matter of fact," but had gone to head up Cessna's Pilot Center program a few years ago, so he was actually a little bit of both the corporate and general aviation worlds.

"Guess we'll see you tomorrow," Justin said as they turned to leave.

"I'll be here. All alone. I hate weekends." She was flirting a little too much for Paul's taste. He was glad to have Christina.

They went back to Paul's apartment, unloaded and cleaned the trailer Paul had had to tow with his tiny car, and returned it to the U-Haul center on North Oak Street, where the guys were much more helpful in taking the illegal trailer hitch off the Dodge Omni then the ones in Ohio had been about telling Paul how to install it.

By then it was nearly dinnertime, and Paul suggested they go grab some of the barbeque that made Kansas City famous. They ended up at Smokestack, just south of the Plaza, where K.C. Masterpiece was located. "*Masterpiece* is for tourists. It's done to death," Paul bragged as they passed by, as if Kansas City was Disneyland. "One of my Captains told me about this place—it's like crack for your taste buds. It's like, what you'd ask to eat before they execute you!"

Neither of them had eaten lunch or much of a breakfast, so the sweet, smoky smell greeting patrons at the simple, tiny strip-mall restaurant's door took their simmering stomachs to a full boil. They ordered some huge, succulent onion rings with horseradish ranch dip for an appetizer and three-meat combo plates for dinner, with cole slaw, baked beans, cornbread, and fried okra for sides.

Paul did most of the talking at first. They hadn't spoken at any length since Paul's last visit to Wichita, which was by then five months ago.

"Her family's really taken me in, made me the butt of all kinds of stupid jokes. At first I thought they were kind of an unruly mob, really rowdy, you know, but now that I've gotten to know them a little better, I think I underestimated them that night we first met. They're kind of the closest things to heroes left in the civilian world.

"They've got all these stories of having saved people from car wrecks, infernos, and all kinds of catastrophes, but then they'll practically kill each other in a pickup football game, hide disgusting things in each other's food, and carry on like teenagers even as old men.

"They all talk about their Grandpa, The Chief, who I haven't met yet, like he spits nitroglycerin and pisses battery acid or something. He got a Medal of Honor for taking out a German machine gun emplacement singlehandedly on D-day, and when he came home, he married his girlfriend over her parent's objections and took her to Cleveland. I guess after you survive something like D-day, there's not a whole lot left to be afraid of.

"Words like *murder, tear, gouge, bludgeon, snuff,* and *stalk* seem to get used an awful lot about things he's said or done, and from the pictures I've seen, I believe it's all true. Looks like one scary son of a bitch. Not an old man you want to piss off.

"Since I'm living out here now, I guess I'm not going to have to meet him until the wedding, which seems kind of odd. I know if I had a granddaughter who was about to get married, I'd want to at least meet the guy first, but Christina said since he and her grandma eloped, he wasn't in any position to withhold consent. She's got him completely buffaloed. It's hilarious. All the guys are scared shitless of him, but she just does whatever she wants. She says he has no idea how to handle women.

"It's kind of funny how it all worked out, timing-wise, I mean. I had that emergency the day we met, and I never bothered to tell you this, but the General who runs Rickenbacker seemed kind of impressed by what we'd done, and I think he was trying to get me to join the Guard or the Air Force."

"What do you mean?"

"He just told me point-blank he wished the Air Force had more pilots like me, and he asked if I'd ever considered joining."

"Did you tell him, 'only about twenty-five times a day since I was six'?"

"No, but something like that. I told him about my vision, and he started up with the whole 'join as a back-seater and then transfer later' thing. Said he could 'help me'."

Justin's eyebrows went up as he took another of the now-lukewarm onion rings.

"Paul, you know Generals don't 'help.' They make things happen."

"I know. At the time, I was actually thinking about it. Well, I mean, I was thinking about thinking about it."

"So why didn't you?"

"I met Christina that night."

"So?"

"She was the first woman on the CFD. She's really proud of that, and I can't blame her. Back when I proposed to her, we talked about me moving to Cleveland so she could keep her job, be part of her Granddad's legacy and all that, and I just told her I really don't want to commute forever. If it was Maui or something, I could kind of see it, but really, who commutes from Cleveland?

"So she said she'd make a deal with me. She'll move to wherever I can be based with Wingspan, and she'll try to get a job wherever that is—which is here. But she said once she gets that first job, she's done. No more Traveling Prator clan."

Justin put his hands up in a full-mouthed mea culpa.

"She's on a union seniority list, like me, so we just can't pull up roots every two or three years. She couldn't take it, and I wouldn't be able to either, if I were her.

"So, meeting her that night kept me from doing something that would have made it pretty much impossible for us to ever be together, and it all worked out for the best without me having to make any decisions at all. I'm happier than I ever thought I'd get to be, and it's all because of that one 'bad day'. That's why I asked her to marry me in what seemed like such an impulsive move.

"It's what's meant to be. I just know."

With most of the meat and about half of the slaw, beans, and okra devoured, Paul finally seemed to have said about all he had to say, and Justin took a deep breath, loosened his belt, sat back and smiled in perfect satisfaction with his boy, who it seemed only a few years ago was sitting on a booster seat next to him, with legs too short to touch the rudder pedals, asking if he could try a landing.

"You've been on a wild ride the last few months, Paul, and I just can't tell you how proud I am. You're doing what I wished for you more times than I can count when you were growing up, and the really cool thing is, you know exactly what you've got. There's going to be rough times too, but for now you just need to try to suck the juice out of every day; this is the best time of your life, I guarantee."

Paul grunted with a smile, holding back a mouth full of coleslaw, "You can say that again." He wiped a stray bit of dressing off his mouth, grunted again, swallowed a drink of Coke, and started to put together a meat-and-beans-combo bite, anticipating his father had yet to come to his point.

"With everything you've had going on these past few months I haven't really felt the time was right to tell you this, but I've had some really incredible things happening too, and it all started about the same time as yours."

Justin was leaning his elbows on the table now with his hands clasped, as if in prayer, in front of his still-chewing face. Paul, genuinely interested, told him he knew something weird was going on back when he got the call for the interview, but admitted that he'd kind of forgotten about it.

"Are 'they' female?" Paul managed to raise only one eyebrow.

"Well, as a matter of fact,"

"Dad, let me make this easy for you. You and Mom have been divorced a long time now, and—"

"Paul—"

"No, Dad, please. I think it's great, I mean, you can't just live alone the rest of your life. You deserve somebody, and she deserves you. I can't wait to meet your 'sh-pecial sh-omeone'." Paul's baby-talk wasn't amusing his dad at all.

"Neither can I."

Again, the eyebrow.

"I'm not talking about a woman I'm seeing. I mean, I'm not seeing her." Justin shook his head at his clumsiness. *All this time waiting to tell him, you'd think I'd be able to say it better,* he thought.

Paul's face was the picture of a badly confused, bemused, conspirator.

"What. The hell. Are you talking about?"

"OK. I guess I don't have any idea how to tell you this, and it's not even that big of a deal anymore, but," he paused, mouth open and without breathing. "I've gotten in touch with my birth mother—your real grandmother."

"No shit?"

Justin nodded.

"Dad, that's fantastic!" he chuckled. "How?"

"She spent months trying to find me and then just called out of the blue the day after you went home from Wichita last June. We actually had lunch together the day you damn near burned the wing off your plane."

"Hey! I just want to clarify—*I* didn't *burn* anything," he pointed a mock warning. "I *kept shit* from burning, ok? Why didn't you tell me? This is huge!"

"Well, let's see. You had that emergency, the investigation, your interview, the waiting, you've been seeing Christy, you're hired, you're getting married. Jesus, Paul, you need two mouths and one ear these days!"

Paul sheepishly bowed his head. The two were quiet for a second, then Paul raised his glass of Coke.

"To the best of times. Isn't it about damned time?"

"Hear, hear," Justin said, clinking his just-refilled glass against his son's.

8

Ploesti was an unmitigated clusterfuck. After weeks of training in the vastly different tactics required for the low-level attack executed by the 93rd Bombardment Group that August 1st, the mission was almost completely ruined by a very few simple but critical navigation and formation flying errors. At the end of a fourteen-hour round-trip, eighty-eight of the one-hundred seventy-eight airplanes returned to Benghazi, fifty-five of which required repair to fly again.

Ploesti's damaged oil refineries were back at full pre-raid production levels in less than two months.

The remains of "Ted's Travelling Circus" returned to Hardwick later in August. The pride of the 409th squadron managed to get her crew back home safely, but was damaged beyond repair. As her sister ship, *Wary Canary* lifted the eight surviving members of

Barfly's crew off the Libyan wastes for the last time, Wes couldn't help but stare back at her, sitting so alone and forlorn, even in the company of several other proud birds that had done their jobs and brought their boys back home that sad day.

One of her tires had been hit with an anti-aircraft round and made them ground-loop out of control on landing; their faithful plane now sat where she had finally come to rest. Her number two engine was utterly destroyed by a direct hit, the others were run-out from overheating, and half her airframe seemed to be shot away. Wes hated that she had to be left to rot, and he tried without success to reassure himself that, despite all appearances to the contrary, *Barfly* had always been, and would forever be, just a machine—a tool with which to bring the bloody war to an end.

To the Air Corps, she was utterly expendable. Even before her crew arrived back at Hardwick, ten shiny new B-24J's stood—like so many more human replacements—to greet Ploesti's survivors, eager "to get into the war."

Not so eager, however, were the boys lucky enough to return from the disastrous raid, least of all *Barfly's* Flight Engineer, Randall Twomey.

Before their arrival over Ploesti, Twomey had been quiet as usual, and initially took frequent shots at the anti-aircraft guns mounted on towers that were, as advertised, often taller than their insanely low altitude. But, as they arrived inside Ploesti's deadly defensive perimeter and penetrated the thick black smoke, they began taking serious damage in the wilting crossfire.

Left with nothing to shoot, like no other member of the crew, Twomey had an unobstructed view of the plane ahead of them as it took a direct hit and pulled up sharply, slowing markedly in an effort to attain a safe bailout altitude. As it passed directly above them, he saw three burning, flailing bodies dive out the bomb bay, the inside of which he could see was engulfed in flame. Each of them knew, like Twomey did, they were far too low to survive bailing out. He continued to watch transfixed as the plane's right fuel cell ignited, at which point the plane went from a climb to a steep dive, skidding hard to the right and straight into one of the hundreds of storage tanks scattered beneath them.

His gun remained silent thereafter.

This seemed completely normal at first, since his dual role as flight engineer and turret gunner often demanded he be in two places at once. With all eyes focused outside the plane, it didn't occur to anyone that Twomey was manning his gun in body only until they too took a direct hit from one of the German guns.

The eighty-eight millimeter shell, about the size of a large man's fist, came from a gun beneath their left wing, no more than a quarter mile ahead. It began to detonate on contact with a steel cylinder head at the bottom of the number two engine, which then careened into the bottom of the left wing's nearly empty inboard fuel tank as the exploding shell itself slammed into Chuck Allred's radio console before its explosive charge was fully spent, killing Allred and navigator Billy Marshall instantly and severing dozens of wires, including those for the intercom and bomb release.

With nothing to see or shoot through the dense smoke, and suspect of Twomey's damage control, Wes focused on the plane and knew immediately they had serious problems. He'd seen engine fires before, and they'd all gone out fairly quickly. This one seemed to be getting worse.

Looking forward to Twomey's position, Wes' temper flared when he saw him standing motionless in his turret instead of at his console. Screaming "I'm coming!" to his ship, he ran forward, bashing his head in some turbulence along the way, the pain detonating his anger. He hit Twomey as hard as he could in the most convenient place, his ass, as he passed and set about shutting off fuel to number two.

While at the console, Wes took a quick look around at the other gauges to see if anything else needed immediate attention, then checked in with Warwick and Newhart, who were unaware Twomey had abandoned his gun since they'd expected to hear it go quiet when number two was hit. Twomey never said much anyway unless he needed help, so their larger concerns of flying the crippled airplane through a man-made black cloud with dozens of other planes only yards away, seemingly coming from all directions, had all their attention.

With the fire out on number two and their target behind them, Wes manually jettisoned the bombs and resumed his position at the waist gun. Now headed south with Ploesti behind them, enemy fighters would come to gnaw on the survivors. They'd need every gun and every round they had to fight their way back to the Mediterranean, gathering strength only from each plane that managed to rejoin the tattered formation.

The fighters never came, however, at least not to Wes' squadron. There were more than enough other bombers behind them to keep the short-range fighters busy. He'd never forget the blue of the Mediterranean finally coming into view ahead and, having yet to fire a single round at any fighters, going forward to check in with Tommy Warwick and hearing him shout over the din of their engines, "We're going to make it after all, just you wait. *Barfly's* got it made now, buddy!"

Twomey remained silent in his turret all the way back to Benghazi, despite repeated attempts to get him to talk. Wes filled in for him as de facto engineer, nursing *Barfly* along and keeping a steady mechanical dialogue with her: adjusting fuel mixtures, turbocharger wastegates, oil cooler bypass valves, cowl flaps, monitoring a dozen other functions, and talking, always talking, to comfort and reassure her as she carried her men to safety, and herself to her grave.

On the ground, Twomey had to be physically pulled from the turret, catatonic and crying. He was placed on the mile-long casualty list as "battle fatigued" and taken back to England, where he ultimately recovered and was placed in a non-combat staff position in another unit. No one alive would ever hear or have to ask what had gotten to him. In the carnage of that mission, any guess would do.

The "Circus" resumed flying from Hardwick with their new planes after a brief furlough. Wes used the break to try to catch up on his mail and make up for lost time with Melody, since he'd been so busy in the weeks leading up to their African junket, but his experience at Ploesti had left him emotionally barren and unable to enjoy time with her as much as he'd looked forward to it.

Melody couldn't ignore the stark change in his demeanor. Put off at first, she was afraid he might have fallen out of love with her or, worse, into it with someone else. After a few conversations with him however, doing a rough count of how many men had been lost, watching him with his friends and them around him, she began to understand what an indescribably hellish experience they'd been through. The 93rd Bombardment Group lost well over a hundred men on that mission. More than a hundred more were killed in the last quarter of 1943, compared to just over a hundred in the entire year before Ploesti. She pitied him for his losses, including his beloved airplane, loved him all the more for his brave perseverance, and wanted more than anything else to be able to take him away from the war and keep him safely to herself, once and for all.

The change in Wes was also clearly visible in his letters home, which bore markedly fewer "blackouts" from where Army censors had stricken sensitive information that never occurred to him as anything "Jerry" could use against them. It wasn't that he was now taking any greater care to keep his comments on the safe side, only that he was no longer writing anything about the Army, his job, the war, or even the airplanes he used to love to talk about so much. Going into the holidays of 1943, after weeks back in civilization, he managed to write only two pages of drivel about the differences between the English and American Christmas.

Charlotte Hutchinson noticed the sharp difference in the tone of his letters home. She was, of course, ecstatic that he was safe, at least as of the two to three week lag in each letter's arrival, but she worried when his letters, which used to have her practically hearing his laugh from behind the paper, turned into a series of pulpy second-section newspaper articles. Not wanting to talk about it herself, she didn't share her concerns with Levi, but he too had noticed, and would pray as he read each letter that this man he missed so much, who was once his son but had become more like a brother, would have the wits and the luck to get back home soon. And he knew the odds were decidedly against it.

Early 1944 brought England's infamous gloom, and the men and machines of the mighty Eighth Air Force coiled like a spring under the oppressive weather. Fuel and ordnance inventories piled up, maintenance was fully caught up, and flight crews rested and recreated as never before, sometimes to the point of excess.

Wes and Melody were able to spend more time together than ever, going out for dinners, taking long walks, attending hangar dances, and, yes, even spending a few nights together when opportunities arose. As frowned upon by the brass as it was commonplace among the men, the evil of illicit sex paled in comparison to those found in combat. England's cold nights cast a great many eyes blind to grammar school morality, for the simple reason that any one or one-thousand men might not live to grope their way through the next.

When they did return to the sky, the character of the bombers' missions had changed for the better in one regard; They were now afforded the luxury of fighter escort for some distance into Occupied Europe, which was comforting, at least until the Germans learned not to bother attacking the bombers until they were farther from home. Then, with an uncanny knack for knowing exactly when their "little friends" would have to abandon them to "search and destroy" their way back home, the Messershmitts and Focke-Wulfs would seem to come from everywhere at once, faster and more numerous than they could count.

This melee would last until they reached the next Dantean level of Hell, to which they were long accustomed—in which the enemy fighters would abruptly depart, making the deafening roar of the four engines and two-hundred mile-per-hour slipstream seem an eerie silence, only to be shattered by thousands of anti-aircraft guns taking their own brand of butchery to the skies over the target. Those emerging from the barrage intact would face freshly-refueled fighters bent upon letting none return to England. The missions could run over eight hours, with only the first and last hours free of hostile fire.

A Silver Ring

Unlike Frank Lawton's 1st Infantry, airmen wounded in flight had no "rear area" or aid station to evacuate to, no medics to scream for, no choice but to fight on untreated for what could be hours—getting tossed around like pebbles inside a tin can, flying through air cold enough to freeze blood at the wound, and thin enough to turn its normal vibrant red color to a washed-out pastel. Such was the combat life of the "prima donna" American bomber crews.

With Twomey's exit, Wes became flight engineer of their as-yet-unnamed new airplane, referred to simply as "248," the last three digits of her serial number. Warwick asked his crew if they should name her *Barfly II* in homage, but the men unanimously felt that there'd be no honor for *Barfly* in it. That was a name and a plane that would best live and die one-of-a-kind, like her casualties.

Wes was glad to be out from under Twomey's shadow, faint and vague though it had been, and away from the gaping waist windows in the side of the Liberator. In the top turret, the temperature was still well below zero at altitude, but without a hurricane blowing all around him, his heated flight suit actually made him hot. He could talk to Warwick and Newhart without using the intercom, which made him feel even closer to doing the job he so coveted.

Wes' crew flew only four missions in January, 1944 due to bad weather. February saw them fly no less than ten times, culminating in what would come to be known simply as "Big Week," during which the Eighth Air Force as a whole dropped 10,000 tons of bombs in six days, including some on Berlin.

With Big Week over and Berlin stricken, the men became certain the war was as good as won. Hitler was running out of resources for his Luftwaffe almost as fast as combat-qualified pilots. With air superiority, thick supply lines, and a fearsome industrial complex now humming along at a frenetic pace, the Allies would soon be bombing Germany mercilessly. The shell of Europe's "nut" had been cracked.

With this in mind, Wes and Melody began, for the first time, to talk about Peace. For his part, Wes had no doubt whatsoever that he would take her home with him and live the rest of his days a happy man, if only she could be talked into leaving. Melody's family proudly traced their lineage back to feudal times, and they were all deeply enmeshed in each others' lives.

There were times, on the rare sunny days he wasn't fighting for his life, that he thought perhaps he could be the one to expatriate to this quirky but not unattractive country, but his folks were sounding more and more desperate about the situation between Eileen and Frank Lawton.

Good friends with Caney's Postmistress, Charlotte was secretly kept apprised of all Lawton's letters to Eileen, with a just-credible number of the envelopes arriving "damaged," allowing her to preview their contents. Confrontation with Lawton was inevitable if he survived the war, and Wes knew his father wouldn't stand for the loss of his only daughter after what he saw as his failure with their wayward firstborn, Lee. Wes prayed nightly not just for survival, which he felt obvious, but for God to show him the way to get Melody to forsake her grand Kingdom, and for his father and Lawton to make peace, or for Lawton to get out of Eileen's life somehow, before somebody got killed.

Melody knew, too, that their relationship was far deeper than the hormone-fueled affairs of the day, and she longed first and foremost for Wes' safety. Unbeknownst to him, she also secretly wished for her own ties to her homeland to somehow weaken.

Civilized, established, "dreadful" England was all she'd ever known, and the stories Wesley told of his childhood, simple and hardscrabble as it was, had such an air of adventure and potential to them that she began to fantasize about how she might be able to secure her family's blessing to emigrate.

Snobbishly patriotic, her father couldn't fathom any reason why a born-and-bred Briton would ever be attracted to the "colonies," as he called them. Meeting Melody's "unabashedly simple" Yank had done little to convince him otherwise, and though he wished "the daughters of England had more of their own kind around from which to pick and choose," he knew well the power Love has over a young heart, and bore her no real malice for her choice, so long as she "held prime in her judgment the honor of her family and her King."

The second waxing moon since her last menstrual period shone through a thin fog over Hardwick as March, 1944 drew to a close. There'd been rumors of a long mission on April Fools' Day, but since it hadn't yet officially been announced, Wes caught a ride into town to have dinner with Melody before passes could be cancelled.

Melody said she had something for him the week before, but Wes had been unable to get a pass. He was more preoccupied with his need to talk to her in person than whatever gift she had for him. Everyone could sense the invasion looming, and his next mission would be his twenty-third; twenty-five was the magic number to get sent home to sell war bonds. One way or another, he wasn't going to be in England much longer.

Wes wanted to take her somewhere they could have a serious talk without the noise and interruptions of a pub—somewhere privacy and hushed conversation were implicit and wouldn't garner attention. He took her to the library.

Hardwick's library was old and established, but small and often deserted. Wes had gone there once just before their detachment to Libya, just to kill time while waiting to see Melody, but he had become one of its most frequent patrons since their return. They had a few books about aviation, as well as subscriptions to *Popular Mechanics, Popular Science,* and *Air Progress* magazines, and something about the place just agreed with him. The old librarian was rather hard of hearing and given to grumpiness with women and soft-spoken men, but he'd always been kind and patient with Wes, who'd found his voice in Oklahoma's oilfields' racket.

Wes spent entire rainy days educating himself about flying, and he secretly began to cobble together plans to become an airline pilot or, if he was too tall for that too, at least flight engineer when the war was over. The technology on the B-24 and the new B-29 bomber was more than adequate for civilian applications, and the skies over America were being predicted to fairly darken with all the airplanes once the war's stranglehold on resources was broken.

The old librarian, Mr. Littleton, looked up and smiled when he saw Wes open the library's door for Melody, but his expression dimmed considerably when he realized his young friend was showing more than polite kindness to one of Hardwick's more prominent daughters. Nevertheless, he managed to almost bellow a "Good day, Miss Thompson, Sergeant. May I assist you with anything today?"

"No, thanks Mr. Littleton. Melody here was wanting to show me some of her favorite books, and I've got a couple I wanted to tell her about too, so we just thought we'd come in and have a look around for a bit. We both know right where we need to take the other, but I sure appreciate the offer. How are you doing today?"

His smile returned when he saw Wes' usual respectful demeanor and courtesy didn't degrade into a young man's bluster with a pretty girl at his side, and the reverent way Wes touched the back of Melody's shoulder as he mentioned her didn't go unnoticed either.

"Suffering from a slight headache," he replied, "and to be frank old boy, dangerously close to falling asleep at the switch the moment you arrived. But I envision our Mr. Hitler with rather more pressing problems at the moment, which bolsters my forbearance considerably."

Melody was embarrassed for him when she saw Littleton's long-winded joke fail to plant even the seed of a smile on Wes' deadly serious face.

"You poor dear. I could trot over to the pharmacy to fetch you a bottle of aspirin, if you like."

He shook his head. "Sorry?"

Melody caught Wes' wry grimace and remembered the old man's hearing was shot, then repeated herself, louder, "Would you like me to fetch you some aspirin?"

"Oh, that's terribly kind of you, my young lady, but completely unnecessary, I assure you. Like all things, pleasant and not, it's here for a reason and will pass in due time. Now please waste no more of the day on an old man, but do call on me if you have any difficulty finding what you need."

They thanked him and disappeared into the stacks, holding hands and talking far too quietly for him to hear.

Once they were a few aisles deep into the small library, Wes stopped her at the end of a bookshelf, well out of sight from the desk, and spent a long moment drinking her in with his eyes, a small, perhaps sad smile on his face.

"So, Sergeant Hutchinson, whatever are we doing in the Hardwick "Hard Luck" Library at three of a Wednesday afternoon? Surely you don't propose to have your way with me in a library..."

"I wanted a quiet place to talk to you, and I don't know any better place." His smile had disappeared again and his eyes bore a pleading sadness she'd never seen before that sent a chill through her.

"Is something wrong, Wesley?"

"No, nothing. Nothing at all. I just..." He looked away from her to the wood floorboards beside her feet. She followed his gaze and lifted her right foot to brush it against his left leg, playfully.

"Are you wondering what I have for you?"

"No, not really. I know I'll love whatever it is, and to tell you the truth I've got bigger things on my mind lately."

"Like what?"

"Like the end of the war. It might be here for me pretty soon. Our next mission's my twenty-third, and Jerry's not going to have a pot to pee in that hasn't been blown to hell in another few weeks."

He looked up from the floor to her eyes, which were flicking back and forth between his own, searching for the real meaning behind his vague expression.

"I want to know what comes next before it gets here."

She stared up at him, her heart pounding at the sight and sound of this tall, strong, brave American, begging her with tasteful indirectness to tell him what he must do to have her. She laughed aloud and tears welled up in her eyes at the adorable silliness of it.

"What on Earth does that mean?"

She threw her arms around him without a word, hugging him hard for a long time and weeping into his class A uniform tunic, the Air Medal he'd received for Ploesti, and its Oak Leaf Clusters from Big Week poking into her cheek. She gently caressed his back and the short hair at the top of his neck she remembered playfully tugging on the night they met.

"I think what I have for you here might help you figure that out." She pulled away from him and began fishing through her purse, pulling out a blue velvet jewelry box.

"I think we might have this backwards," Wes said, his own heart pounding as she handed him the box.

"Don't get your hopes up," she looked coyly up at him, "it's but a trinket."

Wes opened the box and saw a ring like those he remembered mentioning in his letter from Benghazi, with an Air Corps wings and propeller insignia cast into its table. Among Ploesti's losses had been his desire for such a display of the pride so many men's blood had dulled. He hadn't mentioned the rings since. In fact, many were being sold second, sometimes even third-hand, though still at a premium, to bright-eyed replacements.

Melody's Uncle Percy had sold out of them while the 93rd was in Libya and, with rationing, was unable to secure enough silver to produce another lot. When Wes returned, Melody begged him to make just one more. He had to melt down some earrings and other inventory to do it, so it cost far more than the rest he'd made, but Melody swore she'd make it up to him somehow.

"Oh my. You did read my letters, didn't you?" He kissed her. "Thank you, doll."

Do you still like it? I haven't heard you mention them at all since you've been back. I was afraid perhaps they've become trite with your chums."

"No, no. I just…I just haven't thought about it that much, I guess."

"What do you think now?"

"I love it! It's absolutely beautiful." He kissed her again, longer, then added another "thank you."

"So. Now. Let's finish what you wanted to talk about, and then perhaps I'll have something more to tell you," she toyed with him.

"Well, whenever I have to leave here, for good, I just want to know if you'll still be my girl. I mean, I still want you to be."

"Wes, I've been thinking more about this than you may ever know. My family, my life, everything I've ever known or loved is in England." At that his face fell again, but she took his chin in her hand and made him look at her as she added, "but only until you leave."

They heard the library door open and Mr. Littleton say "Good day, Sergeant, may I help you at all?"

"I'm actually looking for a friend of mine. Have you seen any other Americans in here today?" Wes knew the voice well—it was Ed Worley.

"Well as a matter of fact, there's one here now, but I can't believe it could be the exact person you're looking for."

Wes walked out to the front of the library to meet Worley, with Melody close behind.

"I'm back here, Ed. What's going on?"

"Oh, hi Wes. Hi Melody." He inhaled.

"Passes are revoked. They've got us locking down for tomorrow, lights out at 2100, brief's at 0500. Sounds like the long one came through. I told Warwick I thought I might be able to find you, and when you weren't at the Ransom I figured you might be here. We need to get back."

A Silver Ring

Wes looked back at Melody with a strained smile, and gave her a polite kiss, then asked, in a library whisper so faint even she almost couldn't hear, "so you'll go home with me, then?"

She nodded bravely, fighting every instinct to grab him and refuse to let go.

"Right! We'll have a look at your picks next, then," he said with his practiced English accent, and she laughed for a moment before covering her mouth, then, punching him softly in the chest she said, "Take care of that airplane, Yank."

He gave her a long kiss on her forehead, a short one on her cheek, then walked out with his friend, telling Mr. Littleton he hoped his headache went away soon as he gently pushed the door closed.

9

Paul stood outside the Cessna Pilot Center at Cleveland's Lakefront Airport watching a small plane's approach, which was a little high, even with the strong wind. After a lifetime spent around airplanes, he still couldn't resist the urge to watch the miracle of flight in action and left for the airport a little early, just to take in the sights and sounds of Lakefront's private airplane traffic pattern.

Dipping the right wing slightly while kicking hard left rudder to keep the plane from turning, the pilot put the plane deep into a forward slip, quickly, if not quite gracefully, bleeding off the excess altitude then executed a picture-perfect full-stall landing near the runway threshold. He needed no brakes, and actually had to add a touch of power to maintain a reasonable taxi speed to the runway turnoff.

"That was interesting," Paul mumbled to no one.

Paul was so busy appreciating how the little plane seemed to still be flying as it taxied in, he didn't notice until well after the pilot jumped from its long, low wing that it was his father.

Paul helped him tie it down, determined not to give his dad the satisfaction of asking about the gorgeous new plane, but finally, as they walked inside to check in, he relented to his curiosity.

"What would Clyde Cessna say if he knew one of his people was out flying around in a Mooney?"

"Clyde's got no use for me anymore. Nor I, him," came the curt reply.

"Whose is it?"

"Mine." He said it like he was talking about a dirty dish left sitting out.

Paul stopped dead in his tracks. "Say again?" The plane's value was deep in six-figure territory.

"It doesn't even have a Hobbs meter." Justin, smiling deviously, was referring to the simple hour meter in almost every rental airplane in the world.

"How?"

"Ever hear of something called a "signing bonus?"

Justin had told Paul Cessna was pulling the plug on its Pilot Center program, with a product liability crisis looming that would force it, like most other major airplane manufacturers, to cease production of the small airplanes it had built for decades, but with typical secrecy, or lack of forethought, he hadn't mentioned what he was going to do next.

With his management experience at Cessna, Justin was able to get a new job heading up a similar program with Mooney Aircraft, in Kerrville, Texas. The difference was that Mooney was hedging its bets, focusing on training the pilots that were actually ordering their famously fast airplanes, not just trying to create pilots who may or may not be brand-loyal if they bought one later, like Cessna. The plane, a brand-new "252", named for its top speed, along with an expense account for up to 100 hours per year, was Mooney's enticement to get Justin to leave a job it didn't know Cessna was about to cut anyway.

"Took me a while," Justin said, "but I think I finally got this 'career' thing licked."

"How the--" Paul spun around for at least the third time, looking back at the beautiful airplane, incredulous.

"I have to admit I couldn't have done it without my mum's help. She knew somebody that knew somebody at Mooney, and brought up that she sure wished she could get me to move to Texas somehow. Next thing I knew, I was flying back from Kerrville wishing to God that damned Cessna would get out of its own way so I could start packing."

"No shit." Paul was still stunned. He stopped at the door to the FBO, started to take a step back toward the plane, but then realized he was getting married in a little over a day, and much remained to be done. There was no time for a joyride. Unless—

"When did you say her flight's getting in?"

"She said 2:35. Can you loan me some wheels, or do you want to go with me to pick her up?"

"Shit. It's almost two now. I want to go, but I've still got a lot to do today." He was still staring at the plane.

"What I really want is a ride in that fire-breathing dragon you've got there."

"There'll be time later, Paul. It's not going anywhere, well, except back home with me, and I'll be coming out to see you every chance I get. It's only a day's flight to anywhere in this thing, for God's sake. You won't believe it." Paul had never in his life seen his dad gloat this way.

"Oh, I'll believe it, all right." Paul sighed sharply, shook his head, and opened the door for his dad with an exaggerated flourish, in homage.

Their arrangements made, they walked through the parking lot, and Paul ogled his brand new white '87 Trans Am convertible gleaming in the summer sun with the covetous, assaying look of a man with a lovely wife who's just met one prettier. They set Justin's bags on the useless back seats and got in.

"I may just have to toss you the keys and meet up with you guys later, but I'm dying to meet her." Paul looked out at the Mooney one more time. "I'm a little nervous about letting you drive my *Alyssa*, but if you can fly that thing, I guess you can probably drive a TA."

"Your what? Oh, the car. No, I won't abuse your mistress. Some nice set of wheels. You rich airline pilots." Justin laughed self-consciously as Paul started the car and began backing out.

"Yeah, we've got it really good compared to you poor management types with your, holy shit, FREE AIRPLANES!"

"Well, she's dying to meet you too, but you just worry about what you've got to do. There'll be time for visiting at some point, I'm sure. Are you staying at Christy's folks' place, or what?"

"Yeah. I was just going to stay with her, but we didn't want to piss the Chief off. This way we don't risk me seeing her in her dress before the wedding, either."

"Good. Her Grandpa doesn't sound like he'd take too kindly to any 'funny business', certainly not right under his nose like that. I'm glad you're being respectful."

"I still have yet to meet the guy. I think I've seen about everybody else in the family by now at least twice, but he and I just kept missing each other. His wife's real nice, though; I can't imagine he's that bad. I think they might just be full of shit, trying to scare me. They're the biggest bunch of jerk-offs you've ever seen." Justin perceived a touch of tolerant admiration for his heroic soon-to-be in-laws in there somewhere.

"Sounds like it's going to be a fun weekend. Guess where I'm going from here when I leave Sunday?"

"Well, I was assuming you'd be heading back to Wichita, but then I was assuming you'd be flying a piece of shit Skyhawk that reeks of ass and gas too, you lucky bastar--" Paul was a little envious, but mostly just happy for his dad, who seemed to have more going right for himself right now than he'd had in his entire previous life put together. He was glad he wasn't the only one having dreams come true.

"Not anymore, I'm not..." Justin mused, just audibly, well aware that Paul had just embarrassed himself with the dreaded "bastard" utterance, which, of course, was what Justin considered himself all his life, until very recently.

"...renting Cessnas, I mean." He passed Paul a wink.

"I'm flying down to Leesburg, Virginia to talk with a guy who knew my dad."

"You tracked him down finally?

"Yep. It took some digging, but the info mum gave me was all I needed to get a detailed report from the Air Force. I just got it last month and tracked the guy down. There was a big fire in a records warehouse in the seventies that destroyed a lot of the written records of their missions, but this guy, Worley's his name, is going to tell me the whole story, and I'm going to tape it."

"Wow. So, he really was on a B-24?"

"He was the waist gunner when he and my mum met, but they promoted him right before he got killed; he was in the top turret on their last mission."

Justin waited for Paul to look at him before continuing, "Flight Engineer."

"No shit? That's awesome. But you don't know what happened at all?"

"Nope. My mum wasn't next of kin, and his parents wouldn't talk to her about it when she came to the states carrying me. That's another subject altogether. I'd love to be able to find them somehow. Although judging by how they treated her when she talked to them, I'm not so sure they'd react very well to it. But, it's been a long time, who knows?"

"So, how weird is this, to find out who your mom and dad really were when you're almost a grandfather yourself?"

"Grandfather? Is there something you're not telling me?"

"You know what I mean."

"I'm still trying to process it all, really. The thing that's really amazing is he wanted to be a pilot. He was just too tall, so he had to do something else. And then here I am, my whole life wanting to fly too, never knew a thing about the guy, and then there's you. You were crazier about airplanes than I ever was. There's something in our blood for it, Paul; it's just what we're here to do."

Paul didn't answer, but gave his father a huge grin. Justin admired his son's handsome face, tan and unblemished, his blue eyes shielded from the glare by the brown-lensed Ray-Ban aviator sunglasses he'd never known another pilot to wear, and his spiked brown hair just vibrating in the sixty-mile-per-hour breeze, thanks to the three or four handfuls of ultra-hold styling gel he used for the decidedly unnatural style.

"I want a copy of that tape, ok?"

"Sure. It's going to clear an awful lot of mysteries up I hope."

"I want to know everything there is to know about him."

"I know."

After a few more minutes of driving in silence, they arrived at Christy's parents' house, but no one was home. A note was on the front door. Paul read it, walked back to the car and told Justin to go on and pick his mom up without him, and that he'd come to get the car after either his best man, Mark Rogers, or any of Christy's family showed up.

Rogers arrived from Detroit an hour later, his lifelong girth compressed into a brand-new Mustang GT he'd helped build himself at Ford. He had a twelve-pack on ice in the Detroit Lions cooler that lived in his trunk and immediately began the same relentless goading with which he'd gotten Paul and himself into what little trouble they'd found in high school. He insisted Paul start drinking immediately, and refused to take him to get his car, so he'd have no way to drive.

"Tonight you don't have a fucking car. Tonight you don't even fucking *drive*. Tonight you fucking *drink*; for tonight your life as you know it fucking *ends*, my friend."

"But I don't want my car spending the night in a hotel parking lot! Besides, I told my dad I'd be over later, and his mom said—"

"Whoa, whoa, whoa. His mom? I thought your dad's an orphan."

"His real mom tracked him down a few months ago. She's been really cool to him; even helped him get an awesome new job with Mooney Aircraft down in Texas. I haven't even met her yet. C'mon, man, I've got to get over there!"

"Ok, but if it weren't for that…we'll get going right after you down a brew." He opened a can and handed it to Paul.

"Come on, man, let's hurry up and get over there before the other guys get in. I'll bring you up to date on the way over. We've got the whole night to drink."

"Drinkmotherfucker."

Fifteen minutes, two beers, and three burps later, Paul was inspecting his car and noticed the keys still hanging in the ignition. With a silent grimace, he tucked them into his pocket and went to his dad's room.

Justin looked more like a father than a proud son as his mother checked her hair and dress before they answered the door. She couldn't smile wide enough when she first set eyes on Paul.

"Well now, would this be my grandson, the hotshot airline pilot?"

"Only if you'd be my long-lost Limey-Texan Grandma! How are you?" They hugged warmly.

"I'm fine, darling, just fine. Oh, just let me look at you." She sized him up, 25 years of grandmotherly doting compressing into a few seconds.

"Why, I must say, you are the very image of your grandfather when we met. What a delightfully handsome young man." She sighed, "And a pilot. He would be so proud of you—and jealous." She welled up and hugged him again, quietly saying, "Oh, darling, this is so wonderful. I couldn't have dreamed this one tiny bit better."

She noticed the intrigued expression on Rogers' face, realized she might be embarrassing her young grandson, and released him saying, "And this would be one of your chums, then?"

Paul politely turned to introduce her to Rogers. "This is Mark Rogers, my oldest friend still speaking to me. He's going to be my Best Man."

They shook hands, "Pleased to meet you, Mrs…"

"'Grandma' is fine, Mark. Or 'Mum,' if you prefer something shorter. There's not much point even knowing my married name; it has no bearing here. Today I'm just Paul's Grandmum, and very proud at that, I must say."

Paul wanted to bring Justin into the conversation, but decided to take him down a peg while he was at it.

"Dad, I trust you and *Alyssa* got along well. Got my keys?"

"Yep." Justin reached into his pocket and pulled out his own set on a "Mooney" key ring. He then reflexively tapped the breast pocket of his shirt and turned to search the pockets of his sport coat hanging on the rack near the bathroom. Paul called to him, "Hey Einstein," holding the keys up.

"A real nice guy named 'Tennessee' hanging around by the dumpster outside told me where you left them. He said he just couldn't see getting another 'grand theft-auto' on his record, but if I was into it, he had dibs on the stereo."

Justin deflated by half.

"Sorry, kid. Not thinking well today with all this going on."

Paul moved on. "Well, we don't have time to visit, really. My friends are all supposed to get in soon, and I don't want them to have to leave a message over at Christy's and wonder when they're getting picked up, so we need to get going. I just was dying to meet you," he paused slightly, as if trying the name on for size, before finishing the sentence, "Grandma." She tapped her hand, already over her heart, against her chest and whispered an indulging "Oh..."

"I can't wait to introduce you to Christina; we all have so much to talk about, it's going to take a lot more than just this weekend to get it all out."

"Yes, yes. You boys go and enjoy yourselves, but be careful. I want to get some of that talking done tomorrow, and it will be quite difficult if you're in jail or vomiting every half-hour." They all laughed, except for Justin. Paul hugged and kissed her on the cheek again, and they said goodbye.

Having heard more than she needed to know about Mark Rogers in the months leading up to the wedding, Christina wasn't expecting to see Paul's hung-over face much before ten the next morning, but when it was nearly noon and he had yet to even call, she began to worry. The rehearsal was at four p.m. She called his hotel room, but got no answer. She had no other idea how to reach him and was more than concerned and rather angry when her grandparents arrived just before lunch; too angry, in fact, to conceal it from her grandfather, Frank Lawton.

10

On another summer afternoon forty-odd years before, eighteen-year old Private Frank Lawton reread a letter to Eileen Hutchinson, against his own policy. The sun wasn't yet touching the Mediterranean's endless horizon outside the troop ship U.S.S. *Cardinal*, and he was fresh out of things to do on the eve of the invasion of Sicily.

His "no-rereads" policy had its genesis in the second week of basic training, when he'd written a short letter to Eileen, then reread it to make sure it "sounded ok." He found places in it where he thought he came off sounding like a "panty-waist," as his dad would have taunted him, and ended up wadding up the letter and throwing it away, hoping to have an opportunity to write again later in the week.

When one of the other men in his platoon drew garbage duty, the crumpled letter fell out of the can by chance, and Don Higgins recognized the fancy stationery Eileen had given Frank when he left for training. Higgins straightened out the paper and started to read it silently, but when it got good, he began reading aloud to the platoon:

"...I miss you like crazy my sweet rose, and I wonder how long it might be before I can again look into those beautiful eyes of yours without Uncle Sam tapping me on the shoulder saying, 'C'mon Mac, get a move on.' I dream about you every night, and half the time wake up wondering..."

It took a few seconds for what he was hearing to register, but then Frank wasted no time, jumping down from his bunk and charging full speed at Higgins, who began to dance around, thinking he was playing a good-spirited joke on his new "buddy." But Frank Lawton wasn't laughing.

Still evading his "victim" Higgins chided, "Gee, Lawton, you really wake up half the time wondering where you are? Remind me to pay attention when you're up on point!"

By now the whole platoon was attentive and amused, many of them chuckling aloud at the whole situation. Sensing the opportunity to get him to drop his guard, Frank softened his expression, smiled, and shook his head in a mock tacit acknowledgment of his being had, then slowly walked the last two steps to Higgins.

He put his left arm around the prankster's shoulders as he fixed his gaze on the letter, then quick as a snake's strike locked Higgins' head in the crook of his left elbow and began punching with his right.

Higgins was a far better clown than brawler, and fatigued as he already was from the day's exertions, he truly had no idea what hit him. Knocked out cold, Lawton let him drop at his feet, looking not much better than the discarded letter now splattered with his blood on the floor next to him, which Lawton picked up, carried into the latrine, and flushed down the toilet.

As Frank turned to go back to his bunk, however, his Drill Sergeant Terry Allison plugged the door, arms crossed, eyes aflame. Behind him, Frank could see a few men tending to Higgins, giving him a rag to hold over his gushing nose. Allison stepped into the latrine and kicked the doorstop out of the way, letting the door slam closed behind him. Exactly what happened behind that door would never be disclosed, but Frank Lawton came to in the stockade looking like death warmed-over, with three broken ribs and a nasty knot on his freshly shorn head from where he had "slipped on the floor and fallen onto one of the commodes." Higgins cut Lawton a wide berth from then on; almost as wide as that Lawton gave Allison. Frank swore he'd never again re-read another letter, or beat the living shit out of someone just to make a point, as long as he lived.

But now he lay on his side in his bunk, his head propped up on his cramped right hand, the first page of his latest letter in his left. His lips moved as he read at first, but then he noticed one of the other men in his platoon watching him, gave him a "what are you lookin' at?" sneer, then started over.

Dearest Eileen,

Finally a lull in the action long enough for me to be able to sit down somewhere quiet, have a smoke, and write you a decent letter! Of course I can't say much about where we are, where we've been, or where we're going, but I can tell you that this outfit is shaping up to look like some real hell for Jerry, I'll tell you.

The difference between when we first got here and us now is just amazing. Near as I or anybody else can tell, it's all come from a simple change of command. We came as scared but eager kids ready to kick some kraut ass, but without the first idea how to do it, or anybody offering to tell us. But now, with some real combat under our belts and a real man's man for a. commander, we're still plenty eager, maybe even more scared, but way more ready, just for different reasons.

We want to kill the bastard Huns for what they've done to our guys, and to the Brits, and for what they'll do to all of us if they get the chance, instead of just wanting to "win" a war. I guess you'd say it's gotten personal. And now we know a little more what to expect, and what's going to be expected of us, and a lot of the stuff they drilled into our heads back in basic that we'd kind of forgotten about just shows up when we need it. Our new C.O. has a reputation for being a real hard ass, but I think the guy's got a few tricks up his sleeve to help us get to the krauts, so I'm not going to complain. If he gets us all home faster, so much the better, I don't care how many pretty toes he steps on along the way.

Speaking of home, I got the newspaper clippings you sent me and I laughed so hard I about died! If only I could have seen the look on Leon's face when he got called to get his own daughter out of the drunk tank in Coffeeville. She never was much to look at, but I never would have figured her for a boozer. Guess maybe she's having a harder time with Chuck being gone than anybody knew. Good thing they don't have any kids yet, huh? I know it's got to be hard on you girls to have all the fellows gone to fight, but I just can't see you getting into a state like that over it. I sure don't want you to, anyway. Like we've all heard so many times, this war's going to be fought somewhere, sometime, one way or the other, and now and here's better than later at home! You know I'm a loose cannon, but you also have to know how much I love you and how bad I want to come home to you and pick up where we left off what seems so long ago.

By the way, do you think your folks suspect anything about us keeping in touch like this? It was a great idea you had getting that post office box to get my letters. I wish there was some way we could all just start over with a clean slate, so you didn't have to feel like you're sneaking around behind their backs just to write to me. Maybe when the war's over we'll all look at each other with older eyes and just wonder if what we were fighting about was really all that bad that we need to keep it going or just let it go and get on with our lives.

Have you heard anything new about my dad? I've written a couple letters to him and they came back as undeliverable with no forwarding address. I wonder where the old bastard went. Zach's written me a few times, probably just because Granny made him when she was writing though, and he sounds ok despite being basically an orphan. I told him if Dad never came back he'd be better off, but I don't guess he'd believe me, at least not for a few years yet.

Bobby's on a destroyer out in the Pacific, last I heard. I got a letter from him before our last operation and he sounded real good. I guess the cooking thing didn't work out, so they made him a Boson's Mate, whatever the hell that is. If the Navy's found something he can do without killing himself or any friendlies, I sure hope to God they keep him there at least till the war's over.

I suppose your brother and I might be crossing paths at some point in all of this, not that we'd ever know it probably. I haven't seen any flyboys for quite some time now and it doesn't look likely for a while, either. Samuel's probably going to wish he'd gone into the Air Corps too, if he ever sees some of the garden spots we've been through the last few months. We had some engineers pass through a while back on their way to building an airstrip somewhere, and they weren't exactly what I'd call happy campers. They kept looking at us like we were all loonies or something. I guess that's what happens when you got a padded chair at a desk somewhere and nothing sharper than a pencil for miles around and then -boom- you're in no man's land, the chow's in a can, and you're shitting in it when it's empty.

Anyway love, on that note I think I'll leave you laughing (I hope!) and close this up for you. I'm sure we're going to have some rough times again soon, but we're ready for whatever Jerry's got for us now. Whatever you hear about us, just remember you can't believe everything you read—unless it's about Janie Darby!

All my love,
Frank

Lawton folded the letter up and stuck it in an envelope, then put his boots on and went to the mailroom to send his letter. When he got close, he saw the line was nearly a hundred men long. "You'd never guess we were about to hit the beach again," he said to himself and got in line.

After a few minutes, someone ahead called out to him He turned and made eye contact with a man from his platoon, Ray Hinman, roughly twenty feet in front of him. Hinman motioned for him to come up, so Frank left his place in line and walked up to his friend, which of course set those behind them to grumbling.

Frank exchanged pleasantries with Hinman for a few moments, ignoring the comments from behind them. Just as he figured, they died down, perhaps a bit too suddenly. Then he felt a strong tap, more like a series of pokes, at his right shoulder. Turning toward it, he came chin-to-forehead with one of the smallest Sergeants-Major he'd ever set eyes on, shifting a long-dead, spit-soaked cigar in his mouth.

"Back of the line. Move it!" Standing barely five feet tall and not particularly well-built, the forty-ish man nevertheless had a no-bullshit air about him, and Frank could do little more than breathe and swallow as he wrestled with his impulses. The men around him were utterly silent.

Having seen the calculating look on Lawton's face many times on many others', the Sergeant-Major stepped toward Lawton without shifting his glare, putting the rancid, tarred end of his cigar right under Frank's nose, and said, "Get your cock-sore ass out of these men's way and to the back of the line, Private, before I kick the shit out of it and shove it down your fuckin' throat—one, sorry, piece, at a time. Move."

Lawton's restraint began to unravel as the near-midget taunted him. A year ago, he would have taken the man down without regard or fear of any consequence in this world. But in less than 12 hours they'd be fighting and dying together, and a single man of any size could save, or get killed, many others—others with wives and girlfriends like Eileen, and little boys and girls like they once were.

While these thoughts all streaked through his mind, he became aware his arms were at his side, where they belonged, and that his friend Ray Hinman was immediately behind him. Eileen's letter was in his right hand, and as the Sergeant Major drew out the words, "one, sorry, piece, at a time," Frank curled that hand up and behind him at the wrist, putting the letter right into Hinman's sight and reach. Hinman gingerly took the letter and mixed it with his own outgoing mail, then barely succeeded in keeping a smile from his face as Frank took a step to the side, turned, and went to the end of the line. After standing there a few minutes, making challenging eye contact with as many of the other men as he could to refresh his dominance, he pretended to have forgotten something, stepped out of line again, and returned to his berth for the night.

When the boatswain's whistle blew well before dawn the next morning, it became in Frank's dreaming mind an *Atchison, Topeka, and Santa Fe* locomotive slowing to a stop at Caney's humble station. Dressed in his Class A uniform, medals and ribbons on his left chest placket, he stepped onto the platform and searched the small crowd for Eileen. Someone was saying something over the loudspeaker, but he didn't care what it was. The war was over, we had won, and he was home.

"Where could she be?" he thought.

"Frank! Frank!" another voice was yelling at him, but it wasn't Eileen's. "Who's that?"

Something was squeezing and tapping his left foot now. "What the hell?"

He looked down to see a shoeshine boy, an amenity tiny Caney had never had, buffing his pristine boots and popping his rag. Something about him reminded him of Eileen's brother Jim, but it wasn't him, or anyone else he recognized. "Jesus, kid's a real go getter - didn't even ask me for a shine..."

Another voice again, louder than before, "LAWTON! Roll your ass out! We're goin'!"

His eyes popped open to see his lieutenant standing over his berth and slapping his feet, careful not to get within arm's reach of a combat veteran when awakening him.

"I'm up, I'm up, damn it," Frank growled as he half-fell out of his bunk. He wiped his eyes and face for a moment, trying to remember whether he'd seen Eileen or not, but then forgot about it, grabbed his pack and rifle, and fell into line with the rest of his Company as they made their way into the landing craft.

What little talking went on was related only to the tasks at hand, and the sound of officers and non-comm's barking orders to their men could be heard in all directions, shattering the tranquility of 3 a.m. on the soft, warm bed of the mid-summer Mediterranean.

Casualties from the invasion of Sicily saw Frank Lawton promoted to Sergeant, and not quite a year later he led his platoon up Omaha Beach and, through a twenty-man gun emplacement, all the way to Germany.

That next generation of Lawtons grew up in appropriate awe of their war-hero father. Two of them even stayed around to work for him after they grew up. Christina was the youngest daughter of the eldest and, in an irony everyone but Frank and his equally headstrong granddaughter found humorous, to say she was afforded "princess" status in her grandfather's eyes would have been a grave underestimation.

Those eyes could see the strain on Christina's face when Frank and Eileen arrived at her house just before noon, and he was, for the moment, helpless to do anything about it. No one knew where Paul Prator, his friends, or his father were.

11

Wes' crew met for breakfast and briefing at 0500. A fog was unforecast, but too thin to prevent safe takeoff, and the chemical works of Ludwigshafen, Germany had been left unmolested since January. The mission was a go.

Normally, Wes would awaken to the typical late night sounds of the base mobilizing for a "show," as the Brits called their missions. Activity would begin before midnight sometimes, and before Ploesti, Wes was invariably wide awake by the time the orderly came to roust them, having spent the better part of the night thinking, dreaming, and praying about his plane, his Love, and his life. Today, however, he actually had to be awakened from a dream.

He'd been at his house in Caney, playing tag in the back yard with a little boy he was calling Jim, but it wasn't his little brother with the missing finger. Running after him in the dream, he was just reaching out to tag the boy when he heard that scoundrel Frank Lawton call "Hutchinson," from the edge of the yard. Lawton was calmly smoking a cigarette and smiling at him, like they were old friends long apart. As Wesley walked over to him, he noticed Lawton kept calling his name, as if he couldn't see him. This seemed very curious, until Wes realized that Lawton was indifferent to his presence entirely, and was actually calling to the little boy, who was standing motionless, staring at him, completely unaware of who the man was and clearly afraid of him.

Lawton's voice in the dream melded into that of the orderly come to wake Warwick's crew, so Wes missed the chance to see how Frank Lawton knew the boy in his dream, or who he was in the first place. In his rush to get dressed for chow and briefing, Wes forgot to take off his new ring, but the orderly reminded him to do so on his way out the door.

Wes pulled the ring off, and, studying it for a moment, decided there and then that he was going to buy Melody a ring of her own when he got back, and ask her to marry him when the war ended for him, and he'd do whatever he had to do to make her say yes, including staying in England himself if her family made her balk. He couldn't be around to protect Eileen her whole life; if Lawton made it through the war, he could have her as far as Wes was concerned. Worse things could happen.

The weather forecast for the target was for clear skies, making for accurate bombing and anti-aircraft fire, which they were told to expect to be "moderate." The men had long ago realized reliance upon intelligence reports and weather forecasts was only for the uninitiated or stubbornly dimwitted among them, and more than a few cynical looks were exchanged across the room as they listened with minds about as open as so many Catholic priests at a Tarot reading.

The Air Corps had long since adopted the practice of designating a secondary target to bomb in the event that weather or other conditions over the primary were unfavorable to accurate bombing. In this event, the lead ship in the lead formation would simply leave its bomb bay doors closed and turn toward the secondary, bringing the rest of the formations along with them with no words spoken over the radio. Today their secondary target was Strasbourg, even further south in Germany, where a Messershmitt aircraft factory was due for a little touch-up. Limited production had somehow resumed though several bombardments during Big Week very nearly blew the place off the map.

Since Strasbourg was, at least by way of Ludwigshafen, so much deeper into Germany, their fighter escorts would be unable to accompany them there if they diverted from the primary. The fighters were to provide escort to the primary or, in the event of an early diversion to the secondary, no further away in point of time; at this "bingo fuel" point, turning back to base would be mandatory. If at any point during the inbound flight the escorts encountered opposition intense enough for them to have to jettison their external fuel tanks to maneuver better, those aircraft would have to abandon the bombers even sooner or risk fuel exhaustion over France or the English Channel, where a downed pilots' chances of survival were slim at best.

For any, or perhaps all, of these reasons, Tommy Warwick watched with disdain as the lead formation turned south, away from what had all the appearance of a crystal clear-blue sky over Ludwigshafen, when they were still over a hundred miles out. With no choice but to follow, he let fly with a "Here we go, boys, 'wilkommen au Strasenbourgen. Fuck."

Their escorts turned with them, as expected, but several hundred men aboard scores of bombers now nearly simultaneously checked their watches and made a mental calculation as to how much longer their "little friends" would stay with them. The unspoken consensus was thirty minutes, leaving the Circus to fend for itself over three-hundred miles deep and going deeper into German airspace, on a morning God himself couldn't have created any better for bombing Jerry.

As expected, they'd experienced light but accurate anti-aircraft fire at sporadic intervals since making landfall over France, taking two planes out of the formation with engine or fuel tank damage, but they had yet to see any enemy aircraft. No doubt the P-51s were keeping all but the best-supplied units on the ground, saving their thinning fuel stocks and fraying nerves for softer targets.

Right on time, however, the Mustangs' empty drop tanks fell carelessly to German soil, perhaps smashing an unlucky cow or kraut, but having met their obligation as bodyguards, the fighters eagerly began an hour or so of predatory mischief, reveling in their hard-won air superiority by destroying targets of opportunity all the way home.

It took about ten minutes, but the Luftwaffe finally got some fighters up to meet them, and what fighters they were. Messershmitt 109s arrived from two different directions, one group from the west and slightly above them, and another larger group from the east, still climbing to their altitude. Their coordination was, in classic German form, magnificent, with the higher force attacking immediately while the lower group continued climbing out of gun range to form a second wave.

The German pilots had become adept at attacking the bombers head-on. This frightening technique exposed them to far less fire than a more leisurely lateral attack across the formations, which had been shown repeatedly to be a suicide run for the merciless crossfire it drew from multiple bombers' fields of fire. Side benefits of the head-on attack included the relatively good chances of taking out the bombardier in the glass "greenhouse" at the nose of the airplane, or at least his bombsight, without which the American bombers were as inaccurate as Germany's. It was also a good bet that one or both of the pilots could be killed with a lucky shot, since what little armor plating the bombers had was in the floors to protect against anti-aircraft fire. Finally, the impact energy of any bullets or cannon shells fired was nearly doubled by the closing speed of the fighter plane and its target, making any direct hits devastating.

The higher fighter group, three dozen strong, made a sweeping left turn to attack the bombers in this manner. Wes' hands curled around the handles of his turret's .50-caliber machine guns as he narrowed his choice of targets to the one he thought would finish his turn closest to them.

When he first entered combat, Wes was overwhelmed by the level of chatter on the interphone. It seemed he could scarcely process the information being given out by his fellow crewmembers, with their various fields of vision and fire, in time to react effectively. Over time, however, as the crew became more experienced, they quickly developed an ear for each other's voices, making textbook prefaces like "pilot to tailgunner" and other calls alerting others to problems they could already see superfluous. These men had lived and fought together for months and could nearly read each other's minds, so the chatter was far more familiar, and there seemed less of it with each mission as the men's knowledge of their individual strengths and weaknesses became second nature and they came to function, with their airplane, as an organism with deadly defenses.

Wes was still getting used to the turret, with its unnatural, motor-driven movement, and was not at all sure he liked it, toasty though it was out of the ferocious slipstream. It was far more difficult to maneuver than the simple .50-cal aimed second-nature by his ever-obedient arms. He had difficulty lining up his shots and had to pre-position the turret to point where he thought the target would be in a second or two, then stop and wait to fire, hoping to score a hit as the target flew into the sights, rather than precisely tracking it. It was hard enough to lead a target accurately, and leading them by twice or three times the normal amount then hoping for the enemy to just fly into the right position before firing, was maddening. Wes loved having Twomey's engineer's console to himself, but he'd give it up to be out of that clunky turret and back at the waist with Ed Worley when the shooting started.

He chose his target, the third Messershmitt from the bottom of its formation, eyeballed its flight path, positioned the turret, and fired just before the plane would fly into his sights, but the pilot pulled up abruptly, so his shot went low. Seeing the Me109's machine guns flashing as he came in at what seemed only inches above them, Wes instinctively ducked a little in his turret. As he did, bullets ripped into the left wing, the number two engine, and the plane's nose just behind the greenhouse, shattering Tommy Warwick's left shin. Growling in pain, he motioned for copilot Newhart to take over as he saw to his wound. No actions on the part of any pilot could help them get through a fighter attack—Newhart could only do what Warwick had been doing before he was hit—try to hold formation and let the gunners do their jobs.

Doing so was about to become impossible for Wes however. The number two engine, closest to the fuselage on the left side, was missing badly. Having taken a direct hit to one of its carburetors, it was leaking fuel which hadn't yet caught fire. No one aboard the plane could know about the fuel leak, but the engine's miss was unmistakable.

"How bad is it, Tommy?" Newhart asked, afraid of hearing the truth.

"My damn leg's hamburger. Shit!" Warwick was rolling up his pant leg and taking off his belt to use as a tourniquet to stop the profuse bleeding. The shattered bone had pierced an artery deep inside the leg, and there was no good way to elevate it. Feeling the engine on his side missing, Warwick looked back, but couldn't see the problem.

He called into the interphone for Wes, forgetting for a moment that he was right behind him in the turret instead of back at the waist gun. "Wes, what's with number two—you see anything?"

From his perch atop the fuselage, Wes had already heard the miss, and could see holes in the cowling, but no smoke, fuel, or other signs of damage. Meanwhile, another section of fighters were beginning their attack run, and Wes was frantically trying to line up his next shot.

"It got hit, but I can't see a fire or any leaks. What do the gauges show?"

Wes had been firing when Warwick got hit, and was too busy trying to shoot to step down and have a look himself. More fighters were coming in at their one o'clock position, and some of those that had already passed were turning around just outside gun range to make another, more accurate pass from behind. In a matter of minutes, the lower formation coming from the west would be at their altitude and ready to attack also.

"Hell if I know. I took a hit up here myself, Hutch, so I'm a little busy. Looks like the CHT's down a little, manifold pressure and EGT's way down, RPM's are steady, but she's got a bad limp, so there's no way it's making normal power, and we're slowing down. Get up here and help us out, would you?"

"Sir, as bad as I'm shooting with this thing, I really don't think you want me to quit trying. Those krauts are coming back for seconds. Try the mixture, run the prop to low pitch, cross your fingers, pray, whatever you've got to do, but if I get out of this turret, we're dead."

As if to punctuate that, Wes opened fire on the next plane he'd lined up in his sights, scoring several good hits to its engine and cockpit. The engine belched a plume of flame and the plane dove out of Wes' sight beneath them, where it drew fire from several other planes and continued to burn in a long spiral dive earthward. The pilot, killed by Wes' shot, never even tried to get out.

With the second wave of fighters now tearing through the rest of the formation behind them, and the eastern group not yet in range for what would have to be a risky attack on their rear quarters, Wes had a minute to triage their stricken plane, unaware that its pilot was in far worse shape.

Slipping out of the turret to brace himself against the engineer's panel, Wes just caught a glimpse of something in the slipstream behind the number two engine. A look at the panel confirmed his suspicions: fuel pressure was near zero, cylinder head and exhaust temperatures were well below normal, and manifold pressure was low. The engine couldn't have been firing on any more than a few cylinders, if that, and was only still turning because of the propeller "windmilling" in the slipstream, creating drag that was slowing them down.

Poking his head into the cockpit, he noticed Warwick's leg and the blood-soaked clothing around it, then stole a glance out the side window, where he could now see a fire had begun in the stricken engine.

"Fellas, we've got to shut it down. Now. Fuel pressure's zero, and it's on fire!"

"Kill it then," Warwick said distractedly to Newhart, who briskly pulled the fifth of eight black levers on the control quadrant all the way back, feathering the propeller blades, then the second of four red ones, shutting off fuel at the carburetors.

"I'll get the firewall," Wes said, turning off the engine's fuel supply at the tank. They were already thirty miles per hour slower than the planes behind them and had no choice but to descend out of the formation, jettison their bombs, and run the two-hour gauntlet across occupied France to get back home.

"Maybe those Mustangs will pave a way back for us," Max Newhart offered as he swung into a gentle right turn back to England. Tommy Warwick was obviously in a great deal of pain, and his blood was beginning to pool on the cockpit floor.

"Yeah, sure they will," he countered, dryly. "Take a 300 heading to start with, and let's get rid of these bombs while we're still over Germany." Warwick was turning pale, his eyes glazing over as shock set in.

"Jettisoning bombs," he said over the intercom as he flipped the red guard from a switch on the pedestal, then flipped the switch itself. Behind and beneath them, the bomb bay doors rolled open, and two by two, twelve five-hundred pound bombs fell from the racks to the Schwartzwald below.

His engineering duties complete, Wes resumed his position in the top turret and scanned the huge view afforded him as Newhart turned them northwest. Warwick's crew had been in bad positions a few times before with *Barfly*, but never so deep inside enemy territory. It had always been a comfort to Wes and some of the others to be in their own plane when things got dicey. Even though 248 was "theirs," every plane ran, and handled differently. After a few missions, each one even smelled a little different; this one still felt strange to them, offering no comfort whatsoever.

A tidal wave of dread rose among the crew, realizing they were, by virtue of being down an engine, unlikely to run three-hundred miles across the channel safely. Wes and Newhart were the only ones yet aware Warwick was wounded, a fact they chose to keep to themselves for now. Wes called out to the others to expect company from stragglers from the second group of fighters, which he could now see beginning their attack runs on the formation. The short-range fighters would concentrate their efforts upon those bombers still droning on to their target so long as they remained healthy and well-positioned, but any that sustained damage or were otherwise indisposed to continuing their attacks would find a stray, damaged bomber irresistibly easy prey on the way back to base. If they managed to leave Germany behind them, there were still several Luftwaffe bases in France, well within range of their best route back to Hardwick.

For the next three hours, they would swim, utterly alone and trailing blood, through a shark-infested ocean of crystal clear sky.

12

Paul and his other groomsmen were still out cold when Alan Hinkson awoke around 12:40 and pulled the curtains open, squinting as the noon light flooded the room. No one had yet made a sound. Paul's hangover was in full bloom beneath the anesthetic of sleep, and he was dreaming the incoherent gibberish of a pickled subconscious. Those dreams came to an abrupt end as a still-drunk Mark Rogers didn't just knock, but damned near pounded down the door, jolting all three awake.

"Open the Goddamn door, assholes. We gots us a wedding to rehearse!" The temperature, mild in the 60's when they left him passed out in his car, was now in the high 80's. Rogers' clothes were drenched, and the sight and smell of the sweaty, hung-over fat man holding a brown suitcase at the door was a study in male repugnance.

"Well, did you have a nice little nap, boys?" he began as he pressed past Hinkson, traversing the room as he ranted, "Thanks a hell of a lot for leaving me in the car. I just love new car smell, and mixed with alcohol, skank funk and beer farts, it's a real treat for the senses, let me tell you." Unfastening his pants as he neared the tiny bathroom, he blurted out, "Jesus Christ. My dick's a dam on the Pississippi River!"

He turned left into the bathroom, relieved himself for what seemed like several minutes, without closing the door first, then came out and briefly regarded Paul, holding his head in his hands at the side of the bed.

"And how are *we* feeling, Pauly-boy? Need some Tylenol do ya? Got some in my bag here, still 'sealed for your protection,' even." He kicked his suitcase next to the sink, then turned on the shower and began to undress, tossing his sweaty clothes onto the suitcase. Alan Hinkson briefly considered getting the Tylenol out for his friend, but recoiled when the huge, sweaty, off-white Fruit-of-the-Looms landed on it.

Paul looked at his watch and fell back over into his pillow, moaning a little. He was still drunk, so the headache had yet to reach its zenith, and vomiting--again—was still a distinct possibility. Breakfast time was long over, and lunch was out of the question. He wanted only a glass of water, three or four of those Tylenol, and maybe the grace of God to help him keep it all down long enough to get through this day.

He couldn't remember if the rehearsal was set for 3 or 4 p.m., and he figured Christy would be worried about him if he hadn't at least called by lunchtime, so he dragged himself out of bed and went to urinate, asking Rogers exactly where in the suitcase the Tylenol was as he steadied himself with the towel rack above the toilet.

Paul found the pills and took them and a glass of water back to the nightstand. "Got to take my medicine," he said to his friends, holding the pills and the phone up together. They smirked and began to talk amongst themselves as he discovered the phone had been left unplugged by the room's previous occupants. He dialed Christy's parents' place. The Chief answered.

"Hey, this is Paul. Is Christy there?"

"She's upstairs. Where the hell have you been, son? She's been pacing around all morning worrying about you."

"Yeah, I figured, I mean, I know. Uh, is this her Grandpa?"

"That's right."

"Hi, sir. We did my bachelor party last night, and we didn't get back till really late, and I guess I got kind of drunk, so, um, anyway, I just woke up a little bit ago and I wanted to let her know I'm ok and sorry if I worried her or, and, everything."

"Is this something you see happening often, Paul?"

"No, sir. It was definitely not something I'd want to repeat." Paul looked at his friends and feigned passing out from pain.

"I really hope not, for both your sakes. I know what being a young man's about, and what goes on at a bachelor party, and I didn't see Christina getting upset about it the way some women would until your ass went off the radar. You seem to make her very happy, but not so much right at the moment. You get my meaning, don't you Paul?"

"Yes, sir, I do. Really. We really didn't set any new records or anything, just stayed out too late is all. I'm really sorry she was worried though. Can I speak with her, please?"

A Silver Ring

He heard the phone get set down then made the same apology made to millions of women by millions of men each year and promised to be at the house by two, having confessed his being there for lunch would not be a good idea. Paul and his motley entourage hit a Burger King drive-thru to feed the three not-morbidly-nauseous members of the party and arrived at the house just after two. His headache was under control by then, but his stomach was still on edge, and the smell of the "little smokies" Christina's mom had cooked up made him have to go dry heave in the guest bathroom.

Feeling the stressful, task-oriented estrangement most couples do on the eve of their wedding and also some simple guilt for having spent so little time with his father and grandmum thus far, Paul spent most of the night after the rehearsal with them, and he learned a great deal about his grandfather. Toward the end of the evening, having shown Paul the two pictures she had of him and some letters he'd written, she took a tiny blue velvet box out of her purse and said that she had one final trinket to show them.

From the box she pulled out a small, simple, sterling silver ring. It had been polished only days before, and would have looked new if not for one side of it being very badly worn, almost as if it had been sanded down, but without scratches. On its face was a set of U.S. Army Air Corps wings, which were identical to the present-day Air Force insignia, except the wings had a propeller crossing their center from top to bottom, nearly as tall as the wings were wide. The wings were exquisitely detailed, with tiny engraved feathers and heavy lines where a real bird's wing feathers change texture. It was a stunning antique.

"This is the ring he was talking about in that letter." She pointed at the one she'd read to them last. "I had my Uncle Percy make it for him while he was in

Africa that second time. He came back in August of 1943, and couldn't talk about where he'd been or what they'd done, but he was so different, I know it must have been very trying for him. He was never the same after that. They'd raided a refinery complex in Ploesti, Romania, I found out later. You probably have never heard of the place, but it was—"

"I know about Ploesti," Paul interrupted, "I just read a book about it a year or so ago. It was incredible. They gave out more Medals of Honor for that raid than D-Day!

"You're telling me my grandfather was *on that raid?"* Paul's face was intense, his mouth half open, his gaze distant as he remembered the nightmare he'd had the night before the engine fire.

"What is it Paul, what's wrong?" Justin was out of the loop.

"When did you two first meet? What day?"

"Jeez, I don't know. It was last summer sometime, right Mum?"

"I have it in my planner, I can look it up for you. Why, Paul? You seem frightened."

"I'm not sure. Can you just look that up for me? Please?" His eyes were wide and he was turning pale, looking down and to his left, recalling the dream in perfect detail.

"Around the same time you two met, I had a big thing happen at work. We had an engine catch fire and damned near burn the wing off. "

"Yeah, we know. That's what you think got you hired at Wingspan, right?"

"Right. But the night before, I'd been reading a book about the Ploesti raid, and I had a really long, vivid nightmare about it, like I was there, you know? I never thought much about it, but now that I know he was on that raid…"

A Silver Ring

"'June 20th, 1986—meet with Justin in Wichita,'" she read from her planner.

"That was the day. Holy shit." Paul's legs folded him onto the bed.

"That's creepy." Justin had goosebumps.

Paul was staring at the desk – his face no longer wore surprise, but instead a dreadful knowing. "So, he never told you what happened on that raid?"

"No, he couldn't discuss operations. But I read some things about it in the newspapers, and it began to make sense. Weeks later, his unit was awarded Air Medals for their performance, and he told me it was over that mission. They'd been one of the lucky few to make it back. He said the target was extremely heavily defended, but it was as if their ship sacrificed herself for them. He loved his plane so much. I often wonder if he'd been on it instead of the one in which he was killed, perhaps things would have turned out differently."

"He wasn't in his regular plane when he was killed?" Paul was consumed with curiosity. His head was swimming. He wanted to tell them everything he knew about Ploesti, everything from his dream, but was derailed by her remark about the airplane.

"No, they'd had to leave her in Africa because they hadn't the facilities to repair such serious damage. They were in a new plane when he was killed, which was also his first mission as an engineer."

"I thought you said he was a gunner," Justin asked.

"He began as a gunner, and also assisted the engineer, who manned the top turret gun in combat. Their engineer suffered some kind of a breakdown on the Ploesti mission, and Wes was promoted to take his place. He was very proud to be put in charge of the plane, but he never told me what had gone wrong with the man he replaced. I got the feeling he was rather unpopular with his mates."

The ring still lay on the bed where they'd been sitting, and Paul picked it up without asking.

"Paul," his father chided. He looked up from the ring and immediately apologized. It was, for each, as if they'd just buried him.

"Oh, I'm sorry, I…"

"No, no, please. I brought it to give to you, well, first to your father, actually, but for him to pass on to you someday. It's the closest thing to an heirloom I can offer either of you, but I thought you might like to have it. You're grandfather was so enamored with airplanes and flying, and when I learned you both were pilots in your own right, it just seemed so very noble to me that you all clearly share a gene for it. I thought it was time for the ring, which symbolized the things he loved most in the world, the thing that bonds us as his family, to spend the rest of my life not just sitting in a drawer full of meaningless trivia, but with his men, of whom he would be so very proud."

Justin and Paul were utterly silent. Paul stared at the ring a moment more, then handed it to Justin, who held it reverently as tears welled up in his eyes and cascaded down his cheeks. She hugged him as he sat silently crying, decades of unreasoned shame having just turned to bursting, swollen pride; forty years of existence as Nobody finally explained and justified, all in a half-ounce of silver.

"How did you end up with this, Grandma? I mean, if he was wearing it—"

"The men were told to leave their jewelry and other valuables behind when they flew, so that they wouldn't be lost with them or stolen if they were taken prisoner. The rest of his effects went home to his family, but one of his friends who knew me brought it back to me when," she choked up but quickly recomposed herself, "when he didn't come home. Dear God, it was so awful. I've never cried like that. I cried for hours at a time, for days on end." They huddled up around her, all emotional wrecks, staring at the ring as if it were a light at the far end of a tunnel, in which each saw clearly a different version of the same phantom.

"I was already a month late when he was killed. I'd been having difficulty finding the right moment to tell him, but I made up my mind while he was out that day that I'd tell him that night no matter what, so if anything ever did happen to him, he'd know something of him was left behind."

"Grandma," Paul quietly asked, "do you know how he died, I mean, what exactly happened?"

"No, darling, I don't. I'm sorry. My life became quite complex afterward, as I'm sure you can imagine, and with the war on and thousands of men dying every week, it just didn't seem important. I learned later that one of his shipmates, Ed Worley, survived and was taken prisoner, but I never felt strongly about asking him to dredge up the war just to satisfy some morbid curiosity. Truth be told, I still don't care to know. He's gone. How or why has never mattered."

"That's why I'm going to talk to him day after tomorrow. I'm his son. I never knew him, and I feel like I need to know what happened. He said on the phone he wouldn't mind at all talking with me about it. Said any son of his deserves to know what he did; that he was a 'true blue' hero."

Justin tried the ring on first his right, then his left finger, but the ring was too small for any but his pinkies. He offered it to Paul to try on. It slipped with perfectly minor difficulty onto his left ring finger, but his grandmother quickly pointed out, "That one's reserved now." He laughed nervously, pulled it off the left finger and with only slightly more difficulty pushed it onto the right and extended his fingers, admiring it.

Justin looked at her and said, "Maybe we shouldn't wait to pass it down then." She nodded, tentatively at first, but then looked at her grandson and smiled and hugged him again.

"Two rings in two days, Paul. That seems like it might be some kind of record."

"Yeah." Paul was absolutely awestruck by it, so much that his own wedding, now scarcely 18 hours in the future, seemed a sideshow in comparison.

"You better tell Christy what that's all about before she sees it tomorrow. It's unwise to surprise a woman on her wedding day," Justin said.

"Would you tell her, Grandma? I mean, I'm not supposed to be seeing her before she walks down the aisle to me, and I'm not sure she'd take too well to me springing anything on her right now anyway. She's a little mad at me still for being out so late last night."

"I'd be delighted to dear, but it's a bit late for anything like that now, don't you think?"

"Yeah, maybe you're right."

"Why don't you just have us hold it for you until tomorrow night, and we'll tell her about it at the reception?" Justin asked. Paul considered it, staring at the ring, as if it would speak the answer to him if only he asked.

"That'll work. She's got enough going on right now that anything I tell her before our honeymoon's just going to go in one ear and out the other. I'll get it back from you one way or another before we head out tomorrow night, ok?" Justin nodded.

Paul pulled the ring off and scrutinized it carefully then asked, "Why is it so worn down on this left side here? Did he rub it when he was stressed out or something?"

"I'm afraid that was my fault." She was looking down at Paul's shirt buttons, remembering.

"I wore it for years after. It was a very dark, lonely, and guilty time for me. I was all alone in a strange country, I'd lost the love of my life to that Nazi son of a bitch, and then had to give up the only part of him left in this world. I can't tell you how painful it was. The only thing that kept me going was knowing someday I'd find his boy and tell him how very badly I wanted to have kept him—that he wasn't just some damned inconvenience." She pulled herself closer to Justin and patted his chest as she pressed her head against his shoulder.

"Somehow, I developed a habit of rubbing it whenever I thought of him, and before I knew, the damage was already done. I'm very sorry."

Her eyes went dark and hollow as she apologized for "damaging" the ring, and Paul could find no words for this old woman actually apologizing to him for making an otherwise merely priceless heirloom absolutely sacred.

At precisely noon the next day, in front of nearly two-hundred people, many in Cleveland Fire Department uniform, seated on both sides of St. Paul's Episcopal Church to hide the fact that only ten of them were there for the groom, the organ began the prelude to the Bridal March. The doors at the rear of the church swung open, and Christina Lawton appeared to claim her mate.

Her nearly transparent lace veil and an ivory gown with a low neckline perfectly complimented her dark complexion, if not her less than ample bust. A fitted waist, ornate textured flourishes around the hips, and an elegant eight-foot long satin train completed the vision, and her practice sessions in her three-inch heels paid off with a glide up the aisle that could not have been more gracefully executed by a Queen.

Awaiting her, with his mind fully absorbed with his next life-altering event, Paul was relieved to see her radiant smile beneath the veil and, as she slowed to a hover next to him, a wink that seemed to say, "all is forgiven, this time." He was glad he hadn't worn the ring; it would have been a terrible shame to let something so utterly irrelevant to their banns become a distraction at this, arguably the most celebrated moment of her life as a woman.

The minister addressed the congregation and gave a rousing if predictable introduction, expounding on the sanctity of marriage, its lofty ideals of unwavering companionship, emotional security, and joyful continuation of the family's life in a new generation. With this obligation fulfilled, he informed the crowd that Christina and Paul had written their own vows, keeping their verbiage secret from each other until this moment, and that the time had come for them to be exchanged.

Christina went first, as was her desire to keep her from losing her composure and forgetting her vows should Paul write as beautifully as she knew he was able. Her own talents as a writer could only be conjured through the catalyst of speech, and she had composed her vows by speaking them into a tape recorder dozens of times until she was satisfied, then, on the morning of the wedding, hurriedly writing the words on stationery she bought for this purpose alone, having put off the chore of writing them as long as possible.

"Since I was a little girl, I have dreamed of this moment, living it in my imagination as perfectly as anything can be envisioned. Yet as thrilling and perfect as any of these dreams were, none of them held for me the one thing that makes pledging my unending love to you today so easy for me, and that is the utterly certain calm I feel in giving you my heart." Paul smiled knowingly at this, having discussed with her at length dozens of times during their courtship the total unjealous security they both felt.

"I learned long ago that love can be thrilling beyond words, leave you breathless with excitement, and at times even take away your ability to think about anything else, but until we met I never imagined that it could also be calming, soothing, and emboldening, making me feel that whatever life brings to our door, with your hand in mine, we can at least withstand, and likely triumph over it all.

"Today I become your wife, but I have been and will be your mate for eternity; one side of a perfect soul that we, together, form. I am yours to love, yours to depend upon, yours to cherish, yours to take with you forward on this journey that we know began long before we ever met, and I hope and pray never ends."

That said, the minister instructed her to put the band on Paul's finger, which she was able to do much easier than at the rehearsal, when Paul's fingers were swollen from his hangover. Then, she'd had so much trouble, and was still so angry with him, she twisted his finger after giving up on getting the ring over the knuckle. She smiled as she did it, letting him know she was angry but forgiving him with the penance. His knuckle was still a little sore, and he almost whispered, "Easy now," as she pushed the ring gently into place, and they both giggled before she looked up at him with her eyebrows raised, saying "Well? Your turn."

Paul had written his vows on his last trip before the wedding, and felt strange about referring to a copy, so he'd memorized them. It wasn't difficult since they were, after all, his own words, but the uncanny similarity between his and those he'd just heard come out of Christy's mouth made him even more self-conscious and uncomfortable than before. He decided to wing it now and show her the original vows he'd written in private that night. So what came out bore little similarity to the eloquent speech he'd written.

"I also knew right away our love was different from anything I'd ever felt before. All the good elements were there, all the fun, all the magic, all the compatibility, but none of the bad stuff. None of the anxiety, the insecurity, wondering whether I was as much a part of your life as you are of mine."

At this point she already knew what he was saying wasn't what he'd written, and she even suspected why. This wasn't his soulful, expressive "writing voice," with which he'd penned a hundred silly notes left around her apartment, postcards from cities he'd been to, and a few thoughtful cards, and letters from training at WingSpan.

Paul had learned as a boy that the more eloquently he spoke, the more reviled he was by his ever-new classmates, so he'd developed what he'd called a "dumb kid" speaking style that made him less of a target, and years of practicing this defense had created an impenetrable partition between his intellect and his mouth, which was often inconvenient as an adult. It certainly was now, as he struggled nearly dumb before his bride and her friends and family.

"Everyone feels like their love is special somehow, that they and they alone have what it takes to go the distance, so there's not much point in saying it, but I'm going to anyway."

Now she knew he was making this up as he went along and was hoping he could just get through it; that whether he'd forgotten or forsaken what he'd written, he'd at least sound loving and sincere to her family.

A Silver Ring

"The word 'soulmates' is really big these days, and I for one am getting a little tired of it, so I'm going to make it obsolete. When we're together, everything works. When we're apart, nothing does. I never thought I'd wish I wasn't flying until I had you waiting for me on the ground. But it doesn't feel like we're soul *mates*. It feels like we're two halves of *one* soul, and I never knew the other half was even out there. What I used to think was my heart has been broken lots of times, but now I know that wasn't my heart— it was just my ego. I never really knew before, because we hadn't met yet; but my heart—is you."

With that Christina, most of the women, and even some of the men in the church went into estrogen meltdown. Tears cascaded down her painstakingly made-up face, and she instinctively threw her arms around Paul in the biggest hug she'd given since he first proposed, making it impossible for him to put her ring on her finger. The minister, more than a little uncomfortable with this turn of events, addressed the guffawing crowd saying, "I hate it when they write their own vows." Everyone, including the ones crying, laughed with the moment of blissful catharsis Paul had just given them, in pure spontaneity.

The minister continued, "Now, to keep the state of Ohio happy, let's pretend we didn't just hear all of that for a moment, and ask these young people a few simple questions, as if we didn't know the answers.

"Do you, Christina, take Paul Prator to be your lawful wedded husband, to have and to hold, in sickness and in health, for richer for poorer, till death do you part?" Christina composed herself somewhat, but remembered halfway through the traditional vow that she hadn't given Paul a chance to give her the ring, so she was almost oblivious to what she heard, wondering when would be a good time to remind him .

She said nothing right away when the word "part" left the minister's mouth, but was smiling proudly at Paul, who, having forgotten exactly what he'd said that made such a fuss, had been paying closer attention to the minister, and was now trying to cue Christy to speak by conspicuously pointing his eyes to the right and smirking.

"Yes! Yes! I do, I do!" burst out of her mouth as she realized she was holding up the show.

"Do you, Paul, take Christina to be your lawful wedded wife, to have and to hold, in sickness and in health, for richer and for poorer, till death do you part?"

Paul feigned indecision for a half second, pursing his lips together and furrowing his brow. Christina glared at him briefly, but then, with the helpless, resigned, proud, and contentedly final tone of a man admitting to a sanctioned addiction, Paul deadpanned the words "I do."

The Reverend began, "By the power vested in me by the Church of our Lord, Jesus Christ the Nazarene and the…"

Christina was looking directly at him and bouncing in her heels like a child in the grocery store candy aisle, with her ring finger extended in front of her.

"The ring, Norman, the ring!" he said aloud to himself. He then nodded at Paul, who prolonged, seeming to almost revel in the moment of slipping the band on her finger.

"Let these rings symbolize the bond between Christina and Paul, which we here today have witnessed—bonds which no one on Earth may break. And *now*," he briefly stood on his tiptoes as if he had just stopped short of a cliff. "By the power vested in me by God's Church and the state of Ohio, I pronounce you man and wife. Please…kiss your bride."

A Silver Ring

They kissed softly, as they'd rehearsed privately, for several seconds, both pairs of eyes closed, drinking in the moment fully and without regard for appearances, then hugged for almost as long before turning to face the crowd.

"Ladies and Gentlemen, I present to you, Mr. and Mrs. Paul Prator."

The exit music thundered from the organ, the boisterous congregation cheered, and they triumphantly promenaded down the aisle to a white limousine waiting just outside.

13

"I wish we could have had a party half this size when we were married," Christy's grandmother said to The Chief as the last score of guests crowded into the VFW hall, the cheering crowd already inside quickly filling the dance floor as the DJ cued up the B-52s' new hit, "Love Shack."

"Hell, I'd have settled for just a proper wedding," came his gruff reply with an accommodating smile.

"So am I correct in assuming you to be the gentleman responsible for so many firemen being under one roof without there being any danger of its impending collapse?" Paul's grandmother joked in her persistent English. She was seated at a round table across from the Lawton patriarch.

"Well, now we are watching the Baked Alaska suspiciously," he replied with a chuckle. "Everybody knows firefighters get some good benefits, but no one ever mentions the part about never even having to bother with fire insurance. You must be Paul's 'new' grandmother."

"Well, there's nothing about me that could even kindly be described as 'new', but yes, I did only recently meet your new grandson—perhaps not a moment too soon. My name is Melody. I'm delighted to meet you, Chief Lawton."

"Please, Frank. This is my wife, Eileen."

"Christina said you tracked Paul's father down over some period of years?"

"Yes, when my husband passed away I became acutely curious about the fate of my firstborn," she pointed lovingly to Justin, "whom I ensured the others knew nothing about, out of respect for their father. With him at rest and time on my hands, I got in touch with a service that researches such things, and within a matter of weeks they found not just one, but several leads. Unfortunately, I apparently chose a rather popular American name for him, and the war had caused its share of orphans. There actually were nine other Justins born on the same date in 1944, if you can believe that, but further investigation found that they had in fact been born to American girls.

"The adoption agencies of today will make it so much easier for adoptive children to be reunited with their parents in the future. They keep excellent records. But it wasn't so in 1944—I knew it would be difficult to find him, but I just had to try."

"It seems like it would be impossible. How did you manage it?" Eileen asked.

"Well, obviously I knew Justin's father's surname, and the orphanage to which I had given him, and so that was how I began the search. That orphanage closed in the 1970's, so I went to the courthouse in Kansas City where the orphanage had been and searched manually through hundreds of pages of records until I finally found it. Like most adoptive parents, his had elected to change his name to their own, so there was no way to look for him by his birth name, not that that would have been much help anyway, it's so common."

"And what was that?" Eileen asked.

"He was born Justin Francis Hutchinson."

"Hutchinson! Well, I can tell you what a popular name that is," Eileen mused, "that was my maiden name!" She bore the expression of a woman who had just heard a very juicy bit of trivia.

"Really? Well isn't that a funny coincidence? Justin's father was actually the only Hutchinson I ever knew, and now here sits you, the second."

"Well, there are still quite a few of us left, actually—in my family, anyway. I had four brothers, so there's still plenty of stock to carry on the name. I have, what, 13 nieces and nephews, and two great-nieces and three great-nephews running around driving them crazy."

"You must have been a bit crazy yourself growing up in a home full of boys like that." The two women became engrossed in their conversation, and Frank went to get a beer, leaving Justin to listen idly to the old hens cluck away. Gloria was mingling, as was her way, and he didn't much mind the respite from having to talk anyway.

His mind drifted to thoughts of his next day's trip to meet Ed Worley, the only survivor left of his grandfather's bomber crew. The weather was good enough, but a cold front was forecast to pass overnight, and the thunderstorms associated with it would likely lie across his route to Virginia the next day. The Mooney had a new kind of crude lightning detector he'd never used, but no radar.

"Times were a bit harder when you two were married," Melody and Eileen continued their friendly banter.

"Oh, heavens yes! We were married right after the war, but my family didn't much care for Frank, so I ended up leaving home in the middle of the night and we just had a Justice of the Peace marry us on our way to Cleveland, out on old Route 66.

"No, it wasn't much of a wedding, but the marriage sure has been good." She looked lovingly at Frank, who had returned with his beer, and gave his other hand, already holding hers, a squeeze.

"Were any of your brothers or Christina's cousins able to make it to the wedding, or are they here somewhere?"

"Well, ever since what happened back then, my family's always been more distant, geographically and otherwise, than I'd like. I'm the only one here in Ohio, most of them are out in the Midwest, near where Justin lives, but spread out over a few states, and a couple of them have health problems now that have slowed them down. We sent them all invitations, but I honestly didn't expect any of them to show up. It's kind of a long drive for the older guys, and like I said, we're not as close as we could be, I'm sad to say. Family can be very difficult."

"Indeed, they can."

"I think there's still a chance my baby brother might come for a visit, but not today. He had a conference in Chicago and was talking about dropping in afterwards."

"What does he do?"

"He's an insurance agent with State Farm in a little town called Coffeeville, Kansas."

"I know where that is. I passed through there one day, right after I came to the U.S., in the summer of '45. I was actually looking for Justin's father's family, hoping they might help me get settled and perhaps help care for their grandchild, but they wouldn't hear anything of it."

"You must have been beside yourself. Did they ever get to see him before you, I mean, before he, well…"

"No, no. They were absolutely convinced that their nice boy couldn't possibly have gotten a girl into trouble like that, and they were already so distraught over his loss, I just had to let it go."

"Oh, that's just awful. I don't think there's a person in the world that wasn't affected, I mean very seriously affected, by that war. I still can't believe Frank lived through it."

"Will your brother be here tomorrow, or later in the week?"

"Well, if he comes at all, it will probably be Monday. His conference wraps up tomorrow, and knowing Nubs he'll spend that last night with his buddies instead of driving tired."

"What did you call him?"

"Oh, that's just my pet name for him. He had a terrible accident when he was a little boy and lost most of his middle finger on one hand. Lucky he didn't lose more than that. But I've always called him 'Nubs' or 'Nubsy' since then. He used to hate it so, I'd call him that just to rile him, but he's a big boy now and doesn't much mind." Eileen smiled, remembering the tantrums she'd induced.

Melody politely smiled with her, even as a memory surfaced from so deep in her mind she wasn't sure if it was valid or a figment of her imagination.

"What do your other brothers do?"

"Well, Lee is the oldest, and quite infirm now, actually. He's had a hard life, mostly of his own making." She smiled warmly again, remembering her parents' problem child. "He always was a pistil—about drove my folks to the funny farm. He lives in Oklahoma on a ranch he's had for about twenty years now. Poor fellow can hardly walk, he's got arthritis so bad, so I don't know how much longer he can stay out there like that. But his pride will kill him before he'll come off that land.

"Then there's Samuel. He's an engineer with Douglas Aircraft in St. Louis; and Jacob, he's a school principal in Wichita. Then there's Jim, who I already told you about, and me."

"You said you had five brothers, though, didn't you?"

"Did I? Well, that's just," she paused with her eyes closed, as if she'd misspoken. "I had five, yes. We lost Wes in the war. That was Hitler's little contribution to our lives," she winced. "He was our family's hero, although I think if he'd come home either he or Frank would've killed the other. He and Frank didn't care much for each other—mostly over me, I'm afraid."

"Oh, we didn't hate each other or anything, it's just that her pop didn't like me, so neither could Wes. He was the original daddy's boy." This Frank Lawton was no old man with scars and gray hair, but a dashing young suitor, sticking his chest out and deriding his mate's protectors, even though they had all long since abandoned the cause.

"Now, dear," Eileen began, but was interrupted by Melody.

"Did you say 'Wesley'?"

"Well, yes, Wesley was his full name, but just about everyone called him Wes."

"Yes, of course. You Americans do love your one syllable nicknames.

"I believe I need to go freshen up a bit, if you'd excuse me. Justin, would you be a dear and show me to the ladies' room, please?"

"How you doin', Tommy?" Max Newhart asked Warwick.

"I'm pretty sure I've got the bleeding stopped, but it hurts like hell. You think we ought to get up to bailout altitude, so we can get out if we need to?"

Warwick was still in command, and he knew if he ordered Newhart to climb, or the men to bail out, they would obey him. He'd lost a lot of blood, but was still coherent enough to know he was well into shock and may not be thinking clearly much longer. Their escape from combat left him unsure of their exact position, and he couldn't bear to think of getting his men killed trying to get back to base, when bailing out and accepting getting taken prisoner while they were still in pretty good shape might save them.

"Tom, even if we could get you out of here with that leg, you'll lose it for sure if you have to land on it and end up in a kraut hospital."

"You ready to die, and take these guys with you, to save me from a little limp?" Warwick looked directly into his copilot's eyes, back into the bomber's fuselage, then gave Newhart a ghastly, dying man's smile, his thinking too sluggish to look away after the appropriate length of time. His complexion was pallid, his eyes glazed.

"Let's talk about it over France. At least there we'll have half a chance of staying out of the Stalags." Newhart gave Warwick a cursory look, but pretended to be too busy flying to look longer. The Air Corps had lost track of hundreds of crewmembers who, wounded too badly to make it back to base, had been "dropped" by their friends, so they'd have some chance of survival, even if as a prisoner, after a short parachute ride to the relative safety of Earth. Newhart considered that their first option, but for now, in a quiet sky devoid of any other planes, it seemed alarmist. For twenty-two missions now, some more difficult than this, they'd always found a way to get everyone alive home, if not everyone home alive, and he wasn't about to watch his best friend die.

As if on cue, Wes Hutchinson appeared between them and asked about Warwick. He looked at the leg, still dripping fresh blood, and at the man's ghostly complexion, then asked Newhart how long he thought it might take for them to reach "the Kingdom."

"At this speed? If we don't have to take any 'detours,' I'd say two, two-and-a-half hours." The hopelessness in his expression and Warwick's appearance told Wes they would be saying goodbye to their Captain, one way or another, before then. It made him sick.

"We over France yet?" Wes asked as quietly as he could in the din of the cockpit.

"We will be soon if we're not already. You think you can help him get back there and get that leg elevated? He's not doing anybody any good up here."

"Sure. Ok, Cap, what do you say we take you back to the club car and get you something to drink, buddy?" Warwick smiled faintly, and nodded, but didn't move. Wes grabbed him around the middle with his right arm and, bracing against the seat with his left, pulled the nearly two-hundred pound man out of his seat like a sack of potatoes, trying as hard as he could to keep any weight from bearing on the wounded leg. Warwick flailed his arms weakly, trying to help.

Newhart almost broke with pity for the man with whom he had cheated death a hundred times, in a hundred different ways, and a wave of horror that perhaps it was already too late, even if they got him out now, spread over him. His voice shook as he spoke.

"Wes, get him into a chute and get him out of here while he's still conscious. I'll get the doors."

Wes stopped moving him and looked at Newhart. That was it. Almost two years of tearing around the world with their lives in Warwick's hands, living second-to-second with him, sometimes because of him, as they fought their way through a thousand hells, now were going to come to this undignified end, delivering him like one of the hundreds of bombs they'd dropped. For Tommy Warwick, there was no better alternative now than to bet his life on the presence of some basic goodness in men whose wanton disregard for humanity had brought them all to Europe in the first place.

"Cap'n. You hear me? Captain Warwick? Come on, Tommy, look at me, Joe."

Sitting with him on the floor next to the bomb bay, Wes strapped the parachute on, but Warwick had to be conscious to pull the rip cord. France's warm sun bore down on him through the turret like a spotlight, just as Oklahoma's did that day so long ago, when he picked up his injured little brother Jim and, ridden with guilt for not keeping him safe as they played, carried him back home, wailing and bleeding like a stuck pig, unsure of just how badly he was hurt .

He hadn't thought of that accident that cost Jim his finger in a long time; it now seemed almost comical that he'd actually been so worried for him with just a smashed finger. The situation with Warwick was far more desperate, his love for the man every bit as strong, and, once again, it was his fault for not getting the kraut son of a bitch that got him before he took that shot.

"Tommy!" he screamed, and Warwick opened his eyes wide. Wes smiled warmly at him. "We're thinking maybe it's time you tried some of that fine French food tonight. Can you do that for us and let us know what you think?"

Warwick mumbled something Wes couldn't make out. Time was short. Worley had come up from the waist when he saw Wes carrying Warwick, and was helping get him into position.

"Cap, I'm going to put your hand on your rip cord. You feel that?" Warwick's eyes were still half open, but frighteningly distant. Wes felt sure the man was going to die right in front of him, right here in the bomb bay of his own Godamned plane.

He nodded and, startlingly lucid, repeated one of his favorite clichés, "You'll never get me to jump out of a perfectly good airplane, Hutch." Then he looked over at Worley and smiled, "This one will do just fine."

With that, Wes called to Newhart and gave the signal to open up the bomb bay doors, and they were enveloped in a dry hurricane as the serene countryside beckoned below. Wes clenched his hand around Warwick's, which was holding on loosely to the rip cord lanyard on his parachute harness. His grip tightened on it when he felt Wes' hand close around his, and, giving Wes a smoky gaze, said "Au revoir, amis." As gently as they could, they helped him scoot to the edge of the bomb rack and watched him tumble like a rag doll into the furious slipstream.

Max Newhart had coordinated with tailgunner Dick Lindstrom to look for Newhart's chute. None of the men wanted to think about having to write a letter home to Warwick's wife about how they threw him out of his own plane and never saw his chute open.

Although logically he'd have surely died if they didn't get him help in time, it would have seemed to them such a better death to be in his own plane, with his crew around him.

"He's got it open!" Lindstrom shouted into his intercom, just as Wes returned to the cockpit to check back in with Newhart. "He's drifting into a fencerow, it looks like. Come on, Jean-Paul, Pierre, somebody, go get him."

"He's ok!" Newhart shouted to Wes, who promptly turned around to give a relieved thumbs-up to Worley, who was already returning to his station at the right waist gun.

"You up to flying this thing yourself, Lieutenant?" Wes asked Newhart as he returned to the cockpit.

"You know it—but just in case you're wrong, get up here."

Justin hadn't been keeping up with the conversation very closely, but was preoccupied with what questions to ask his father's old friend the next day. He turned in his seat and pointed to the large sign above a short hallway that led to the restrooms, saying "Well, Mum, the restrooms are just over there down that hall."

"Justin, dear, my eyes aren't what they used to be," she insisted. "Would you please just indulge your old Mum this time and show me?" She was hoping for just a shard of the quick wit she had so appreciated in his father to show up in his son.

"Yeah, ok, sure." Justin had no idea what was going on, but his mother's concern was clear.

They walked together to the hallway with the restroom sign above it, and she took her son's arm once they were deep enough inside it to not be seen.

"Justin, I don't know how to say this, and I don't know if I believe it myself, but I'm fairly certain these people are relations of your father. Do you know what I'm saying? Do you understand who these people are?"

"What?"

"Christina's family. Do you know who they are, to you?"

"I was under the suspicion they're Paul's in-laws, as of about an hour ago, but unless you've had too much champagne, that can't be all you mean."

One of the bridesmaids came down the hall, smiled at them as she walked past, and disappeared into the ladies' room.

"Justin, I think, I think they're your father's sister and her family!"

"What? How?"

"Your father talked a great deal about his family. He told me he had a sister, some brothers, I can't recall how many, and one baby brother who lost a part of his finger when he was playing with him in an oilfield one day. His name was Wesley Hutchinson, her maiden name was Hutchinson. He was from Caney, Kansas, and most of her family seems to be from the Midwest."

Justin's mouth was hanging open, silent.

A fireman in uniform, one of the guests, brushed past them on his way to the men's room.

"What does that mean, if you're right?"

"Well," she smiled a devilish grin, "I guess it means my grandson may have more English 'tradition' in him than one might otherwise assume."

They stood there together as two or three more guests pushed past them, struggling to understand the enormity of the situation. Convinced the Lawtons suspected nothing, she began to consider how, if at all, to get her suspicions confirmed and tell them. The wedding had already occurred, it was fairly obvious that it had long since been consummated, and it was certainly more than possible such a revelation could easily cause a huge, embarrassing scene.

"What do we do?" Justin asked.

"I haven't the first idea." The old girl was enjoying this.

The bridesmaid came out of the restroom and made a comment about how hot she was in her dress and how her makeup was melting off her face. They laughed courteously, but she could tell there was a serious conversation going on. "Is everything alright?" she asked them.

"Yes, dear, we just have some plans to make, that's all, thank you for your concern." The girl smiled, said 'k', and walked back into the hall.

"Well, should we maybe head back? I feel really funny here."

"Yes, I suppose. Just don't say anything for a while. Let me try to see if this isn't an old woman's imagination gone wild first, before we do something terrible on Paul's wedding day."

He agreed, and they walked together back to the table, their minds reeling. Justin had only recently met his mother, learned that his father had been a war hero, and confirmed he was illegitimate. Had he just now also learned his son had just married his cousin? Was it legal? Was it safe? What would happen if she became pregnant?

When they returned to the table, Christy was there, visiting with her parents and Paul's mother and sister. Justin and his mother greeted everyone, looked briefly at each other, and sat down.

"Well, what have you two been up to?" Christina said. "My friend Jill said she saw you two talking really quiet by the restroom. I hope you're not hatching any schemes to leave early. We have way too much alcohol around for that!" She laughed, then remembered her father-in-law was a recovering alcoholic.

"And a lot of great food, too."

"No way, honey, we're here for the duration," Justin piped up. "How much longer till the dollar dance anyway? I haven't had my arms around a pretty girl in a long time now!" Justin stole an appreciative look at his ex-wife, who rolled her eyes, gave him a demure smile, and looked away.

For the first time since he hopped on the wagon, Justin wasn't expending any energy whatsoever to resist drinking, despite its proximity and the strong call for it at a wedding. It seemed getting to know his mother and, through her, his father, had put something terribly ugly and restless deep in his soul to rest.

Looking at his son's beautiful, funny bride, his own daughter he had yet to give away, their devoted, patient mother, and his own classy, deeply caring mum, and thinking about the rich man's toy waiting for him at the airport, for the first time in his life he was in total bliss. From this lofty new perspective, his life looked more like a journey, bumpy though it had been, than a disaster.

"Dollar dance is coming up, I guess. I don't know. We never decided who was going to run this show, so it's just on autopilot."

"Well, you better get on it, before people start falling down."

She laughed and looked around. "True. Well, you want to just go right now? Oh, but my dad's supposed to start it though, isn't he?" She looked the question at her father, Doug, possibly the quietest and most difficult person to read at the table. He grimaced.

"I think that's the idea, yeah, but maybe I could abdicate?" He gave a friendly look to Justin, who put his hands up in deference.

"I'll get my turn. Weddings are all about the bride"

Paul snuck up from behind and put his arms around Christina, and she snuggled into the embrace with a glowing smile. From her bare, supple shoulder, Paul addressed the table, "Hey guys! Fun meters pegged-out yet? So, who do you think is the hardier partiers, pilots or firemen?" No one answered, and Frank Lawton gave a clearly hollow smile to him.

Sensing the tension, Justin tried to send a message to his son, "I think we'll know in a few hours, but my money's on whichever is the larger group."

"Yep. Sorry babe, but I think the CFD's got your flying buddies outnumbered and out of their league," Christina ribbed him, and he let her go.

She looked first at Justin and then her father, "Well, anyway, I'll grab the old man and drag him out there, and you can come cut in any time after the kicking and screaming stops. He hates dancing—he really is wrapped up way too tight, especially for a fireman. Maybe a pilot's family somewhere got the wrong baby."

She was still radiating beauty in her gown, and there wasn't the slightest hint of pretense about her as she put out her hand for her father to lead her out to the dance floor, with Paul and his mother right behind. Justin realized his boy couldn't have found a more perfect partner in a thousand lifetimes—he didn't care who her grandmother was.

With the bride and groom and their father and mother gone from the table and the soft rock of "Head Over Heels" cued up on the sound system, Paul's grandmother sensed the opportunity to put her chips on the table.

"Eileen, when we were talking about your wedding, I was about to ask you if you ever reconciled with your parents after. I mean, were there raw feelings for a long time?"

"Oh, heavens, yes. I just don't know for sure how much of it was over what we had done and how much of it was just sorrow over Wes. I wrote them regularly, and my mother would always write back, but it took some years for my father to come around. But it all worked out. We came to visit them with Doug, who was our first baby, a year or so later, and it was tense at first, but Frank and Dad seemed to get things ironed out well enough. I think my dad felt a lot better just knowing that Frank Lawton hadn't embarrassed his girl."

"I didn't need to—she does just fine herself."

"Yes, I don't recommend that experience." Melody was clearly fishing with potent bait, but a little afraid of what she'd catch.

"Oh, it must have been awful. You were so brave to deal with it all alone like that. How did you do it?"

"Well, when Justin's father went missing, I was, of course, inconsolable. He and I had been together for nearly a year and were inseparable, but for the Army. It was such a dark time. It seemed everyone knew someone who'd been killed in the last month, and we were just so in love it seemed more wrong than right to resist temptation, knowing what could happen. I knew we would marry, perhaps after the war, which seemed near at the time, but...

"I waited until the second month, to be sure, but—you *know*. And I further knew that I would have to leave soon before it became obvious. I borrowed some money from my Uncle Percy, who somehow suspected it and didn't want me to shame 'his' family by having to admit to being put upon by a damned Yank. I packed what I could into a small trunk, and came to the U.S. to make contact with W——, what remained of his family."

"Oh, so you knew where they lived?"

"Yes, he had told me and all his friends in the squadron. We were all like a big family. Everyone knew where everyone else came from."

"So what did you tell them, I mean, how could you put it?"

"I tried to think of some good way to say it, but in the end I just told them the truth right out, without much sugar around it at all. They were terribly distressed over his loss already, and I think they simply couldn't handle any more strife in their lives right then. Denial was a matter of survival for them.

"They told me I had to be mistaken, and closed their door to me."

"Oh, how awful. So you had to go to 'plan B' then. Well, at least you did the right thing, and now just look at how wonderful it turned out in the end."

"I can't tell you how wonderful it is. I feel as if I've lived two lives, and now they've finally merged again and I can look back and consider the whole, and it's absolutely beautiful. I was so well loved by two wonderful men and had four wonderful children. I only wish I could have been a better mum to the first."

"He doesn't seem to be holding any grudges," Frank said.

"No, he's intensely proud, actually. I swear he stands four inches taller now than when we met in Wichita. You can see it in his whole demeanor. He finally feels as if he was born of good stock, and not just some accidental, unwanted waif. I can only imagine how proud his father would be."

"What did he do in the Army, anyway, and I don't believe I heard you say his name."

Melody's already well-trained posture straightened even more, she looked at the centerpiece, took a deep breath, and cleared her throat. The moment had come. Soon she'd know if this incredible apparent coincidence could possibly be true.

As badly, and for as long, as Wes had wanted a seat in the cockpit, this wasn't what he'd had in mind. In the hundreds of hours he'd spent flying in Liberators, working on them, studying complex schematics in their manuals, he'd never once touched the hallowed control yoke while airborne, not even when all was well and they were completely free of danger. Now they were down an engine and a Captain, shot up badly, and trying to limp undetected across Hitler's front yard in broad daylight.

Taking care not to step in the pool of Hardwick's blood on the floor made getting into the seat difficult, and sitting in Warwick's place seemed somehow blasphemous to Wes. Nowhere in any of his Walter Middy-esque daydreams of sitting there had there been a single drop of blood; now a pool of it stood drying on the floor, the only evidence Tommy Warwick had ever been there. He had to ask Newhart if he thought they should change seats.

"I wouldn't be able to fly us out of a brown paper bag from that seat—this is where I sit. Just take it easy and don't do anything with the wheel or pedals unless I ask for help. You can run the props, throttles, and mixtures better than I can anyway, so those are all yours."

Newhart looked out his window at the two engines throbbing at full throttle on his wing. The bare metal propeller hubs always seemed to spin so slowly to him, their bottom halves reflecting the green of Life just out of reach below, while their top sides reflected the infinite blue of which they were now a part.

"Just help us get home, Wes." He said it like he was praying, both to God and this still-unfamiliar new plane, with Wes as the intercessor in some bizarre, only partly-Holy Trinity, which was far from normal for stolid Newhart.

Until then, he'd always managed to keep his game face, but losing Warwick the way they did had rattled him. Sweat was visible under the stained, flattened officer's cap of which he was so proud, and his eyes seemed to be open wider than Wes had ever seen them. In command and separated from his partner for the first time since flight school, flying a plane he couldn't yet trust, Newhart was scared shitless.

"I feel helpless up here without a gun in front of me," Wes jibed, trying to lighten the mood a little as he perched himself uncomfortably in Warwick's seat, still taking care not to tread in any of the blood.

"Yeah, well, if we see any more fighters you may have to go back, but even then, keep an eye on me. If I get hit like Tommy did, you'll have to get everybody out."

"How the hell do I do that?"

Newhart glared at Wes with an insulted half-smile. "You don't honestly expect me to believe you don't know, do you Wes? I wish to God we had you beside us in one of those Mustangs right now. I bet you'd see us home just fine."

Wes hadn't kept his dreams of becoming a pilot a secret, but out of respect for Warwick and Newhart, he hadn't ever made it a point to mention either. Now he realized Newhart had divulged the real secret—the whole crew had always known.

A Silver Ring

Wes flushed with pride and idly tweaked the mixture on number one, avoiding eye contact with Newhart in self-conscious embarrassment. A pilot to his core, Max Newhart had set into motion his contingency plan for the failure of the next most critical piece of equipment on the plane—himself.

Max settled into his seat somewhat after hearing Warwick's chute had opened, and they rode on without incident for nearly a half-hour afterward. Wes spent his time tweaking and talking to the plane, riding it harder than he'd have ever done with *Barfly*, even leaving Warwick's seat twice to get a better look at the oil and exhaust temperatures, fuel and various other gauges on his engineer's panel, trying to get the ship to go as fast as possible with no concern whatsoever for its longevity. If they made it back and Mike Lewis dared to say a fucking word about "his" plane, Wes would deck him. They had three more missions to finish their tour, and they could bring back three more airplanes all shot to hell, for all he cared.

The next time he returned to Warwick's seat, he completely forgot to avoid stepping in Warwick's now-dried blood on the floor.

"There's a shudder on the left side, sir, do you feel it?" Wes hadn't said anything about it at first, but he'd been trying for the past ten minutes to identify and stop a sensation only he could perceive coming from number one, which in fact was burning an exhaust valve, making one of the engine's nine cylinders misfire. If that outboard engine on the same wing failed, they'd be lucky to get the plane down without it rolling over.

"I don't feel anything, Wes. What do you think it is?" Newhart had his hands full already and no interest in or talent for Wes' subtleties. He just wanted the condensed version, and even then only if there was something he could do about it.

"I can't tell for sure, but it feels like maybe a miss in One."

Newhart glared at Wes but said nothing.

Approaching Reims, with Wes staring back at his engineer's panel, Newhart called out to him, "Wes, get up in that turret and tell everybody to look sharp. We're going to have company—190's." He was pointing at a group of the Luftwaffe's deadliest fighters, Focke-Wulf 190's, climbing away from their base northwest of town, with the leaders turning their direction.

Wes popped into his turret and flushed pale when he saw them. There were already five or six airborne, more than enough to finish them off, with who knew how many more coming down the runway. The krauts were going to have to guess at whom to credit with the kill.

"Engineer to crew: man your guns. We've got 190's coming in at nine o'clock, level. Looks like a lot of them, Joes." He exercised the turret and cleared his guns with a brief burst, as did the others, except Lindstrom, who typically used more ammunition than the others and was always low on the way home. They grimly smiled to themselves at Wes' theft of Colonel Timberlake's term. Each knew he'd be lucky ever to hear him address them that, or any other, way again.

"Copilot to crew," Newhart paused at realizing he was no longer the copilot. He thought of correcting himself, but decided against it. Warwick was still with them, in each of them.

"Wes is going to be keeping an eye on me up here. If I get hit, he's going to give you all the bailout order and try to keep it upright long enough for you all to get out. If something makes you want to get out sooner, screw 'Miss Manners.' Just call it and get the hell out. I'll be right behind you."

"Sir, if that's the new standard, then I left with Warwick," came the voice of Ed Worley. Every man aboard knew they were guaranteed not to survive the onslaught, certainly not intact. They donned and checked their parachutes, mentally rehearsed the bailout drill, and prayed they'd somehow find a way to live through the next five minutes.

Wes practiced moving his turret, concerned more with not letting his novice in the position get any more of his friends hurt or killed than with mere survival. If he'd been better with that turret, he thought, Warwick might still be with them. He might have picked a different way home, perhaps found another shot-up bomber to pair up with. Warwick had found them a way out of some pretty sour pickles. Hell, they might not even be in this mess in the first place if he just would have been nicer to Twomey, or if…

He forced himself to stop indulging in any more guilty fantasies about what might have been. He'd screwed up before, he'd seen plenty of others do it, and God willing, they'd all screw up again and again before it was all over. Right now, he just had to keep those Focke-Wulfs from getting Newhart.

He'd never considered himself a protector with his machine guns. In formation with other bombers, the lethal crossfire he helped create made him feel more like an assassin. But now, entirely alone and about to be surrounded by fighters, with the only man capable of getting the crippled plane back on the ground sitting defenseless beside a tacky bloodstain where their friend had always been, it occurred to him that all along, what he'd really been was a protector, a bodyguard.

With hearts in their throats and their hands and feet ice cold, the men who could see the fighters coming didn't think to tell the others what happened next. When enough time had gone by for them to have fallen under attack and nothing had happened, Lindstrom piped up to ask what was going on; where were the krauts?

"They're turning west, they're still out of range," Newhart deadpanned. Did the fighters not see them, were they perhaps going out on a different mission, or were the sons of bitches just going to let them go, since they were disabled and alone, in some chivalrous brothers-in-arms thing? They'd all heard stories of fighter pilots letting their enemies go if the fight became terribly unfair at some point, but none of them ever expected to witness such old-fashioned courtesy.

"What the hell are you up to, Heinrich?" Wes mumbled to himself. He'd had his turret fixed on the leader, with what he knew would be a perfect lead, and was moments from firing when the Germans turned away.

Wes Hutchinson and his crew had become accustomed to only the German pilots' most aggressive tactics. They had no knowledge of a popular game amongst the Luftwaffe, because no survivors had yet returned to debrief it. With so many inexperienced replacement pilots to train, and so little resources left with which to train them, the trickle of unescorted, damaged Allied bombers struggling to return to England had unwittingly become part of a macabre, unofficial rite of initiation known colloquially to the Luftwaffe as *zielpraxis* or, roughly translated, "target practice."

Wes and his crew didn't know what to make of the Germans' flight away from them until they'd made another half-circle in the opposite direction to come back at them, shallowing out and accelerating through the last third of their turn, to reach their guns' range at top speed, above and heading almost perpendicular to the lumbering bomber's flight path, affording them a luxurious window to fire on the Liberator's long, slender, fuel-filled wings, while exposing them to only three of its guns at a time: the two in Wes' top turret and first the left, then the right, waist guns.

"They're lining up single file; they're going to just take turns until somebody finishes us!" Wes shouted into his interphone. *Thank God they're coming from the left*, he thought. If they'd known the only pilot on board was in the right seat, they might have gone the other way around to kill Newhart, just to see how the plane would crash without a pilot. At least now there might be time for those without a shot to bail out. One was Ed Worley, who, at the right waist gun, would only get a trailing, low-energy shot at fighters flying away from them.

"Dean, I'll take the leaders as they come. You go for the followers before their turns come. Everybody else aboard this plane's a sitting duck. Lieutenant, I think now's a good time to give that order."

Dean Whitcomb, the man who replaced Wes at the left waist gun when he was promoted to engineer, began lining up his first shot at the second Focke-Wulf in the line, determined to buy some time for his mentor Ed Worley to get out.

"Roger, engineer," Newhart piped up without hesitation, "you heard the man. I want everybody that doesn't have a shot out of this hunk of junk, now! Bailout! Bailout! Bailout!"

One by one, Dick Lindstrom, their new radio operator and navigator Buck Talbot and Jason Moore made their way to the bomb bay to bail out, the sound of Wes' gunfire acting as a rather convincing evacuation signal.

"What the hell are you waiting for?" Whitcomb screamed at Ed Worley, who was standing beside him, trying to gauge the fighters' speed, for lack of anything else to do right then. Worley didn't answer him.

"Sir, Worley's not leaving. Get this asshole out of here!" Whitcomb said into the interphone.

"Worley, bail out, that's an order! You've got no horse in this race." Newhart bellowed.

"Sir, when those 190's pass over, I can take out whatever Wes and Dean don't get before they get a chance to regroup."

"Yeah, Ed, that's great. We'll just take out a whole fucking squadron by ourselves, right? Get the hell out of here, now!" Wes screamed at his best friend.

Wes' first shots at the leader hit dead center, shattering the Focke-Wulf's radial engine in a burst of flame, shrapnel, and sooty oil smoke, but not before its pilot fired a burst himself.

A novice, the pilot led the three-engined Liberator a little too much given its reduced speed and hit its long nose and cockpit instead of the wings. Perpetually cool bombardier Larry Wilson had already begun his trek aft to bail out, stopping briefly at the flight deck to give Newhart's arm a squeeze and tell him "Let's go, Max."

Those were the last words Newhart heard before a cannon round tore through the aluminum fuselage and lodged in his head.

Wilson caught his friend's death out of the corner of his eye just as he was turning to Wes, and he stood there for a moment transfixed by the merciful and absolute horror of it, but then managed to scream over the noise, "Max is gone, Wes! We've got to get out of here, now! Let's go!"

Wes couldn't hear a sound over his guns and the heated argument he was having with Ed Worley, however, and he wouldn't look away from the second fighter, whose gun muzzles were now flashing their deadly message to him. Wilson grabbed his leg to get his attention.

The second German, who was an absolutely awful near-washout at flight school, forgot to lead the bomber at all, and hit nothing but French countryside as Wes put a few rounds into his plane, to no apparent effect. But at the same time Wilson grabbed his leg, Wes ran out of up-travel with his guns. Snapping out of his target fixation, he realized the plane was rolling over to the left.

Newhart had used the plane's trim tabs to make it fly hands-off with the dead number two engine, allowing the plane's natural stability to mask his impending death at the controls, but as Wes was firing on the lead Focke Wulf, number one finally swallowed its damaged valve, and no plane had trim tabs big enough to offset two dead engines on the same wing. Without a pilot's constant pressure on the controls, the plane was going to roll over.

Wes jumped from his turret just as it was obliterated by accurate fire from the third Focke-Wulf. Nearly deaf and blind from the new torrent of wind and Plexiglas shards rushing from the turret out the bomb bay, Larry Wilson gave Wes a quick salute and dove through the opening while it and gravity still shared a common direction.

Dean Whitcomb's waist window was fast becoming the floor, and he had to clutch his gun to keep from falling out, with Worley right beside him. Three gunners were the only ones left aboard the dying plane.

Wes screamed and waved frantically at them to bail out, then climbed the short ladder into the cockpit to try to right the plane. As the bank angle steepened, Whitcomb finally stopped struggling to stay aboard. Wes nearly fell into Warwick's seat then flipped himself into position and cranked the yoke with all his might while jamming the right rudder pedal down. The plane staggered back toward level flight so sluggishly,

Wes knew if he let go to bail out, he'd be upside down and trapped inside by the time he made it to the bomb bay.

All he could do now was fly.

Having seen men jumping out of the Liberator and its near roll-over, the more experienced German pilots toward the back of the line elected not to pursue it further and just continued following the leader around in a large circle to the right, waiting to take potshots at the survivors. Each of them had lost at least a few close friends or relatives to the incessant Allied bombardment of the Fatherland. Chivalry had died with them.

It was all surreal to Wes Hutchinson, sitting in Tommy Warwick's seat beside Max Newhart's body, flying their airplane with no one else aboard, and no credible hope left of getting back to England alive. He'd studied the pilots' movements on the controls whenever he could, sometimes for hours, but he never dreamed it could be so easy. Knowing the fighters were watching him, and that he couldn't bail out, Wes turned for the largest field he could see, reducing power on the two right engines to descend for it. If he could just get the Germans to leave him alone long enough…

"His name was Wesley. Wesley Hutchinson. Everyone but me called him Wes. He was a gunner and flight engineer on a B-24 Liberator in the Army's 8th Air Force."

Eileen and Frank Lawton sat silent for a moment, then looked at each other and then at Paul and Christina, both acting like imbeciles, dancing with childish abandon with their mother and father.

"When was this Wesley of yours killed?" Eileen asked, with deadly seriousness.

"April 1, 1944. April Fool's Day, as I learned it's called here."

"You're not fooling us now, are you?" Frank Lawton's face had flushed.

"No, sir. I'm quite sincere."

"Do you have a picture of him?" Eileen's voice was breaking, her eyes filling with tears. The same sickening stew of emotions she'd felt that day so long ago, down the street from Frank's old house, was enveloping her again. She could hardly grasp what she was hearing.

Melody picked her clutch up from the floor, took her wallet from it, and pulled a badly worn sepia-tone photograph of Sergeant Wesley Hutchinson, in full Class A uniform, out of its plastic holder and offered it to Eileen Lawton. She took it, stared wide-eyed at it for a moment, then looked at Christy and Paul and fainted against her husband, who bolted out of his chair and laid her across it and her own in one smooth motion, gently slapping and rubbing her face to revive her.

Were it not happening right in front of him, Justin Hutchinson would have been hard pressed not to laugh as awareness of the situation spread through the ranks of the nearly 100 firemen present in the hall, faster than any blaze any of them had ever battled. Scores of some-time and would-be heroes, tall and short, burly and slight, smart and dull, rushed to the table where the Chief's wife had just collapsed, only to see her come to while being attended by her family, among whom the remnants of a squabble were clear.

"You knew this when you came here? How could you let them do it?" Eileen was overwhelmed, but more concerned for her granddaughter than anything.

"No, no, I swear to you, I didn't know until you told me about him just now. How could I?" Melody had, of course, never even dreamed that Eileen would take it this way and felt terribly vulnerable and guilty for having pursued the truth into this corner.

"But, you…oh!"

"What the heck is going on? What happened?" Christina asked.

"Gammy's just had a little spell, sweetheart, nothing to worry about," Eileen said, in total opposition to and clear betrayal of her true feelings. She looked all around at the crowd that had gathered around her and then back at Frank, who was considering the options— all of them.

He too felt the whole thing was just too freakish to be unplanned, yet Melody gave every appearance of being as stunned by it as they had been, albeit a step or two ahead of them in processing it and not nearly so shocked.

More than anything, the Lawtons wanted to get the crowd to disperse so they could continue the rather sensitive conversation they'd begun in relative privacy. "C'mon guys, take it easy. I know how much you all love to help. *Really,* I do." The obvious understatement had the desired effect, and most of the crowd chuckled and began to trickle back to their tables, comfortable that what they had seen was just an old woman's nerves fraying on a hot, happy, stressful day.

The family, however, wasn't going anywhere, and the dollar dance was suspended while Christina fretted over her grandmother, with her new husband dutifully looking on. An uneasy silence was obvious between the grandparents, and their children and grandchildren could sense something terribly objectionable had been said or done to the Lawtons.

"They weren't supposed to show anyone the bill 'til this whole thing was over," Paul said, trying to get the last stragglers to leave.

Barry Reeder, an oversensitive, underweight, and unsurprisingly still-single fireman in his forties had, of course, come without a date and, perhaps lacking any good reason to return to his table of couples, was particularly stubborn in refusing to take the hint. He was asking Eileen to raise her arms, make fists, squeeze his hand, and even pulled a penlight out of his pocket and attempted to check her pupils for response, convinced he could be the hero who had flagged the onset of a mild stroke. Frank Lawton had to draw a sharper picture for him.

Taking his subordinate's arms in his tight grip, he deftly took the man's attention off of his wife. "Barry, she's ok. Now stop making such a fuss. She just got a little lightheaded and had to get some fresh blood upstairs. Thank you for your concern, but we've got it taken care of. Ok?"

"Ok, Chief, sure. I'm sorry, but, but keep an eye on her. My grandma died from stroke, you know."

"I know, Barry. I remember." Lawton would have been lucky to remember the man's name, much less how his grandmother had died, but for the fact that their uniform included a gold name badge on the breast. "Now, go enjoy yourself. Your date would probably love a dance, so go give her one."

"Actually, Chief, I didn't bring anybody. I was kind of hoping to, well you know, weddings are supposed to be great places to meet people and what not."

Frank let go of Reeder's arms and kindly wrapped his left arm around Reeder's shoulders like he'd done with his platoon-mate back in 1942—and not without briefly fantasizing about putting his right arm to the same use. Looking around the hall, he instead merely gestured, "Yes, Terry, yes, there's a Goddamn cornucopia of eligible bachelorettes here, and I bet there's a few of them would just love to get their hands around a big ol' juicy Reeder-burger."

Letting that mischievous right arm have just a little fun, he used it to tap Reeder's sternum perhaps a little too hard and brought his wilting glare into focus, just to drive his next point home—like a nail through tissue.

"So go, grab a brew, and see if you can't give one of them their big chance and let us have a little family time, here, ok?"

It finally sank in to Reeder that he was the only unrelated person left at the table.

"Ok, Chief, sure. Sorry." He meandered off to follow his orders.

Christina had never heard of her stalwart grandmother doing anything like this. More than anything, she was afraid her grandparents had done something embarrassing to or in front of Melody, who she thought must surely feel somewhat awkward here.

"Now," she said sternly to her grandparents, "would one of you hooligans like to give us the Certified, Lawton-Bullshit-Free version of what just happened here, or do I need to fake fainting myself and get Dudley Do-Right back?"

Frank and Eileen looked at each other, then to Melody, whose face showed pure overwrought guilt. Justin's expression was one of anxious amusement over calm concern. He was confident that once the beans were spilled, everyone would get a good laugh out of this awkward moment that would be relived untold times in the coming years as Paul and Christina's—the Hutchinsons' and the Lawtons'—lives again intertwined. *It's not like it hasn't happened before, for God's sake*, he thought, with a living reminder of Europe's rather knotty family trees sitting right in their midst.

"Christina, dear, we've discovered something just now that you will probably have some difficulty in believing," Melody began.

"Do we have to do this here, right now?" Frank protested.

"Well, where and when do you suggest we do it?" Melody, becoming a little irritated, countered.

"I don't know, but I think chances are pretty good she'll end up on the floor, too, and I really think we've had enough excitement for one wedding already."

"Alright, what the hell's going on? I want to know right now. Nothing can be that bad, unless maybe Paul's already got a wife and kids in Austin and it turns out they're Mel's neighbors."

She leaned into the table as far as she could, pasted on a huge, fake, lighthearted smile, and said with a quiet, deadly serious voice, "See me smiling? This tells everyone around us that we're over here having the time of our lives. What a beautiful wedding, isn't this food great, beer's ice cold, gee, champagne everywhere, aren't they a great couple, this DJ rocks, CFD CFD! Now. What. The fuck. Is going. On?"

Melody beat the Lawtons to the punch.

"Christy, darling, you know your grandmother had a brother who was killed in the War, don't you?"

"Yes."

"I knew him. I mean, I…"

"You what? What is this about?"

"Christy, I was in love with him, and he with me. We would have married had he not been killed."

"Ok, wow. That's wild. What does this have to do with us?"

"Christy, I was pregnant when he was killed."

Christina's face was frozen.

"And, well, I never told anyone. I came to the U.S. and tried to make contact with his parents, but they wouldn't hear of it, so I gave the baby up for adoption. Paul's father is that baby."

"Ok, wait a minute. So, Paul's dad, is my grandmother's…brother's…son. Which makes him her nephew. So what does that make us?"

"It makes you cousins, Christy. Second cousins," Frank Lawton said, rubbing his hand through his thin, white hair, until it stopped at the top of his head. He was convinced the wedding had to be annulled.

Christy turned to Paul, who wore a look of utter astonishment.

"What does that mean?"

"Yeah, what does that mean?"

"It means," Chief Lawton tried to take the chair of this meeting, "that you kids are going to have to do some things you're not going to like, and we're all going to help you through it."

"What's that supposed to mean?" Christina wheeled on him.

"No, no! It doesn't mean anything, dear. It happens all the time, even between people who know in the first place," Melody added her own glare at Frank Lawton to Christina's, catching him in a furious female crossfire. "And there's not a thing in the world wrong with it."

"Nothing wrong with it? Are you out of your mind? Married people have a way of having kids, you know? Do you realize what could happen?"

"Frank, please. None of us knows for certain what this means. Just please let's let them have this night, and first thing Monday we'll find out what we're up against." Eileen Lawton's head was still swimming in all of this, and she had been reliving the last times she'd seen Wes before the war. She could see the resemblance in Justin, and undeniably so, she thought, in Paul.

"Let them have their night? You're off you're rocker, too! Unless you plan on chaperoning them."

"Frank, please. Just calm down." Justin, as the eldest Hutchinson present, felt duty-bound to oppose Lawton, who'd abruptly stood up from his chair, pointing at the couple as he nearly shouted at his wife.

"Frank Lawton! Sit your ass down!" Christina whisper-shouted, her face blood red, her eyes narrowed and piercing.

Frank Lawton's face fairly curdled as he shook his head, walked away from the table, and stormed through the reception hall's doors. Eileen mumbled something no one could make out and followed him at a more casual pace. By the time she caught up to him outside, he'd already lit up a Pall Mall and was drawing on it furiously.

As she closed the door behind her, he turned away and fixed his gaze on the giant flag waving in front of the hall. Eileen walked around and got in front of him, then gently pulled down on his chin when he refused to acknowledge her after a few seconds.

"It certainly seems there's more Frank Lawton in Christy than we ever counted on. Now what's gotten into you?"

"I spend my whole life trying to either measure up to or get the hell away from your family, we finally get a few years' peace, and now this. I swear to Christ, He's got a hell of a sick sense of humor."

"Frank."

"He's one sick fuck, that's what He is. I mean, what are the odds on this?"

"Frank."

As Eileen followed after Frank, Christina's mom told her she should go out there too, but Christina was far too angry.

"I'll deal with him after he settles down, if he ever does."

"What's that supposed to mean?" Her father interjected, suspiciously.

"It means whenever he's ready to talk and not just issue edicts, I'll talk to him, but I'm not going to hold my breath. He can't tell me what to do. The whole world isn't CFD."

"Christy, he cares so much about you, he just has that one horrible way of showing it," her mom said. "He doesn't want anything bad to happen to you, none of us do. Now, you have to admit the safest thing to do is to take it easy for a couple days until we can make a few phone calls and talk to some people who know for sure that what we've got here is absolutely ok. Granted, it would have been nice to have found out earlier on, but it's still better to find out something scary now than later, say when you have..."

"Have what? A kid with three eyes? Eight fingers? Is that what you're all so afraid is going to happen?"

"When you have problems. Look, I don't know any more than you do. None of us do. That's why we just need to take this one day at a time for now. This doesn't happen every day. It's probably nothing, sure, but we don't know."

"It's not going to be nothing. Nothing is ever 'nothing' with this family." She started crying, and Paul instinctively consoled her, but then looked around the table to gauge the reactions, which ran the gamut from Doug Lawton's reserved uncertainty, to Melody's understanding, sympathetic grimace. He asked where Frank had gone, which seemed an odd question to some of them. Christina said, "Don't worry about him.

"I don't care. I just don't. I love Paul and I'm going to be with him, I don't care what anybody says.

I'll go wherever I need to go for it to be ok, God knows that's happened before. It's done, it's over, there's no going back."

"That's not true, Christy. If you find out there could be problems, you can't actually say you're just going to ignore it."

"No, Daddy, you're wrong. That's exactly what I'm saying. There's nothing we can do now. We're going to live our lives."

"What? You act like no one has ever gotten an annulment. This would be understandable to any judge in the country!"

"Well, there's one Judge it wouldn't be understandable to. Not now."

"What do you mean?"

"The toast."

"What?"

"Did you see the toast?"

"Yeah, sure, everyone did. What does that have to do with it?"

"Did you see me drink the champagne?" Her eyes were wild, full of fear, rage, and love.

"Yeah, I saw you drink the champagne, what's that prove? You think once you toast your marriage you can't get divorced? Come on!"

"Dad, did you see me drink the champagne? Did you see me swallow any?"

"I…"

"No, you didn't. Because I didn't. I raised it to my lips, but I didn't drink any. I can't drink any more for a while now. Or smoke, or anything like that." Her glassy eyes had softened somewhat as she released her secret, but they still held that indomitable fury no one but her grandfather had ever seen before.

As Wes feathered the prop and cut the fuel supply to the dead number one engine, making the plane easier to control and less likely to catch fire after landing, a hand on his right shoulder startled him. It was Ed Worley.

"What the hell? I thought you were getting out! You shouldn't be here! Go!"

"*I* shouldn't be here? I hate to break this to you, Ace, but *you're not a pilot*!" Looking around, Worley added, "And this isn't exactly an airplane anymore, either."

"We're close enough. If I get up, she's going to roll over on her back before I could ever get out. Now get out of here while I've still got it all together!"

"Nope. I'm with you, Cap'n. Where are we going, anyway?"

Wes pointed to the field ahead. "I'm going there. You're going down there somewhere," he said, pointing straight down.

"Straight to hell, eh? Guess my mom was right after all." Worley's reserved grin was contagious as ever, and Wes couldn't stifle a laugh.

"Damn it Ed, I don't want to get us both killed, now bail out!"

Worley wasn't going anywhere, and Wes knew it.

"You need me to do anything?" When Wes was promoted to Flight Engineer, Worley had been the logical choice for his assistant, but he'd forgotten almost all his training in aircraft systems by now.

"Close the fuel shutoffs when I tell you to. If we can glide in and not catch fire, we just might make it to the Stalag."

Wes was lined up with the field and less than a thousand feet above it when the German squadron completed its leisurely turn to fall in behind them. The *dumkof* who'd missed the bomber completely on the first pass had been given the lead. He wanted badly to tell his frau he'd shot down an American bomber that day, and he would--or run out of ammunition trying.

They'd planned to tell their families about her pregnancy soon, but not for a few weeks at least, to allow for a storybook wedding and honeymoon to start their fairytale life together. Reality had crashed the party, however, and as her grandparents stood outside in the heat, with Frank Lawton furiously chain smoking the first cigarettes he'd had in months, time itself seemed to career into a solid brick wall as they all sat looking at each other in an awkward silence, despite the well-intended DJ's otherwise timely choice of the Pointer Sisters' "We Are Family" to calm the row.

The next day dawned, however, right on schedule, and Paul and Christina had slipped away, as planned, shortly after the scene at the reception, destination undisclosed. Their families spent the rest of the night avoiding each other but mingling with other guests, trying their best to downplay the situation. Frank Lawton was privately adamant that the marriage be annulled but had no good solution for the pregnancy. Christina's parents and grandmother had a more "wait and see" attitude, wanting more than anything to salvage the night for Christina's sake. Melody couldn't begin to understand what all the fuss was about, knowing full well this kind of thing was commonplace and even desirable in many parts of the world, including the Isles, illicit pregnancy notwithstanding.

Justin Hutchinson's turbulent childhood brought his focus almost exclusively to the fate of his future grandchild, and the relatively petty concerns of those not so inclined reviled him. It seemed that just as he'd finally been able to bury his demons, Frank Lawton and his family were conjuring a new band to torment his son and still-unborn grandchild. He tried at one point to talk calmly with Frank Lawton, but he was rebuffed with a glare that words would only soften. Justin and Melody then found Paul and Christy, said a supportive, loving goodbye to them, and left the reception without so much as mentioning the ring, which Justin had wisely locked in their hotel room's safe before they left that morning, just in case.

Back in their room, Justin and Melody packed their things absentmindedly as they talked till well past three a.m., the storms pounding away outside as the expected cold front passed through. They talked mostly about Paul and Christy and her family, about the incredible odds of it all happening this way, and what it all could mean, but also about Melody's "other" family and Justin's new job and life in Texas. Justin was still excited to meet Worley the next day, but he didn't want to put his old mum through any more emotional recollection. It felt as if they'd already exhumed his father's memory from its unmarked grave, honored him properly, and put him to rest once and for all.

Finally, with their bags packed and the thunder growing faint in the south, they fell asleep, certain there's a reason for even the most trivial coincidence, and eager to see this one's revealed someday.

They said their goodbyes in the hotel lobby the next morning, as Justin's cab arrived to take him to Lakefront Airport while Melody waited for the hotel van to take her to Hopkins for her airline flight back to Texas.

Justin was again preoccupied with seeing Ed Worley, certain he'd find out even more about his dad to share with Paul. His fight against alcoholism had made him a rather spiritual, if not a particularly religious, man, and he wanted badly to be able to impart his sense of the Bigger Picture to his son.

"You'll give him the ring the next time you see him, then?" Melody asked, holding her hat against the cool lake wind.

"Yep." Justin silently wondered if any mother had ever stopped nagging her children.

"And I'll see you back in Texas in a few days?"

"Yes, Ma'am," he drawled in a thick, fake accent. They both laughed and he gave her a lingering kiss on the cheek before climbing into the cab.

For a few minutes just before noon, his Mooney shared Cleveland's sky with an MD-80 taking Melody back to Texas, a 747 carrying Paul, Christina, and their baby, bound and determined to have a happy honeymoon in Hawaii, and a few of the tiniest wisps of cotton-ball cumulus, drifting along on their own affirming journey to bring the rain and thunder to Earth.

Epilogue

Surveying the crumpled, burned fuselage, Ed Worley could hardly believe it had ever been part of a shiny, new airplane. Its tail had separated. The wings, having buckled downward after the plane's tail came off, were folded beneath the fuselage, making the plane look not unlike a bird that had been shot down. The air reeked of avgas, still dripping from the right wing, charred vegetation, and burned leather—or flesh. He couldn't look in the cockpit.

For those long few moments, he didn't know exactly where he was, or how he'd gotten there. Someone came up behind him and, touching his shoulder, asked, "Was this your airplane?"

Worley wheeled around into a defensive posture, cocking his arm back to strike, but in the split second it took him to acquire his target, he realized how utterly futile it would be to resist. He was alone, unarmed, surrounded.

The FAA investigator was more than a little surprised at Worley's combative reaction, and neither man could apologize quickly or profusely enough at Worley's scarred mind snapping—from the scene of the previous day's private plane crash that killed his war buddy's son before he could tell him his father died a hero, to the scene of the crash forty years before that had landed him, his crew's sole survivor, in a German stalag.

"I'm sorry, sir, I didn't mean to startle you like that."

"No, no. I'm the one that should be sorry. You can take a man out of the war, but you can't take the war out of the man, I guess. Seeing this just took me back a little too close to the last time I was in one of these contraptions. Still don't know how I got out alive. Ended up, I was the only one that did."

Worley looked around at the team of investigators, not one of whom was old enough to remember what everyone his age would call "The War."

"I'm really sorry, sir, again. I really appreciate your coming all the way out here like this. We just didn't have any idea who else to call, like I said. You were listed as the destination contact on the flight plan, and we haven't been able to figure out a next of kin. Was this man Hutchinson an associate of yours?"

"Actually, I never got the chance to meet him, but I was good friends with his paw.And his mother."

"Do you know how he came to be flying this airplane yesterday? We have no license record for anyone named Justin *Hutchinson*, but there was one in his wallet with another man's name on it, a "Justin Prator." One's bound to be an alias, so I may need to call the FBI in, unless you know how we might be able to reach someone who knows what's going on here, perhaps his wife or children?"

"Well, sir, I really don't, and I see where you're going with all this, but trust me, you don't need to call the FBI or anything like that. There's no funny business going on here at all, just a real long, kind of sad story.

"I know a lot more about his past than he did, but next to nothing about his present. I know he came from Texas, he never mentioned a wife, but now, wait a minute. He did say he was coming out this way for his boy's wedding in Cleveland, so maybe there's somebody there who might be able to help you. I'm pretty sure he said his son was getting married to the Cleveland Fire Chief's granddaughter. Maybe you can get in touch with his son through him, but let's sit down for a minute first and let me tell you what we've got here, and maybe that'll save you having to jangle somebody's bell.

After the funeral, which awaited Paul when he returned from his honeymoon since he and Christina had purposely kept their destination secret and felt no desire to talk to anyone after the reception, he met Melody in Kerrville to go through Justin's effects.

A two-week accumulation of mail was crammed into the mailbox. Most of it was routine, but a small box from a Cleveland Holiday Inn stood out, both as the only parcel and the only piece addressed to Mr. Justin Hutchinson, a fact which hadn't escaped the attention of Justin's conscientious mailman. It bore a stamp "NEW NAME AT THIS ADDRESS. PLEASE CONFIRM CORRECT DELIVERY."

Inside the cardboard box was a smaller one covered in blue velvet. Inside that was a well-worn but still shiny old silver ring, with a note rolled neatly inside.

A Silver Ring

It read, "*Esto parece decir una historia. Nunca estaria tan lejos de alguien que sabe.* (This looks like it could tell a story. It should never again be so far from one who knows it.)"
Vaya con Dios,
Esmeralda Guttierez
Housekeeper

Acknowledgements

No matter how trite it may sound, the truth remains: many people, myself included, work well enough alone, but no one can do their best relying only upon their own talent, training, and experience to critique their own product. Nor can anyone claim full credit for drawing into their lives the people properly equipped and motivated to provide both the criticism and encouragement needed for success.

In my life, I've been blessed with many miracles, by my definition of the word. Without some of these I might not be a pilot, a father, or a husband, and without a certain one I would literally not be walking this Earth. So my first, most emphatic "thank you" must go to my God, by whom all these miracles were arranged—and sometimes artfully concealed.

Once I'm happy with something I've done, my first instinct is to share it—either with the person I think will love it, or the one I know loves me, the most.

I often have a fortunate difficulty figuring out who that is on any given day, but the clear "winner" in the case of this story was my dear and loving wife, Pamela, without whom it simply wouldn't exist— because neither would my inspiration for it: the second huge miracle of my life, our son Reagan Douglas.

Before I was married, the first to proclaim my worth had always been my parents who, for brevity's sake, I'll just credit with raising five kids between 1958 and 1991, three of whom served honorably, and not one of whom grew up to be an addict, convict, or lawyer. Without my father's patient tutelage, I'd have never learned to fly, and my alternate career as a hobo would have marred their otherwise enviable record as parents.

With my cheering sections convinced of my clear and indisputable genius, it's time for a reality check, and I could list so many names beneath that heading none would seem any more important than any other. But there have been a few key people who've either exposed or edified my family's obvious bias. Chief among them is my editor and cover designer, Cassandra Marshall. Cassandra and I met on Twitter when I was desperately seeking a literary agent to champion my cause, and her frank objectiveness about my plight endeared her to me immediately. One must always find the Truth before one can plot its overthrow.

Before Cassandra, there was once a book by this same title of more than twice its size. I didn't know it then, but it was ridiculous to think anyone would ever buy, much less publish such a tome. Wanting to see it pass muster against a formidable, familiar critic however, I sent it to Mr. Robert Webb, Dean Emeritus of what could easily have been a leading collegiate English Department—concealed within a Marion, Ohio middle school that should bear his name when he's gone. Mr. Webb taught me and anyone else determined enough to earn an A in his class enough about our language in one school year to test out of two semesters of college English. He can never be replaced.

I taxed my share of innocent bystanders along the way, too. Friends from Facebook, Twitter, Absolute Write, and myriad writers' blogs and forums, fellow pilots and passengers, Starbucks denizens, bartenders, guys in bathrooms, women at bus stops, stray dogs, feral cats, anyone who'd weigh in, really, on my pitiable quandary of the decade—something in the vein of whether this story I had was really as half-baked and overcomplicated as the world seemed to think, or if maybe I just needed to take some St. John's Wort. Squarely in the latter camp I found people like fellow aviators Karlene Petitt, Jason Vagim, and Debby Johnson, who refused to let me turn the lights off even when I was convinced all hope was false.

Finally, I must thank formatting guru Jennette Green, of Diamond Press Publishing, for helping me get this book into usable form for print and electronic distribution. She was my lifeline against my deadline.

They say aviation has been made safe by layer upon layer of imperfect rules, regulations, and procedures; that for an accident to happen, each layer must align precisely with the rest so that the tiny gaps in each line up to allow a flight to fall through them all.

I'd say a novel's existence is a similarly rare event. If not for any one of the people in my life at the time I really needed someone just like them, this story would still be floating around like dark matter—fictional yet true, meaningful yet undiscovered—somewhere in the void between reality and romance.